PRAISE FOR

WARM BODIES

"The words Isaac Marion uses to describe his grim near-future are silken smooth. They slip through the mind's grasp easily, pleasurably, leaving hardly a hint of themselves in the images they evoke."

—*The Seattle Times*

"It's got the boarded-up strongholds and mob mentality of *Night of the Living Dead*—but also romance."

—*Time Out New York*

"I never thought I could care so passionately for a zombie. Isaac Marion has created the most unexpected romantic lead I've ever encountered, and rewritten the entire concept of what it means to be a zombie in the process. This story stayed with me long after I was done reading it. I eagerly await his next book."

—Stephenie Meyer, #1 *New York Times* bestselling author of the Twilight saga

"*Warm Bodies* is a strange and unexpected treat. R is the thinking woman's zombie—though somewhat gray-skinned and monosyllabic, he could be the perfect boyfriend, if he could manage to refrain from eating you. This is a wonderful book, elegantly written, touching and fun, as delightful as a mouthful of fresh brains."

—Audrey Niffenegger, #1 *New York Times* bestselling author of *The Time Traveler's Wife*

"Dark and funny."

—*Wired*

This title is also available as an eBook.

"Marion explores the meaning of humanity through R's journey toward personhood, a tale that gets grander in scale as his empathy builds and the book's true villains—cynicism, apathy, and status quo—are revealed."

—*Paste Magazine*

"Isaac Marion has a great new voice that hooks you from page one and accomplishes the impossible: it makes you care about young zombie love. *Warm Bodies* is a terrific read."

—Josh Bazell, *New York Times* bestselling author
of *Beat the Reaper*

"A jubilant story about two star-crossed lovers, one of them dead and hungry for more than love."

—Kirkus Reviews

"Marion is a disarming writer, ruefully humorous, knowingly cinematic in scope. This is a slacker-zombie novel with a heart."

—*The Guardian* (UK)

"*Warm Bodies* is a terrific book—a compelling literary fantasy that is also a strange and affecting pop-culture parable."

—Nick Harkaway, author of *The Gone-Away World*

"R does possess a certain winsome charm, and the upbeat ending will warm many hearts."

—*Publishers Weekly*

"A visually arresting, bleakly Ballardesque world. . . . Wryly playful, cinematic, and ultimately moving."

—*Time Out London*

"A mesmerising evolution of a classic contemporary myth."

—Simon Pegg, *New York Times* bestselling author
of *Nerd Do Well*

"Both tender and lacerating, this zombie novel has more to say about being alive than being dead. 'Love' is not a strong enough word for my feelings about this book."

—Maggie Stiefvater, author
of the Shiver trilogy and the Books of Faerie novels

"Enormous fun."

—*Marie Claire* (UK)

"*Warm Bodies* is a terrific zombook. Whether you're warm-bodied or cold-bodied, snuggle up to it with the lights low and enjoy a dead-lightful combination of horror and romance."

—Examiner.com

"A captivating debut novel that is as romantic as it is terrifying. . . . Marion is an amazing storyteller who writes from his heart, or from his viscera, as the case may be."

—SFScope

"A unique and poignant story about life, love, and change. . . . Marion's writing style is straightforward, funny, and strong, just like his characters. . . . You can't help but be drawn into this post-apocalyptic world and root for love and hope where none should exist."

—Fresh Fiction

"Thought-provoking and highly original. . . . Imaginative characters and quirky dialogue make this a captivating read . . . that readers will devour."

—Dark Faerie Tales

"Has there been a more sympathetic monster since Frankenstein's?"

—*The Financial Times* (UK)

WARM BODIES

A NOVEL

ISAAC MARION

EMILY BESTLER BOOKS

—

ATRIA

NEW YORK   LONDON   TORONTO   SYDNEY   NEW DELHI

ATRIA PAPERBACK
A Division of Simon & Schuster, Inc.
1230 Avenue of the Americas
New York, NY 10020

EMILY
BESTLER
BOOKS

This Emily Bestler Books/Atria Paperback edition December 2012

EMILY BESTLER BOOKS / ATRIA PAPERBACK and colophon are trademarks of Simon & Schuster, Inc.

Interior illustrations adapted by Isaac Marion from *Gray's Anatomy* (public domain)

For information about special discounts for bulk purchases, please contact Simon & Schuster Special Sales at 1-866-506-1949 or business@simonandschuster.com.

The Simon & Schuster Speakers Bureau can bring authors to your live event. For more information or to book an event, contact the Simon & Schuster Speakers Bureau at 1-866-248-3049 or visit our website at www.simonspeakers.com.

Designed by Kyoko Watanabe

Manufactured in the United States of America

10 9 8 7 6 5

The Library of Congress has cataloged the hardcover edition as follows:

Marion, Isaac, 1981–
   Warm bodies / Isaac Marion.—1st Atria Books hardcover ed.
      p. cm.
   1. Zombies—Fiction. I. Title.
   PS3613.A745252011 W37 2011
   813'.6—dc22

                                        2010048583

ISBN 978-1-4391-9231-3
ISBN 978-1-4767-1746-3 (pbk)
ISBN 978-1-4391-9233-7 (ebook)

For the foster kids I've met

You have known, O Gilgamesh,
What interests me,
To drink from the Well of Immortality.
Which means to make the dead
Rise from their graves
And the prisoners from their cells
The sinners from their sins.
I think love's kiss kills our heart of flesh.
It is the only way to eternal life,
Which should be unbearable if lived
Among the dying flowers
And the shrieking farewells
Of the overstretched arms of our spoiled hopes.

—Herbert Mason,
Gilgamesh: A Verse Narrative

"..."

—*The Epic of Gilgamesh,* Tablet II,
lines 147, 153, 154, 278, 279

wanting

I AM DEAD, but it's not so bad. I've learned to live with it. I'm sorry I can't properly introduce myself, but I don't have a name anymore. Hardly any of us do. We lose them like car keys, forget them like anniversaries. Mine might have started with an "R," but that's all I have now. It's funny because back when I was alive, I was always forgetting *other* people's names. My friend "M" says the irony of being a zombie is that everything is funny, but you can't smile, because your lips have rotted off.

None of us are particularly attractive, but death has been kinder to me than some. I'm still in the early stages of decay. Just the gray skin, the unpleasant smell, the dark circles under my eyes. I could almost pass for a Living man in need of a vacation. Before I became a zombie I must have been a businessman, a banker or broker or some young temp learning the ropes, because I'm wearing fairly nice clothes. Black slacks, gray shirt, red tie. M makes fun of me sometimes. He points at my tie and tries to laugh, a choked, gurgling rumble deep in his gut. His clothes are holey jeans and a plain white T-shirt. The shirt is looking pretty macabre by now. He should have picked a darker color.

We like to joke and speculate about our clothes, since these final fashion choices are the only indication of who we were before we became no one. Some are less obvious than mine: shorts and a sweater, skirt and a blouse. So we make random guesses.

You were a waitress. You were a student. Ring any bells?

It never does.

No one I know has any specific memories. Just a vague, vestigial knowledge of a world long gone. Faint impressions of past lives that linger like phantom limbs. We recognize civilization—buildings, cars, a general overview—but we have no personal role in it. No history. We are just *here*. We do what we do, time passes, and no one asks questions. But like I've said, it's not so bad. We may appear mindless, but we aren't. The rusty cogs of cogency still spin, just geared down and down till the outer motion is barely visible. We grunt and groan, we shrug and nod, and sometimes a few words slip out. It's not that different from before.

But it does make me sad that we've forgotten our names. Out of everything, this seems to me the most tragic. I miss my own and I mourn for everyone else's, because I'd like to love them, but I don't know who they are.

• • •

There are hundreds of us living in an abandoned airport outside some large city. We don't need shelter or warmth, obviously, but we like having the walls and roofs over our heads. Otherwise we'd just be wandering in an open field of dust somewhere, and that would be horrifying. To have nothing at all around us, nothing to touch or look at, no hard lines whatsoever, just us and the gaping maw of the sky. I imagine that's what being full-dead is like. An emptiness vast and absolute.

I think we've been here a long time. I still have all my flesh, but there are elders who are little more than skeletons with clinging bits of muscle, dry as jerky. Somehow it still extends and contracts, and they keep moving. I have never seen any of us "die" of old age. Left alone with plenty of food, maybe we'd "live" forever, I don't know. The future is as blurry to me as the past. I can't seem to make myself care about anything to the right or left of the present, and the present isn't exactly urgent. You might say death has relaxed me.

• • •

I am riding the escalators when M finds me. I ride the escalators several times a day, whenever they move. It's become a ritual. The airport is derelict, but the power still flickers on sometimes, maybe flowing from emergency generators stuttering deep underground. Lights flash and screens blink, machines jolt into motion. I cherish these moments. The feeling of things coming to life. I stand on the steps and ascend like a soul into Heaven, that sugary dream of our childhoods, now a tasteless joke.

After maybe thirty repetitions, I rise to find M waiting for me at the top. He is hundreds of pounds of muscle and fat draped on a six-foot-five frame. Bearded, bald, bruised and rotten, his grisly visage slides into view as I crest the staircase summit. Is he the angel that greets me at the gates? His ragged mouth is oozing black drool.

He points in a vague direction and grunts, "City."

I nod and follow him.

We are going out to find food. A hunting party forms around us as we shuffle toward town. It's not hard to find recruits for these expeditions, even if no one is hungry. Focused thought is a rare occurrence here, and we all follow it when it manifests. Otherwise we'd just be standing around and groaning all day. We do a lot of standing around and groaning. Years pass this way. The flesh withers on our bones and we stand here, waiting for it to go. I often wonder how old I am.

. . .

The city where we do our hunting is conveniently close. We arrive around noon the next day and start looking for flesh. The new hunger is a strange feeling. We don't feel it in our stomachs—some of us don't even have those. We feel it everywhere equally, a sinking, sagging sensation, as if our cells are deflating. Last winter, when so many Living joined the Dead and our prey became scarce, I watched some of my friends become full-dead. The transition was undramatic. They just slowed down, then stopped, and after a while I realized they were corpses. It disquieted me at first, but it's against etiquette to notice when one of us dies. I distracted myself with some groaning.

I think the world has mostly ended, because the cities we wander through are as rotten as we are. Buildings have collapsed. Rusted cars clog the streets. Most glass is shattered, and the wind drifting through the hollow high-rises moans like an animal left to die. I don't know what happened. Disease? War? Social collapse? Or was it just us? The Dead replacing the Living? I guess it's not so important. Once you've arrived at the end of the world, it hardly matters which route you took.

We start to smell the Living as we approach a dilapidated apartment building. The smell is not the musk of sweat and skin, it's the effervescence of life energy, like the ionized tang of lightning and lavender. We don't smell it in our noses. It hits us deeper inside, near our brains, like wasabi. We converge on the building and crash our way inside.

We find them huddled in a small studio unit with the windows boarded up. They are dressed worse than we are, wrapped in filthy tatters and rags, all of them badly in need of a shave. M will be saddled with a short blond beard for the rest of his Fleshy existence, but everyone else in our party is cleanshaven. It's one of the perks of being dead, another thing we don't have to worry about anymore. Beards, hair, toenails . . . no more fighting biology. Our wild bodies have finally been tamed.

Slow and clumsy but with unswerving commitment, we launch ourselves at the Living. Shotgun blasts fill the dusty air with gunpowder and gore. Black blood spatters the walls. The loss of an arm, a leg, a portion of torso, this is disregarded, shrugged off. A minor cosmetic issue. But some of us take shots to our brains, and we drop. Apparently there's still something of value in that withered gray sponge because if we lose it, we are corpses. The zombies to my left and right hit the ground with moist thuds. But there are plenty of us. We are overwhelming. We set upon the Living, and we eat.

Eating is not a pleasant business. I chew off a man's arm, and I hate it. I hate his screams, because I don't like pain, I don't like hurting people, but this is the world now. This is what we do. Of course if I don't eat all of him, if I spare his brain, he'll rise up and follow me back to the airport, and that might make me feel better. I'll introduce him to everyone, and maybe we'll stand around and groan for a while. It's hard to say what "friends" are anymore, but that might be close. If I restrain myself, if I leave enough . . .

But I don't. I can't. As always I go straight for the good part, the part that makes my head light up like a picture tube. I eat the brain, and for about thirty seconds, I have memories. Flashes of parades, perfume, music . . . *life*. Then it fades, and I get up, and we all stumble out of the city, still cold and gray, but feeling a little better. Not "good," exactly, not "happy," certainly not "alive," but . . . a little less dead. This is the best we can do.

I trail behind the group as the city disappears behind us. My steps plod a little heavier than the others'. When I pause at a rain-filled pothole to scrub gore off my face and clothes, M drops back and slaps a hand on my shoulder. He knows my distaste for some of our routines. He knows I'm a little more sensitive than most. Sometimes he teases me, twirls my messy black hair into pigtails and says, "Girl. Such . . . girl." But he knows when to take my gloom seriously. He pats my shoulder and just looks at me. His face isn't capable of much expressive nuance anymore, but I know what he wants to say. I nod, and we keep walking.

I don't know why we have to kill people. I don't know what chewing through a man's neck accomplishes. I steal what he has to replace what I lack. He disappears, and I stay. It's simple but sense-less, arbitrary laws from some lunatic legislator in the sky. But fol-lowing those laws keeps me walking, so I follow them to the letter. I eat until I stop eating, then I eat again.

How did this start? How did we become what we are? Was it some mysterious virus? Gamma rays? An ancient curse? Or some-thing even more absurd? No one talks about it much. We are here, and this is the way it is. We don't complain. We don't ask questions. We go about our business.

There is a chasm between me and the world outside of me. A gap so wide my feelings can't cross it. By the time my screams reach the other side, they have dwindled into groans.

• • •

At the Arrivals gate, we are greeted by a small crowd, watching us with hungry eyes or eyesockets. We drop our cargo on the floor: two mostly intact men, a few meaty legs, and a dismembered torso, all still warm. Call it leftovers. Call it takeout. Our fellow Dead fall on them and feast right there on the floor like animals. The life remaining in those cells will keep them from full-dying, but the Dead who don't hunt will never quite be satisfied. Like men at sea deprived of fresh fruit, they will wither in their deficiencies, weak and perpetually empty, because the new hunger is a lonely mon-ster. It grudgingly accepts the brown meat and lukewarm blood, but what it craves is closeness, that grim sense of connection that courses between their eyes and ours in those final moments, like some dark negative of love.

I wave to M and then break free from the crowd. I have long since acclimated to the Dead's pervasive stench, but the reek rising off them today feels especially fetid. Breathing is optional, but I need some air.

I wander out into the connecting hallways and ride the conveyors. I stand on the belt and watch the scenery scroll by through the window wall. Not much to see. The runways are turning green, overrun with grass and brush. Jets lie motionless on the concrete like beached whales, white and monumental. Moby Dick, conquered at last.

Before, when I was alive, I could never have done this. Standing still, watching the world pass by me, thinking about nearly nothing. I remember effort. I remember targets and deadlines, goals and ambitions. I remember being *purposeful*, always everywhere all the time. Now I'm just standing here on the conveyor, along for the ride. I reach the end, turn around, and go back the other way. The world has been distilled. Being dead is easy.

After a few hours of this, I notice a female on the opposite conveyor. She doesn't lurch or groan like most of us; her head just lolls from side to side. I like that about her, that she doesn't lurch or groan. I catch her eye and stare at her as we approach. For a brief moment we are side by side, only a few feet away. We pass, then travel on to opposite ends of the hall. We turn around and look at each other. We get back on the conveyors. We pass each other again. I grimace and she grimaces back. On our third pass, the airport power dies, and we come to a halt perfectly aligned. I wheeze hello, and she responds with a hunch of her shoulder.

I like her. I reach out and touch her hair. Like me, her decomposition is at an early stage. Her skin is pale and her eyes are sunken, but she has no exposed bones or organs. Her irises are an especially light shade of that strange pewter gray all the Dead share. Her graveclothes are a black skirt and a snug white buttonup. I suspect she used to be a receptionist.

Pinned to her chest is a silver nametag.

She has a name.

I stare hard at the tag; I lean in close, putting my face inches from her breasts, but it doesn't help. The letters spin and reverse in my vision; I can't hold them down. As always, they elude me, just a series of meaningless lines and blots.

Another of M's undead ironies—from nametags to newspapers, the answers to our questions are written all around us, and we don't know how to read.

I point at the tag and look her in the eyes. "Your . . . name?"

She looks at me blankly.

I point at myself and pronounce the remaining fragment of my own name. "Rrr." Then I point at her again.

Her eyes drop to the floor. She shakes her head. She doesn't remember. She doesn't even have syllable one, like M and I do. She is no one. But don't I always expect too much? I reach out and take her hand. We walk off the conveyers with our arms stretched across the divider.

This female and I have fallen in love. Or what's left of it.

I think I remember what love was like before. There were complex emotional and biological factors. We had elaborate tests to pass, connections to forge, ups and downs and tears and whirlwinds. It was an ordeal, an exercise in agony, but it was alive. The new love is simpler. Easier. But small.

My girlfriend doesn't talk much. We walk through the echoing corridors of the airport, occasionally passing someone staring out a window or at a wall. I try to think of things to say but nothing comes, and if something did come I probably couldn't say it. This is my great obstacle, the biggest of all the boulders littering my path. In my mind I am eloquent; I can climb intricate scaffolds of words to reach the highest cathedral ceilings and paint my thoughts. But when I open my mouth, it all collapses. So far my personal record is four rolling syllables before some . . . thing . . . jams. And I may be the most loquacious zombie in this airport.

I don't know why we don't speak. I can't explain the suffocating silence that hangs over our world, cutting us off from each other like prison-visit Plexiglas. Prepositions are painful, articles are arduous, adjectives are wild overachievements. Is this muteness a real physical handicap? One of the many symptoms of being Dead? Or do we just have nothing left to say?

I attempt conversation with my girlfriend, testing out a few awkward phrases and shallow questions, trying to get a reaction out of her, any twitch of wit. But she just looks at me like I'm weird.

We wander for a few hours, directionless, then she grips my hand and starts leading me somewhere. We stumble our way down the halted escalators and out onto the tarmac. I sigh wearily.

She is taking me to church.

The Dead have built a sanctuary on the runway. At some point in the distant past, someone pushed all the stair trucks together into a circle, forming a kind of amphitheater. We gather here, we stand here, we lift our arms and moan. The ancient Boneys wave their skeletal limbs in the center circle, rasping out dry, wordless sermons through toothy grins. I don't understand what this is. I don't think any of us do. But it's the only time we willingly gather under the open sky. That vast cosmic mouth, distant mountains like teeth in the skull of God, yawning wide to devour us. To swallow us down to where we probably belong.

My girlfriend appears to be more devout than I am. She closes her eyes and waves her arms in a way that looks almost heartfelt. I stand next to her and hold my hands in the air stiffly. At some unknown cue, maybe drawn by her fervor, the Boneys stop their preaching and stare at us. One of them comes forward, climbs our stairs, and takes us both by the wrists. It leads us down into the circle and raises our hands in its clawed grip. It lets out a kind of roar, an unearthly sound like a blast of air through a broken hunting horn, shockingly loud, frightening birds out of trees.

The congregation murmurs in response, and it's done. We are married.

We step back onto the stair seats. The service resumes. My new wife closes her eyes and waves her arms.

The day after our wedding, we have children. A small group of Boneys stops us in the hall and presents them to us. A boy and a girl, both around six years old. The boy is curly blond, with gray skin and gray eyes, perhaps once Caucasian. The girl is darker, with black hair and ashy brown skin, deeply shadowed around her steely eyes. She may have been Arab. The Boneys nudge them forward and they give us tentative smiles, hug our legs. I pat them on their heads and ask their names, but they don't have any. I sigh, and my wife and I keep walking, hand in hand with our new children.

I wasn't exactly expecting this. This is a big responsibility. The young Dead don't have the natural feeding instincts the adults do. They have to be tended and trained, and they will never grow up. Stunted by our curse, they will stay small and rot, then become little skeletons, animate but empty, their brains rattling stiff in their skulls, repeating their routines and rituals until one day, I can only assume, the bones themselves will disintegrate, and they'll just be gone.

Look at them. Watch them as my wife and I release their hands and they wander outside to play. They tease each other and grin. They play with things that aren't even toys: staplers and mugs and calculators. They giggle and laugh, though it sounds choked through their dry throats. We've bleached their brains, robbed them of breath, but they still cling to the cliff edge. They resist our curse for as long as they possibly can.

I watch them disappear into the pale daylight at the end of the hall. Deep inside me, in some dark and cobwebbed chamber, I feel something twitch.

Bristle passed through left auriculo-ventricular opening.

Passed through aortic opening.

I t's time to feed again.

I don't know how long it's been since our last hunting trip, probably just a few days, but I feel it. I feel the electricity in my limbs fizzling, fading. I see relentless visions of blood in my mind, that brilliant, mesmerizing red, flowing through bright pink tissues in intricate webs and Pollock fractals, pulsing and vibrating with life.

I find M in the food court talking to some girls. He is a little different than me. He does seem to enjoy the company of women, and his better-than-average diction draws them in like dazzled carp, but he keeps a distance. He laughs them off. The Boneys once tried to set him up with a wife, but he simply walked away. Sometimes I wonder if he has a philosophy. Maybe even a worldview. I'd like to sit down with him and pick his brain, just a tiny bite somewhere in the frontal lobe to get a taste of his thoughts. But he's too much of a toughguy to ever be that vulnerable.

"City," I say, putting a hand on my stomach. "Food."

The girls he's talking to look at me and shuffle away. I've noticed I make some people nervous, though I can't guess why.

"Just . . . ate," M says, frowning at me a little. "Two days . . . ago."

I grab my stomach again. "Feel empty. Feel . . . dead."

He nods. "Marr . . . iage."

I glare at him. I shake my head and clutch my stomach harder. *"Need.* Go . . . get others."

He sighs and walks out, bumping into me hard on his way past, but I'm not sure if it was intentional. He is, after all, a zombie.

He manages to find a few others with appetites and we form a small posse. Very small. Unsafely small. But I don't care. I don't recall ever being this hungry.

We set out toward the city. We take the freeway. Like everything else, the roads are returning to nature. We wander down empty lanes and under ivy-curtained overpasses. My residual memories of these roads contrast dramatically with their peaceful present state. I take a deep breath of the sweet, silent air.

We push deeper into the city than usual. The only scents I pick up are rust and dust. The unsheltered Living are getting scarcer, and the ones with shelter are venturing out less frequently. I suspect their stadium fortresses are becoming self-sufficient. I imagine vast gardens planted in the dugouts, bursting with carrots and beans. Cattle in the press box. Rice paddies in the outfield. We can see the largest of these citadels looming on the hazy horizon, its retractable roof wide open to the sun, taunting us.

But finally, we sense prey. The life scent electrifies our nostrils, bright and strong. They are close, and there are a lot of them. Maybe half our own number. We hesitate, stumbling to a halt. M looks at me. He looks at our small group, then back at me. "No," he grunts.

I point toward the crooked, collapsed skyscraper that's emitting the aroma, a cartoon tendril of scent beckoning us *come hither.*

"Eat," I insist.

M shakes his head. "Too . . . many."

"Eat."

He looks at our group again. He sniffs the air. The rest of them are undecided. Some of them also sniff warily, but others are more single-minded like me. They groan and drool and snap their teeth.

I'm getting agitated. "Need it!" I shout, glaring at M. "Come . . . on." I turn and start speed-lumbering toward the skyscraper. Focused thought. The rest of the group reflexively follows. M catches up and walks beside me, watching me with an uneasy grimace.

Spurred to an unusual level of intensity by my desperate energy, our group crashes through the revolving doors and rushes down the dark hallways. Some earthquake or explosion has knocked out part of the foundation, and the entire high-rise leans at a dizzying, fun house angle. It's hard to navigate the zigzagging halls, and the inclines make it a challenge to even walk, but the scent is overpowering. After a few flights of stairs I start to hear them as well, clattering around and talking to each other in those steady, melodious streams of words. Living speech has always been a sonic pheromone to me, and I spasm briefly when it hits my ears. I've yet to meet another zombie who shares my appreciation for those silky rhythms. M thinks it's a sick fetish.

As we approach their level of the building, some of us start groaning loudly, and the Living hear us. One of them shouts the alarm and I hear guns cocking, but we don't hesitate. We burst through a final door and rush them. M grunts when he sees how many there are, but he lunges with me at the nearest man and grabs his arms while I rip out his throat. The burning red taste of blood floods my mouth. The sparkle of life sprays out of his cells like citrus mist from an orange peel, and I suck it in.

The darkness of the room is pulsing with gunfire, and by our standards we are grossly outnumbered—there are only three of us to every one of them—but something is tipping things in our favor. Our manic speed is uncharacteristic of the Dead, and our prey are not prepared for it. Is this all coming from me? Creatures without desire don't usually move quickly, but they're following my lead, and I am an angry whirlwind. What has come over me? Am I just having a bad day?

There is one other factor working to our advantage. These Living are not seasoned veterans. They are young. Teenagers, mostly. Boys and girls. One of them has such gruesome acne he's likely to get shot by mistake in this flickering light. Their leader is a slightly older kid with a patchy beard, standing on a cubicle desk in the middle of the room and shouting panicked commands to his men. As they fall to the floor under the weight of our hunger, as dots of blood pointilize the walls, this boy leans protectively over a small figure crouched below him on the desk. A girl, young and blond, bracing her bird-boned shoulder against her shotgun as she fires blindly into the dark.

I lope across the room and grab the boy's boots. I pull his feet out from under him and he falls, cracking his head on the edge of the desk. Without hesitation I pounce on him and bite through his neck. Then I dig my fingers into the crack in his skull, and pry his head open like an eggshell. His brain pulses hot and pink inside. I take a deep, wide, ravenous bite and—

. . .

I am Perry Kelvin, a nine-year-old boy growing up in rural nowhere. The threats are all on some distant coast and we don't worry about them here. Other than the emergency chain-link fence between the river and the mountain ridge, life is almost normal. I'm in school. I'm learning about George Washington. I'm riding my bike down dusty roads in shorts and a tank top, feeling the summer sun broil the back of my neck. My neck. My neck hurts, it—

. . .

I am eating a slice of pizza with my mom and dad. It's my birthday and they are doing what they can to treat me, though their money

isn't worth much anymore. I've just turned eleven, and they're finally taking me to see one of the countless zombie movies crop-
ping up lately. I'm so excited I can barely taste my pizza. I take an
oversized bite and the thick cheese sticks in my throat. I choke it
back up and my parents laugh. Tomato sauce stains my shirt like—

. . .

I am fifteen, gazing out the window at the looming walls of my
new home. Clouded gray sunlight drifts down through the stadium's open roof. I'm at school again listening to a lecture about salvage safety and trying not to stare at the beautiful girl sitting next
to me. She has short, choppy blond hair and blue eyes that dance
with private amusement. My palms are sweating. My mouth is full
of laundry lint. When the class ends, I catch her in the hall and say,
"Hi."

"Hi," she says.
"I'm new here."
"I know."
"My name's Perry."
She smiles. "I'm Julie."
She smiles. Her eyes glitter. "I'm Julie."
She smiles. I glimpse her braces. Her eyes are classic novels and
poetry. "I'm Julie," she says.
She says—

. . .

"Perry," Julie whispers in my ear as I kiss her neck. She twines her
fingers into mine and squeezes hard. I kiss her deep and caress the
back of her head with my free hand, tangling my fingers in her hair.
I look her in the eyes.

"Do you want to?" I breathe.
She smiles. She closes her eyes and says, "Yes."

I crush her against me. I want to be part of her. Not just inside her but all around her. I want our rib cages to crack open and our hearts to migrate and merge. I want our cells to braid together like living thread.

. . .

And now I'm older, wiser, gunning a motorcycle down a forgotten downtown boulevard. Julie is on the seat behind me, her arms clutching my chest, her legs wrapped around mine. Her aviators glint in the sun as she grins, showing her perfectly straight teeth. The grin is not mine to share anymore, and I know this, I have accepted the way things are and the way things are going to be, even if she hasn't and won't. But at least I can protect her. At least I can keep her safe. She is so unbearably beautiful and sometimes I see a future with her in my head, but my head, my head hurts, oh God my head is—

. . .

Stop.

Who are you? Let the memories dissolve. Your eyes are crusted—blink them. Gasp in a ragged breath.

You're you again. You're no one.

Welcome back.

. . .

I feel the carpet under my fingers. I hear the gunshots. I stand up and look around, dizzy and reeling. I have never had a vision so deep, like an entire life spooling through my head. The sting of tears burns in my eyes, but my ducts no longer have fluid. The feeling rages unquenched like pepper spray. It's the first time I've felt pain since I died.

I hear a scream nearby and I turn. It's her. She's here. *Julie* is here, older now, maybe nineteen, her baby fat melted away, revealing sharper lines and finer poise, muscles small but toned on her girlish frame. She is huddled in a corner, unarmed, sobbing and screaming as M creeps toward her. He always finds the women. Their memories are porn to him. I still feel disoriented, unsure where or who I am, but . . .

I shove M aside and snarl, *"No.* Mine."

He grits his teeth like he's about to turn on me, but a gunshot tears into his shoulder and he shuffles across the room to help two other zombies bring down a kid with an Uzi.

I approach the girl. She cowers before me, her tender flesh offering me all the things I'm accustomed to taking, and my instincts start to reassert themselves. The urge to rip and tear surges into my arms and jaw. But then she screams again, and something inside me moves, a feeble moth struggling against a web. In this brief moment of hesitation, still warm with the nectar of a young man's memories, I make a choice.

I let out a gentle groan and inch toward the girl, trying to force kindness into my dull expression. I am not no one. I am a nine-year-old boy, I am a fifteen-year-old boy, I am—

She throws a knife at my head.

The blade sticks straight into the center of my forehead and quivers there. But it has penetrated less than an inch, only grazing my frontal lobe. I pull it out and drop it. I hold out my hands, making soft noises through my lips, but I'm helpless. How do I appear unthreatening when her lover's blood is running down my chin?

I'm just a few feet away from her now. She is fumbling through her jeans for another weapon. Behind me, the Dead are finishing their butchery. Soon they will turn their attention to this dim corner of the room. I take a deep breath.

"Ju . . . lie," I say.

It rolls off my tongue like honey. I feel good just saying it.

Her eyes go wide. She freezes.

"Julie," I say again. I put out my hands. I point at the zombies behind me. I shake my head.

She stares at me, making no sign that she understands. But when I reach out to touch her, she doesn't move. And she doesn't stab me.

I reach my free hand into the head wound of a fallen zombie and collect a palmful of black, lifeless blood. Slowly, with gentle movements, I smear it on her face, down her neck, and onto her clothes. She doesn't even flinch. She is probably catatonic.

I take her hand and pull her to her feet. At that moment M and the others finish devouring their prey and turn to inspect the room. Their eyes fall on me. They fall on Julie. I walk toward them, gripping Julie's hand, not quite dragging her. She staggers behind me, staring straight ahead.

M sniffs the air cautiously. But I know he's smelling exactly what I'm smelling: nothing. Just the negative-smell of Dead blood. It's spattered all over the walls, soaked into our clothes, and smeared carefully on a young Living girl, concealing the glow of her life under its dark, overpowering musk.

Without a word, we leave the high-rise and head back to the airport. I walk in a daze, full of strange and kaleidoscopic thoughts. Julie holds limply to my hand, staring at the side of my face with wide eyes, trembling lips.

Aᴆᴛᴇʀ ᴅᴇʟɪᴠᴇʀɪɴɢ our abundant harvest of leftover flesh to the nonhunters—the Boneys, the children, the stay-at-home moms—I take Julie to my house. My fellow Dead give me curious looks as I pass. Because it requires both volition and restraint, the act of intentionally converting the Living is almost never performed. Most conversions happen by accident: a feeding zombie is killed or otherwise distracted before finishing his business, *voro interruptus*. The rest of our converts arise from traditional deaths, private affairs of illness or mishap or classical Living-on-Living violence that take place outside our sphere of interest. So the fact that I have purposely brought this girl home unconsumed is a thing of mystery, a miracle on par with giving birth. M and the others allow me plenty of room in the halls, regarding me with confusion and wonder. If they knew the full truth of what I'm doing, their reactions would be . . . less moderate.

Gripping Julie's hand, I hurry her away from their probing eyes. I lead her to Gate 12, down the boarding tunnel and into my home: a 747 commercial jet. It's not very spacious, the floor plan is impractical, but it's the most isolated place in the airport and I enjoy the privacy. Sometimes it even tickles my numb memory. Looking at my clothes, I seem like the kind of person who probably traveled a lot. Sometimes when I "sleep" here, I feel the faint rising sensation of flight, the blasts of recycled air blowing in my face, the soggy nausea of packaged sandwiches. And then the fresh lemon zing of *poisson* in Paris. The burn of *tajine* in Morocco. Are these places all gone now? Silent streets, cafés full of dusty skeletons?

Julie and I stand in the center aisle, looking at each other. I point to a window seat and raise my eyebrows. Keeping her eyes solidly on me, she backs into the row and sits down. Her hands grip the armrests like the plane is in a flaming death dive.

I sit in the aisle seat and release an involuntary wheeze, looking straight ahead at my stacks of memorabilia. Every time I go into the city, I bring back one thing that catches my eye. A puzzle. A shot glass. A Barbie. A dildo. Flowers. Magazines. Books. I bring them here to my home, strew them around the seats and aisles, and stare at them for hours. The piles reach to the ceiling now. M keeps asking me why I do this. I have no answer.

"Not . . . eat," I groan at Julie, looking her in the eyes. "I . . . won't eat."

She stares at me. Her lips are tight and pale.

I point at her. I open my mouth and point at my crooked, blood-stained teeth. I shake my head. She presses herself against the window. A terrified whimper rises in her throat. This is not working.

"Safe," I tell her, letting out a sigh. "Keep . . . you safe."

I stand up and go to my record player. I dig through my LP collection in the overhead compartments and pull out an album. I take the headphones back to my seat and place the big metal cans on Julie's ears. She is still frozen, wide-eyed.

The record plays. It's Frank Sinatra. I can hear it faintly through the headphones, like a distant eulogy drifting on autumn air.

Last night . . . when we were young . . .

I close my eyes and hunch forward. My head sways vaguely in

time with the music as verses float through the jet cabin, blending together in my ears.

Life was so new . . . so real, so right . . .

"Safe," I mumble. "Keep you . . . safe."

. . . ages ago . . . last night . . .

When my eyes finally open, Julie's face has changed. The terror has faded, and she regards me with disbelief.

"What *are* you?" she whispers.

I turn my face away. I stand and duck out of the plane. Her bewildered gaze follows me down the tunnel.

• • •

In the airport parking garage, there is a classic Mercedes convertible that I've been playing with for several months. After weeks of staring at it, I figured out how to fill its tank from a barrel of stabilized gasoline I found in the service rooms. Then I remembered how to turn the key and start it, after pushing its owner's dry corpse to the pavement. But I have no idea how to drive. The best I've been able to do is back out of the parking spot and ram into a nearby Hummer. Sometimes I just sit there with the engine purring, my hands resting limply on the wheel, willing a true memory to pop into my head. Not another hazy impression or vague awareness cribbed from the collective subconscious. Something specific, bright, and vivid. Something unmistakably mine. I strain myself, trying to wrench it out of the blackness.

• • •

I meet M later that evening at his home in the women's bathroom. He is sitting in front of a TV plugged into a long extension cord, gaping at a late-night softcore movie he found in some dead man's luggage. I don't know why he does this. Erotica is meaningless for us now. The blood doesn't pump, the urges don't stir. I've walked in on M with his "girlfriends" before, and they're just standing there naked, staring at each other, sometimes rubbing their bodies together but looking tired and lost. Maybe it's a kind of death throe. A distant echo of that great motivator that once started wars and inspired symphonies, that drove human history out of the caves and into space. M may be holding on, but those days are over now. Sex, once a law as undisputed as gravity, has been disproved. The equation is erased, the blackboard broken.

Sometimes it's a relief. I remember the need, the insatiable hunger that ruled my life and the lives of everyone around me. Sometimes I'm glad to be free of it. There's less trouble now. But our loss of this, the most basic of all human passions, might sum up our loss of everything else. It's made things quieter. Simpler. And it's one of the surest signs that we're dead.

I watch M from the doorway. He sits on the little metal folding chair with his hands between his knees like a schoolboy facing the principal. There are times when I can almost glimpse the person he once was under all that rotting flesh, and it prickles my heart.

"Did . . . bring it?" he asks without looking away from the TV.

I hold up what I've been carrying. A human brain, fresh from today's hunting trip, no longer warm but still pink and buzzing with life.

We sit against the tiles of the bathroom wall with our legs sprawled out in front of us, passing the brain back and forth, taking small, leisurely bites and enjoying brief flashes of human experience.

"Good . . . shit," M wheezes.

The brain contains the life of some young military grunt from the city. His existence isn't particularly interesting to me, just endless repetitions of training, eating, and mowing down zombies, but M seems to like it. His tastes are a little less demanding than mine. I watch his mouth form silent words. I watch his face shuffle through emotions. Anger, fear, joy, lust. It's like watching a dreaming dog kick and whimper, but far more heartbreaking. When he wakes up, this will all disappear. He will be empty again. He will be dead.

After an hour or two, we are down to one small gobbet of pink tissue. M pops it in his mouth and his pupils dilate as he has his visions. The brain is gone, but I'm not satisfied. I reach furtively into my pocket and pull out a fist-sized chunk that I've been saving. This one is different. This one is special. I tear off a bite and chew.

. . .

I am Perry Kelvin, a sixteen-year-old boy, watching my girlfriend write in her journal. The black leather cover is tattered and worn, the inside a maze of scribbles, drawings, little notes and quotes. I am sitting on the couch with a salvaged first edition of *On the Road*, longing to live in any era but this one, and she is curled in my lap, penning furiously. I poke my head over her shoulder, trying to get a glimpse. She pulls the journal away and gives me a coy smile. "No," she says, and returns to her work.

"What are you writing about?"

"Nooot tellinnng," she singsongs.

"Journal or poetry?"

"Both, silly."

"Am I in it?"

She chuckles.

I lace my arms around her shoulders. She burrows into me a little deeper. I bury my face in her hair and kiss the back of her head. The spicy smell of her shampoo—

. . .

M is looking at me. "You . . . have more?" he grunts, and holds out his hand for me to pass it. But I don't pass it. I take another bite and close my eyes.

. . .

"Perry," Julie says.

"Yeah."

We are at our secret spot on the stadium roof. We lie on our backs on a red blanket on the white steel panels, squinting up at the blinding blue sky.

"I miss airplanes," she says.

I nod. "Me too."

"Not flying in them. I never got to do that anyway with Dad the way he is. I just miss *airplanes*. That muffled thunder in the distance, those white lines . . . the way they sliced across the sky and made designs in the blue? My mom used to say it looked like Etch A Sketch. It was so beautiful."

I smile at the thought. She's right. Airplanes were beautiful. So were fireworks. Flowers. Concerts. Kites. All the indulgences we can no longer afford.

"I like how you remember things," I say.

She looks at me. "Well we have to. We have to remember everything. If we don't, by the time we grow up it'll be gone forever."

I close my eyes and let the scorching light blaze red through my lids. I let it saturate my brain. I turn my head and kiss Julie. We make love there on the blanket on the stadium roof, four hundred feet above the ground. The sun stands guard over us like a kind-hearted chaperone, smiling silently.

. . .

"Hey!"

My eyes snap open. M is glaring at me. He makes a grab for the piece of brain in my hand and I yank it away.

"*No*," I growl.

I suppose M is my friend, but I would rather kill him than let him taste this. The thought of his filthy fingers poking and fondling these memories makes me want to rip his chest open and squish his heart in my hands, stomp his brain till he stops existing. This is *mine*.

M looks at me. He sees the warning flare in my eyes, hears the rising air-raid siren. He drops his hand away. He stares at me for a moment, annoyed and confused. "Bo . . . gart," he mutters, and locks himself in a toilet stall.

I leave the bathroom with abnormally purposeful strides. I slip in through the door of the 747 and stand there in the faint oval of light. Julie is lying back in a reclined seat, snoring gently. I knock on the side of the fuselage and she bolts upright, instantly awake. She watches me warily as I approach her. My eyes are burning again. I grab her messenger bag off the floor and dig through it. I find her wallet, and then I find a photo. A portrait of a young man. I hold the photo up to her eyes.

"I'm . . . sorry," I say hoarsely.

She looks at me, stone-faced.

I point at my mouth. I clutch my stomach. I point at her mouth. I touch her stomach. Then I point out the window, at the cloudless black sky of merciless stars. It's the weakest defense for murder ever offered, but it's all I have. I clench my jaw and squint my eyes, trying to ease their dry sting.

Julie's lower lip is tensed. Her eyes are red and wet. "Which one of you did it?" she says in a voice on the verge of breaking. "Was it that big one? That fat fuck that almost got me?"

I stare at her for a moment, not grasping her questions. And then it hits me, and my eyes go wide.

She doesn't know it was me.

The room was dark and I came from behind. She didn't see it. She doesn't know. Her eyes address me like I'm a creature worthy of address, unaware that I recently killed her lover, ate his life and digested his soul, and am right now carrying a prime cut of his brain in the front pocket of my slacks. I can feel it burning there like a coal of guilt, and I reflexively back away from her, unable to comprehend this curdled mercy.

"Why me?" she demands, blinking an angry tear out of her eye. "Why did you save *me*?" She twists her back to me and curls up on the chair, wrapping her arms around her shoulders. "Out of everyone . . . ," she mumbles into the cushion. "Why me."

These are her first questions. Not the ones urgent for her own well-being, not the mystery of how I know her name or the terrifying prospect of what my plans for her might be; she doesn't rush to satisfy those hungers. Her first questions are for others. For her friends, for her lover, wondering why she couldn't take their place.

I am the lowest thing. I am the bottom of the universe.

I drop the photo onto the seat and look at the floor. "I'm . . . sorry," I say again, and leave the plane.

When I emerge from the boarding tunnel there are several Dead grouped near the doorway. They watch me without expressions. We stand there in silence, still as statues. Then I brush past them and wander off into the dark halls.

THE CRACKED PAVEMENT rumbles under our truck's tires. It abuses the old Ford's creaky suspension, making a quiet roar like stifled rage. I look at my dad. He looks older than I remember. Weaker. He grips the steering wheel hard. His knuckles are white.

"Dad?" I say.

"What, Perry."

"Where are we going to go?"

"Someplace safe."

I watch him carefully. "Are there still safe places?"

He hesitates, too long. "Someplace safer."

Behind us, in the valley where we used to swim and pick strawberries, eat pizza and go to movies, the valley where I was born and grew up and discovered everything that's now inside me, plumes of smoke rise. The gas station where I bought Coke slushies is on fire. The windows of my grade school are shattered. The kids in the public swimming pool are not swimming.

"Dad?" I say.

"What."

"Is Mom coming back?"

My dad finally looks at me, but says nothing.

"As one of them?"

He looks back at the road. "No."

"But I thought she would. I thought everyone comes back now."

"Perry," my dad says, and the word seems to barely escape his throat. "I fixed it. So she won't."

The hard lines in his face fascinate and repel me. My voice cracks. "Why, Dad?"

"Because she's gone. No one comes back. Not really. Do you understand that?"

The scrub brush and barren hills ahead start to blur in my vision. I try to focus on the windshield itself, the crushed bugs and tiny fractures. Those blur, too.

"Just remember her," my dad says. "As much as you can, for as long as you can. That's how she comes back. *We* make her live. Not some ridiculous curse."

I watch his face, trying to read the truth in his squinted eyes. I've never heard him talk like this.

"Bodies are just meat," he says. "The part of her that matters most . . . we get to keep that."

. . .

"Julie."

"What?"

"Come here. Look at this."

The wind makes a ripping sound through the shattered plate glass of the hospital we're salvaging. Julie steps to the window's edge with me and looks down.

"What's it doing?"

"I don't know."

On the snowdusted street below, a single zombie walks in a loose circle. It bumps into a car and stumbles, slowly backs up against a

30

wall, turns, shuffles in another direction. It makes no sound and doesn't seem to be looking at anything. Julie and I watch it for a few minutes.

"I don't like this," she says.

"Yeah."

"It's . . . sad."

"Yeah."

"What's wrong with it?"

"Don't know."

It stops in the middle of the street, swaying slightly. Its face displays absolutely nothing. Just skin stretched over a skull.

"I wonder how it feels," she says.

"What?"

"To be like them."

I watch the zombie. It starts swaying a little harder, then it collapses. It lies there on its side, staring at the frozen pavement.

"What's it . . . ?" Julie starts, then stops. She looks at me with wide eyes, then back at the crumpled body. "Did it just *die*?"

We wait in silence. The corpse doesn't move. I feel a wriggling sensation inside me, tiny things creeping down my spine.

"Let's go," Julie says, and turns away. I follow her back into the building. We can't think of anything to say all the way home.

• • •

Stop.

Breathe those useless breaths. Drop this piece of life you're holding to your lips. Where are you? How long have you been here? Stop now. You have to stop.

Squeeze shut your stinging eyes, and take another bite.

In the morning, my wife finds me slumped against one of the floor-to-ceiling windows overlooking the runways. My eyes are open and full of dust. My head leans to one side. I rarely allow myself to look so corpselike.

Something is wrong with me. There is a sick emptiness in my stomach, a feeling somewhere between starvation and hangover. My wife grabs my arm and pulls me to my feet. She starts walking, dragging me behind her like rolling luggage. I feel a flash of bitter heat pulse through me and I start speaking at her. "Name," I say, glaring into her ear. "Name?"

She shoots me a cold look and keeps walking.

"Job? School?" My tone shifts from query to accusation. "Movie? Song?" It bubbles out of me like oil from a punctured pipeline. "*Book?*" I shout at her. "Food? Family? *Name?*"

My wife turns and spits at me. Actually spits on my shirt, snarling like an animal. But the look in her eyes instantly cools my eruption. She's . . . frightened. Her lips quiver. What am I doing?

I look at the floor. We stand in silence for several minutes. Then she resumes walking, and I follow her, trying to shake off this strange black cloud that's settled over me.

. . .

She leads me to a gutted gift shop and lets out an emphatic groan. Our kids emerge from behind an overturned bookcase full of best-sellers that will never be read. They're each gnawing a human fore-arm, slightly brown at the stumps, not exactly fresh.

"Where did . . . get those?" I ask them. They shrug. I turn to my wife. "Need . . . better."

She frowns and points at me. She grunts angrily, and I avert my eyes, duly chastised. It's true, I haven't been the most involved par-ent. Is it possible to have a midlife crisis if you have no idea how old you are? I could be in my early thirties or late teens. I could be younger than Julie.

My wife grunts at the kids and gestures down the hall. They hang their heads and make a wheezy whining noise, but they follow us. We are taking them to their first day of school.

. . .

Some of us, maybe the same industrious Dead who built the Boneys' stair church, have built a "classroom" in the food court by stacking heavy luggage into high walls. As my family and I ap-proach, we hear groans and screams from inside this arena. There is a line of youngsters in front of the entryway, waiting their turn. My wife and I lead our kids to the back of the line and watch the lesson now in progress.

Five Dead youth are circling a skinny, middle-aged Living man. The man backs up against the luggage, looking frantically left and right, his empty hands balled into fists. Two of the youths dive at him and try to hold his arms down, but he shakes them off. The third one nips a tiny bite in his shoulder and the man screams as

34

if he's been mortally wounded, because in effect, he has. From zombie bites to starvation to good old-fashioned age and disease, there are so many options for dying in this new world. So many ways for the Living to stop. But with just a few debrained exceptions, all roads lead to *us*, the Dead, and our very unglamorous immortality.

The man's pending conversion seems to have numbed him. One of the youths latches her teeth onto his thigh and he doesn't even flinch, he just bends over and starts pummeling her head with both fists until her skull dents and her neck snaps audibly. She stumbles away from him, scowling, her head tilting at a severe angle.

"Wrong!" their teacher roars. "Get . . . throat!"

The children back away and watch the man warily.

"Throat!" the teacher repeats. He and his assistant lumber into the arena and tackle the man, forcing him to the ground. The teacher kills him and stands up, blood streaming down his chin. "Throat," he says again, pointing to the body.

The five children exit shamefaced, and the next five in line are prodded inside. My kids look up at me anxiously. I pat their heads.

We watch as the dead man is hauled off to be eaten and the next one is dragged into the classroom. This one is old and gray haired, but he's big, probably a Security officer at one time in his life. He requires three of our males to haul him in safely. They throw him into a corner and quickly return to guard the entryway.

The five youths inside are nervous, but the teacher shouts at them and they begin to move in. When they get close enough they all five lunge at the same time, two grabbing for each arm and the fifth going for the throat. But the old man is shockingly strong. He twists around and flings two of them hard against the wall of luggage. The impact shakes the wall and a sturdy metal briefcase topples down from the top. The man grabs it by the handle, raises it high, and smashes it down on one of the youths' heads. The youth's skull caves in and his brain squishes out. He doesn't scream or twitch or quiver, he just abruptly collapses into a heap of limbs, flat and flush with the floor as if he's been dead for months already. Death takes hold of him with retroactive finality.

The whole school goes silent. The remaining four children back out of the arena. No one really pays attention as the adults rush inside to deal with the man. We all gaze at the youth's crumpled corpse with sad resignation. We can't tell which of the gathered adults might be his parents, since all our expressions are about the same. Whoever they are, they will forget their loss soon enough. By tomorrow the Boneys will show up with another boy or girl to replace this one. We allow a few uncomfortable seconds of silence for the killed child, then school resumes. A few parents glance at each other, maybe wondering what to think, wondering what this all means, this bent, inverted cycle of life. Or maybe that's just me.

My kids are next in line. They watch the current lesson intently, sometimes standing on tiptoes to see, but they aren't afraid. They are younger than the rest and will probably be matched against someone too frail to put up a fight, but they don't know this, and it's not why they're unafraid. When the entire world is built on death and horror, when existence is a constant state of panic, it's hard to get worked up about any one thing. Specific fears have become irrelevant. We've replaced them with a smothering blanket far worse.

· · ·

I pace outside the 747 boarding tunnel for about an hour before going in. I open the jet's door quietly. Julie is curled up in business class, sleeping. She has wrapped herself in a quilt made of cut-up jeans that I brought back as a souvenir a few weeks ago. The morning sun makes a halo in her yellow hair, sainting her.

"Julie," I whisper.

Her eyes slide open a crack. This time she doesn't jolt upright or edge away from me. She just looks at me with tired, puffy eyes. "What," she mumbles.

"How . . . are . . . ?"

"How do you think I am." She puts her back to me and wraps the blanket around her shoulders.

I watch her for a moment. Her posture is a brick wall. I lower my head and turn to go. But as I step through the doorway she says, "Wait."

I turn around. She is sitting up, the blanket piled on her lap. "I'm hungry," she says.

I look at her blankly. Hungry? Does she want an arm or leg? Hot blood, meat and life? She's Living . . . does she want to eat herself? Then I remember what being hungry used to mean. I remember beefsteaks and pancakes, grains and fruits and vegetables, that quaint little food pyramid. Sometimes I miss savoring taste and texture instead of just swallowing energy, but I try not to dwell on it. The old food does nothing to satisfy us anymore. Even bright red meat from a freshly killed rabbit or deer is beneath our culinary standards; its energy is simply incompatible, like trying to run a computer on diesel. There is no easy way out for us, no humane alternative for the fashionably moral. The new hunger demands sacrifice. It demands human suffering as the price for our pleasures, meager and cheap as they are.

"You know, *food*?" Julie prompts. She mimes the act of taking a bite. "Sandwiches? Pizza? Stuff that doesn't involve *killing* people?"

I nod. "I'll . . . get."

I start to leave but she stops me again.

"Just let me *go*," she says. "What are you *doing*? Why are you keeping me here?"

I think for a moment. I step to her window and point to the runways below. She sees the church service in progress. The congregation of the Dead, swaying and groaning. The skeletons rattling back and forth, voiceless but somehow charismatic, gnashing their splintered teeth. There are dozens of them down there, swarming.

"Keep you . . . safe."

She looks up at me from her chair with an expression I can't read. Her eyes are narrowed and her lips are tight, but it's not exactly rage. "How do you know my name?" she demands.

There it is. It had to come eventually.

"In that building. You said my name, I remember it. How the *fuck* do you know my name?"

I make no attempt to answer. No way to explain what I know and how I know it, not with my kindergarten vocabulary and special ed speech impediments. So I simply retreat, exiting the plane and trudging up the boarding tunnel, feeling more acutely than ever the limitations of what I am.

As I stand in Gate 12 considering where to go from here, I feel a touch on my shoulder. Julie is standing behind me. She stuffs her hands into the pockets of her tight black jeans, looking uncertain. "Just let me get out and walk around a little," she says. "I'm going crazy in that plane."

I don't answer. I look around the hallways.

"Come on," she says. "I walked *in* here and nobody ate me. Let me go with you to get food. You don't know what I like."

This is . . . not entirely true. I know she loves pad thai. I know she drools over sushi. I know she has a weakness for greasy cheese-burgers, despite the stadium's rigorous fitness routines. But that knowledge is not mine to use. That knowledge is stolen.

I nod slowly and point at her. "Dead," I pronounce. I click my teeth and do an exaggerated zombie shuffle.

"Okay," she says.

I lumber around in a circle with slow, shaky steps, letting out an occasional groan.

"Got it."

I take her by the wrist and lead her out into the hallway. I gesture in each direction, indicating the small cliques of zombies wandering in the dim morning shadows. I look her straight in the eyes. "Don't . . . run."

She crosses her heart. "Promise."

Standing so close to her, I find that I can smell her again. She has wiped much of the black blood off her skin, and through the gaps I can detect traces of her life energy. It bubbles out and sparkles like champagne, igniting flashes deep in the back of my sinuses. Still holding her gaze, I rub my palm into a recent gash on my forearm, and although it's nearly dry now, I manage to collect a thin smear of blood. I slowly spread this ink on her cheek and down her neck. She shudders, but doesn't pull away. She is, at the bottom of everything, a very smart girl.

"Okay?" I ask, raising my eyebrows.

She closes her eyes, takes a deep breath, cringes at the smell of my fluids, then nods. "Okay."

I walk and she follows, stumbling along behind me and groaning every three or four steps. She is overdoing it, overacting like high school Shakespeare, but she will pass. We bump through crowds of Dead, large hunting parties shambling past us on both sides, and no one glances at us. To my amazement, Julie's fear seems to be *diminishing* as we walk, despite the obvious peril of her situation. At a few points I catch her fighting a smile after letting out a particularly hammy moan. I feel an unfamiliar but pleasant sensation in my lips, tugging them upward.

This is . . . new.

I TAKE JULIE to the food court, and she gives me an odd look when I immediately start moving toward the Thai restaurant. As we get closer she cringes and covers her nose. "Oh God," she moans. The warming bins in front are frothing with dried-up rot, dead maggots, and mold. I'm pretty much impervious to odor by now, but judging by Julie's expression, it's foul. We dig around in the back room for a while, but the airport's intermittent power means the freezers only work part-time, so everything inside is rancid. I head toward the burger joint. Julie gives me that quizzical look again and follows me. In the walk-in freezer we find a few burger patties that are currently cold but have clearly been thawed and refrozen many times. Dead flies speckle the white freezer floor.

Julie sighs. "Well?"

I look off into the distance, thinking. The airport does have a sushi bar . . . but I remember a little about sushi, and if a few hours can spoil a fresh hamachi fillet, I don't want to see what years can do.

"God," Julie says as I stand there deliberating, "you really know how to plan a dinner date." She opens a few boxes of moldy buns, wrinkles up her nose. "You've never done this before, have you? Taken a human home alive?"

I shake my head apologetically, but I wince at her use of the word "human." I've never liked that differentiation. She is Living and I'm Dead, but I'd like to believe we're both human. Call me an idealist.

I raise a finger as if to stall her. "One . . . more place."

We walk to an unmarked side area of the food court. Several doors later, we're in the airport's central storage area. I pry open a freezer door and a cloud of icy air billows out. I hide my relief. This was starting to get awkward. We step inside and stand among shelves stacked high with in-flight meal trays.

"What have we here . . . ," Julie says, and starts digging through the low shelves, inspecting the Salisbury steaks and processed potatoes. Thanks to whatever glorious preservatives they contain, the meals appear to be edible.

Julie scans the labels on the upper shelves she can't reach and suddenly beams, showing rows of white teeth that childhood braces made perfect. "Look, pad thai! I love . . ." She trails off, looking at me uneasily. She points to the shelf. "I'll have that."

I stretch over her head and grab a tray of frozen pad thai. I don't want any of the Dead to see Julie eating this lifeless waste, these empty calories, so I lead her to a table hidden behind some collapsed postcard kiosks. I try to steer her as far away from the school as possible, but we can still hear the wretched screams echoing down the halls. Julie keeps her face utterly placid during even the shrillest wails, doing everything short of whistling a tune to show that she doesn't notice the carnage. Is this for my benefit or hers?

We sit down at the café table and I set the meal tray in front of her. "En . . . joy," I say.

She jabs at the frozen-solid noodles with a plastic fork. She looks at me. "You really don't remember much, do you? How long has it been since you ate real food?"

I shrug.

"How long has it been since you . . . died or whatever?"

I tap a finger against my temple and shake my head.

She looks me over. "Well, it can't have been very long. You look pretty good for a corpse."

I wince again at her language, but I realize she can't possibly know the sensitive cultural connotations of the word "corpse." M uses it sometimes as a rough joke, and I use it myself in some of my darker moments, but coming from an outsider it ignites a defensive indignation she wouldn't understand. I breathe deep and let it go.

"Anyway, I can't eat it like this," she says, pushing her plastic fork into the food until one of the tines snaps. "I'm going to go find a microwave. Hold on."

She gets up and wanders into one of the empty restaurants. She has forgotten her shamble, and her hips sway rhythmically. It's risky, but I find myself not caring.

"Here we go," she says when she comes back, taking a deep whiff of spicy steam. "Mmm. I haven't had Thai in forever. We don't do real food at the stadium anymore, just basic nutrition and Carbtein. Carbtein tablets, Carbtein powder, Carbtein *juice*. Jesus H. Gross." She sits down and takes a bite of freezer-burned tofu. "Oh wow. That's almost *tasty*."

I sit there and watch her eat. I notice she seems to be having trouble getting the clumpy, congealed noodles down her throat. I fetch a lukewarm bottle of beer from the restaurant's cooler and set it on the table.

Julie stops eating and looks at the bottle. She looks at me and smiles. "Why, Mr. Zombie. You read my mind." She twists off the cap and takes a long drink. "I haven't had beer in a while, either. No mind-altering substances allowed in the stadium. Have to stay alert at all times, stay vigilant, blah blah blah." She takes another drink and gives me an appraising look laced with sarcasm. "Maybe you're not such a monster, Mr. Zombie. I mean, anyone who appreciates a good beer is halfway okay in my book."

I look at her and hold a hand to my chest. "My . . . name . . . ," I wheeze, but can't think how to continue.

She sets the beer down and leans forward a little. "You have a name?"

I nod.

Her lip curls in an amused half smile. "What's your name?"

I close my eyes and think hard, trying to pull it out of the void, but I've tried this so many times before. "Rrr," I say, trying to pronounce it.

"Rur? Your name is Rur?"

I shake my head. "Rrrrr . . ."

"Rrr? It starts with 'R'?"

I nod.

"Robert?"

I shake my head.

"Rick? Rodney?"

I shake my head.

"Uh . . . Rambo?"

I let out a sigh and look at the table.

"How about I just call you 'R'? That's a start, right?"

My eyes dart to hers. "R." I feel that upward sensation in my lips again. A slow smile—the first I can remember—creeps across my face.

"Hi, R," she says. "I'm Julie. But you knew that already, didn't you. Guess I'm a fucking celebrity." She nudges the beer toward me. "Have a drink."

I eye the bottle for a second, feeling a strange kind of nausea at the thought of what's inside. Dark amber emptiness. Lifeless piss. But I don't want to ruin this improbably warm moment with my stupid undead hangups. I accept the beer and take a long pull. I can feel it trickling through tiny perforations in my stomach and dampening my shirt. And to my amazement, I can feel a slight buzz spreading through my brain. This isn't possible, of course, since I have no bloodstream for the alcohol to enter, but I feel it anyway. Is

it psychosomatic? Maybe a distant memory of the drinking experience left over from my old life? If so, apparently I was a lightweight.

Julie grins at my stupefied expression. "Drink up," she says. "I'm
actually more of a wine girl anyway."

I take another pull. I can taste her raspberry lip gloss on the rim.
I find myself imagining her dolled up for a concert, her neck-length
hair swept and styled, her small body radiant in a red party dress,
and me kissing her, the lipstick smearing onto my mouth, spreading bright rouge onto my gray lips . . .

I slide the bottle a safe distance away from me.

Julie chuckles and resumes eating. She pokes at it for a few
minutes, ignoring my presence at the table. I'm about to make a
doomed attempt at small talk when she looks up at me, all traces
of joviality gone from her face, and says, "So, 'R.' Why are you
keeping me here?"

The question hits me like a surprise slap to the face. I look at
the ceiling. I gesture around at the airport in general, toward the
distant groans of my fellow Dead. "Keep you safe."

"Bullshit."

There is silence. She looks at me hard. My eyes retreat.

"Listen," she says. "I get that you saved my life back there in the
city. And I guess I'm grateful for that. So, yeah. Thanks for saving
my life. Or sparing my life. Whatever. But you walked me *into* this
place, I'm sure you could walk me out. So again: why are you keeping me here?"

Her eyes are like hot irons on the side of my face, and I realize I
can't escape. I put a hand on my chest, over my heart. My "heart."
Does that pitiful organ still represent anything? It lies motionless in
my chest, pumping no blood, serving no purpose, and yet my feelings still seem to originate inside its cold walls. My muted sadness,
my vague longing, my rare flickers of joy. They pool in the center
of my chest and seep out from there, diluted and faint, but real.

I press my hand against my heart. Then I reach slowly toward
Julie, and press it against hers. Somehow, I manage to meet her eyes.

She looks down at my hand, then gives me a dry stare. "Are you. Fucking. Kidding me."

I withdraw my hand and drop my eyes to the table, grateful that I'm incapable of blushing. "Need . . . to wait," I mumble. "They . . . think you're . . . new convert. They'll notice."

"How long?"

"Few . . . days. They'll . . . forget."

"Jesus Christ," she sighs, and covers her eyes with her hand, shaking her head.

"You'll . . . be okay," I tell her. "Promise."

She ignores this. She pulls an iPod out of her pocket and stuffs the earbuds into her ears. She returns to her food, listening to music that's just a faint hiss to me.

This date is not going well. Once again the absurdity of my secret thoughts overwhelms me, and I want to crawl out of my skin, escape my ugly, awkward flesh and be a skeleton, naked and anonymous. I'm about to stand up and leave when Julie pulls a bud out of one ear and gives me a squinting, penetrating look. "You're . . . different, aren't you," she says.

I don't respond.

"Because I've never heard a zombie talk, other than 'Brains!' and all that silly groaning. And I've never seen a zombie take any interest in humans beyond eating them. I've *definitely* never had one buy me a drink. Are there . . . others like you?"

Again I feel the urge to blush. "Don't . . . know."

She pushes her noodles around the plate. "A few days," she repeats. I nod.

"What am I supposed to do here till it's safe to run away? I hope you don't expect me to just sit in your housejet taking blood baths all week."

I think for a moment. A rainbow of images floods my head, probably snippets of old movies I've seen, all sappy and romantic and utterly impossible. I have to get ahold of myself.

"I'll . . . entertain," I say eventually, and offer an unconvincing smile. "Be our . . . guest."

She rolls her eyes and returns to her food. The second earbud is still sitting on the table. Without looking up from her plate she casually offers it to me. I stick it in my ear, and the voice of Paul McCartney drifts into my head, singing all those wistful antonyms, yes/no, high/low, hello/good-bye/hello.

"You know John Lennon hated this song?" Julie says as it plays, speaking in my direction but not really addressing me. "He thought it was meaningless gibberish. Funny coming from the guy who wrote 'I Am the Walrus.'"

"Goo goo . . . g'joob," I say.

She stops, looks at me, tilts her head in pleasant surprise. "Yeah, exactly, right?" She takes a sip of the beer, forgetting the imprint of my lips on the bottle, and my eyes widen in brief panic. But nothing happens. Maybe my infection can't travel through soft moments like these. Maybe it needs the violence of the bite.

"Anyway," she says, "it's a little too chipper for me right now." She skips the song. I hear a brief snippet of Ava Gardner singing "Bill," then she skips a few more times, lands on an unfamiliar pop song, and cranks the volume. I'm distantly aware of the music—one of those dark, dissonant, brutally clanging chants that dominated the airwaves during the last gasps of civilization—but I have tuned out. I watch Julie bob her head from side to side with eyes closed. Even now, here, in the darkest and strangest of places with the most maca- bre of company, this music moves her and her life pulses hard. I smell it again, a white glowing vapor wafting out from under my black blood. And even for Julie's safety, I can't bring myself to smother it.

What is wrong with me? I stare at my hand, at its pale gray flesh, cool and stiff, and I dream it pink, warm and supple, able to guide and build and caress. I dream my necrotic cells shrugging off their lethargy, inflating and lighting up like Christmas deep in my dark core. Am I inventing all this like the beer buzz? A placebo? An optimistic illusion? Either way, I feel the flatline of my existence disrupting, forming heartbeat hills and valleys.

Supporting cell. Vessel undergoing lymphoid change.

Vessel continuous
with processes of
supporting cells.

Supporting cell.

Small
artery.

Supporting
cell.

"YOU NEED to corner sharper. You keep almost running off the road when you turn right."

I crank the skinny leather wheel and drop my foot onto the accelerator. The Mercedes lurches forward, throwing our heads back.

"God you're a leadfoot. Can you go easier on the gas?"

I come to a jerky stop, forget to push in the clutch, and the engine dies. Julie rolls her eyes and forces patience into her voice. "Okay, look." She restarts the engine, scoots over, and snakes her legs across mine, placing her feet on my feet. Under her pressure, I smoothly exchange gas for clutch, and the car glides forward. "Like that," she says, and returns to her seat. I release a satisfied wheeze.

We are cruising the tarmac, taxiing to and fro under the mild afternoon sun. Our hair ruffles in the breeze. Here in this moment, in this candy-red '64 roadster with this beautiful young woman, I can't help inserting myself into other, more classically filmic lives. My mind drifts, and I lose what little focus I've been able to maintain. I veer off the runway and clip the bumper of a stair truck, knocking the Boneys' church circle out of alignment. The jolt throws our heads to the side, and I hear my children's necks snap in the back-seat. They groan in protest and I shush them. I'm already embarrassed; I don't need my kids rubbing it in.

Julie examines our dented front end and shakes her head. "Damn it, R. This was a beautiful car."

My son lunges forward in another clumsy attempt to eat Julie's shoulder, and I reach back and smack him. He slumps into the seat with his arms crossed, pouting.

"No biting!" Julie scolds, still inspecting the car's damage.

I don't know why I decided to bring my kids to today's driving lesson. Julie has been attempting to teach me for a few days now, and today I just felt some obscure urge to *father*. To pass on knowledge. I'm aware it's not exactly safe. My kids are too young to recognize Living speech patterns, much less savor them like I do, and I've refreshed Julie's gruesome camouflage several times, but at close range her true nature still seeps into the air. Every now and then my kids smell it, and their slowly developing instincts take hold. I try to discipline them lovingly.

As we circle back toward our home terminal, I notice the congregation emerging from a cargo-loading gate. Like an inverted funeral procession, the Dead march out in a solemn line, taking slow, plodding steps toward the church. A clutch of Boneys leads the pilgrimage, moving forward with far more purpose than any of the fleshclad. They are the few among us who always seem to know exactly where they're going and what they're doing. They don't waver, they don't pause or change course, and their bodies no longer either grow or decay. They are static. One of them looks directly at me, and I recall a Dark Ages etching I've seen somewhere, a rotting corpse sneering at a plump young virgin.

Quod tu es, ego fui, quod ego sum, tu eris.

What you are, I once was.
What I am, you will become.

I break away from the skeleton's hollow stare. As we cruise past their line, some of the Fleshies glance at us with disinterest, and I see my wife among them. She is walking alongside a male, her hand woven into his. My kids spot her in the crowd and stand up on the backseat, waving and grunting loudly. Julie follows their gaze and sees my wife wave back at them. Julie looks at me. "Is that like . . . your wife?"

I don't respond. I look at my wife, expecting some kind of rebuke. But there is almost no recognition in her eyes. She looks at the car. She looks at me. She looks straight ahead and keeps walking, hand in hand with another man.

"Is that your wife?" Julie asks again, more forcefully. I nod. "Who's that . . . *guy* she's with?" I shrug. "Is she cheating on you or something?" I shrug. "This doesn't *bother* you?"

I shrug.

"Stop shrugging, you asshole! I know you can talk; say something."

I think for a minute. Watching my wife fade into the distance, I put a hand on my heart. "Dead." I wave a hand toward my wife. "Dead." My eyes drift toward the sky and lose their focus. "Want it . . . to hurt. But . . . doesn't."

Julie looks at me like she's waiting for more, and I wonder if I've expressed anything at all with my halting, mumbled soliloquy. Are my words ever actually audible, or do they just echo in my head while people stare at me, waiting? I want to change my punctuation. I long for exclamation marks, but I'm drowning in ellipses.

Julie watches me a moment longer, then turns to face the windshield and the oncoming scenery. On our right: the dark openings of empty boarding tunnels, once alive with eager travelers on their way to see the world, expand their horizons, find love and fame and fortune. On our left: the blackened wreckage of a Dreamliner.

"My boyfriend cheated on me once," Julie tells the windshield. "There was this girl his dad was housing while the foster homes were being set up, and they got blackout drunk one night and it just happened. It was basically an accident, and he gave me the most sincere and moving confession of all time, swore to God he loved me so much and would do anything to convince me, blah blah blah, but it didn't matter, I kept thinking about it and running it through my head and just *burning* with it. I cried every night for weeks. Practically wore the binary off all my saddest MP3s." She is shaking her head slowly. Her eyes are far away. "Things are just . . . I feel things *so hard* sometimes. When that happened with Perry, I would have loved to be more . . . like you."

I study her. She runs a finger through her hair and twists it around a little. I notice faint scars on her wrists and forearms, thin lines too symmetrical to be accidents. She blinks and glances at me abruptly, as if I just woke her from a dream. "I don't know why I'm telling you this," she says, annoyed. "Anyway, lesson's over for today. I'm tired."

Without further comment, I drive us home. I brake too late and park the car with the bumper two inches into the grille of a Miata. Julie sighs.

. . .

Later that evening we sit in the 747, cross-legged in the middle of the aisle. A plate of microwaved pad thai sits on the floor in front of Julie, cooling. I watch her in silence as she pokes at it. Even doing and saying nothing, she is entertaining to watch. She tilts her head, her eyes roam, she smiles and shifts her body. Her inner thoughts play across her face like rear-projection movies.

"It's too quiet in here," she says, and stands up. She starts digging through my stacks of records. "What's with all the vinyl? Couldn't figure out how to work an iPod?"

"Better . . . sound."

She laughs. "Oh, a purist, huh?"

I make a spinning motion in the air with my finger. "More real. More . . . alive."

She nods. "Yeah, true. Lot more trouble though." She flips through the stacks and frowns a little. "There's nothing in here newer than like . . . 1999. Is that when you died or something?"

I think about this for a moment, then shrug. It's possible, but the truth is I have no idea when I died. One might try to guess my deathday by my current state of decay, but not all of us rot at the same rate. Some of us stay funeral-parlor fresh for years, and some of us wither to bones in a matter of months, our flesh slough-ing away like dry sea foam. I don't know what causes this inequity. Maybe our bodies follow our minds' leads. Some resign themselves easily, others hold on hard.

Another obstacle to estimating my age: I have no idea what year we're in. 1999 could have been a decade ago or yesterday. One might try to deduce a timeline by looking at the crumbling streets, the toppled buildings, the rotting infrastructure, but just like us, every part of the world is decaying at its own pace. There are cit-ies that could be mistaken for Aztec ruins, and there are cities that just emptied last week, TVs still awake all night roaring static, café omelets just starting to mold.

What happened to the world was gradual. I've forgotten what it actually was, but I have faint, fetal memories of what it was like. A smoldering dread that never really caught fire till there wasn't much left to burn. Each sequential step surprised us. Then one day we woke up, and everything was gone.

"There you go again," Julie says. "Drifting off. I'm so curious what you think about when you daze out like that." I shrug, and she lets out an exasperated huff. "And there you go again, shrugging. Stop shrugging, shrugger! Answer my question. Why the stunted musical growth?"

I start to shrug and then stop myself, with some difficulty. How can I possibly explain this to her in words? The slow death of Qui-xote. The abandoning of quests, the surrendering of desires, the settling in and settling down that is the inevitable fate of the Dead.

"We don't . . . think . . . new things," I begin, straining to kick through my short-sheeted diction. "I . . . find things . . . sometimes. But we don't . . . seek."

"Really," Julie says. "Well that's a fucking tragedy." She continues to dig through my records, but her tone starts to escalate as she speaks. "You don't think about new things? You don't 'seek'? What's that even mean? You don't seek what? Music? Music is *life*! It's physical emotion—you can touch it! It's neon ecto-energy sucked out of spirits and switched into sound waves for your ears to swallow. Are you telling me, what, that it's boring? You don't have time for it?"

There is nothing I can say to this. I find myself praying to the ghastly mouth of the open sky that Julie never changes. That she never wakes up one day to find herself older and wiser.

"Anyway, you've still got some good stuff in here," she says, letting her indignation deflate. "Great stuff, really. Here, let's do this one again. Can't go wrong with Frank." She puts on a record and returns to her pad thai. "The Lady Is a Tramp" fills the plane's cabin, and she gives me a crooked little smile. "My theme song," she says, and stuffs her mouth full of noodles.

Out of morbid curiosity, I pull one off her plate and chew it. There is no taste at all. It's like imaginary food, like chewing air. I turn my head and spit it into my palm. Julie doesn't notice. She seems far away again, and I watch the colors and shapes of her thought-film flickering behind her face. After a few minutes, she swallows a bite and looks up at me.

"R," she says in a tone of casual curiosity. "Who did you kill?"

I stiffen. The music fades out of my awareness.

"In that high-rise. Before you saved me. I saw the blood on your face. Whose was it?"

I just look at her. Why does she have to ask me this. Why can't her memories fade to black like mine. Why can't she just live with me alone in the dark, swimming in the abyss of inked-out history.

"I just need to know who it was." Her expression betrays nothing. Her eyes are locked on mine, unblinking.

"No one," I mumble. "Some . . . kid."

"There's this theory that you guys eat brains because you get to relive the person's life. True?"

I shrug, trying not to squirm. I feel like a toddler caught finger-painting the walls. Or killing dozens of people.

"Who was it?" she presses. "Don't you remember?"

I consider lying. I remember a few faces from that room; I could roll the dice and just pick one, probably some random recruit she didn't even know, and she would let it go and never bring it up again. But I can't do it. I can't lie to her any more than I can spit out the indigestible truth. I'm trapped.

Julie lets her eyes auger into me for a long minute, then she falters. "Was it Berg?" she offers, so quietly she's almost talking to herself. "The kid with the acne? I bet it was Berg. That guy was a dick. He called Nora a mulatto and he was staring at my ass that entire salvage. Which Perry didn't even notice, of course. If it was Berg, I'm almost glad you got him."

I try to catch her gaze to make sense of this reversal, but now she's the one avoiding eye contact. "Anyway," she says, "whoever · killed Perry . . . I just want you to know I don't blame them for it."

I tense again. "You . . . don't?"

"No. I mean, I think I get it. You don't have a choice, right? And to be honest . . . I'd never say this to anyone, but . . . ." She stirs her food. "It's kind of a relief that it finally happened."

I frown. "What?"

"To be able to finally stop dreading it."

"Perry . . . dying?"

I instantly regret speaking his name. Rolling off my tongue, the syllables taste like his blood.

Julie nods, still looking at her plate. When she speaks again her voice is soft and faint, the voice of memories longing to be forgotten. "Something . . . happened to him. A lot of things, actually. I guess there came a point where he just couldn't absorb any more, so he flipped over into a different person. He was this brilliant, fiery kid, so weird and funny and full of dreams, and then . . . just quit all his plans, joined Security . . . it was scary how fast he changed. He said he was doing everything for me, that it was time for him to grow up and face reality, take responsibility and all that. But everything I loved about him—everything that made him who he *was*—just started rotting. He gave up, basically. Quit his life. Real death was just the next logical step." She pushes her plate aside. "We talked about dying all the time. He just kept bringing it up. In the middle of a wild make-out session he'd stop and be like, 'Julie, what do you think the average life expectancy is these days?' Or, 'Julie, when I die, will you be the one to debrain me?' Height of romance, right?"

She looks out the airplane window at the distant mountains. "I tried to talk him down. Tried *really* hard to keep him here, but over the last couple years it got pretty clear to everyone. He was just . . . gone. I don't know if anything short of Christ and King Arthur returning to redeem the world could have brought him back. *I* sure wasn't enough." She looks at me. "Will he come back to life, though? As one of you?"

I drop my eyes, remembering the juicy pink taste of his brain. I shake my head.

She is quiet for a while. "It's not like I'm not *sad* that he's gone. I am, I . . ." Her voice wobbles a little. She pauses, clears her throat. "I really am. But he wanted it. I knew he wanted it." A tear escapes one eye and she seems startled by it. She brushes it away like a mosquito.

I stand up, take her plate, fold it into the trash bin. When I sit back down her eyes are dry but still red. She sniffs and gives me a weak smile. "I guess I talk a lot of shit about Perry, but it's not like I'm such a shiny happy person either, you know? I'm a wreck too, I'm just . . . still alive. A wreck in progress." She laughs a quick, broken laugh. "It's weird, I never talk about this stuff with anyone, but you're . . . I mean you're so *quiet,* you just sit there and listen. It's like talking to God." Her smile drifts away and she is absent for a moment. When she speaks again her voice is cautious but flat, and her eyes roam the cabin, studying window rivets and warning labels. "I did a lot of drugs when I was younger. Started when I was twelve and tried almost everything. I still drink and smoke pot when I get the chance. I even had sex with a guy for money once, when I was thirteen. Not because I wanted the money—even back then money was pretty worthless. Just because it was awful, and maybe I felt like I deserved it." She looks at her wrist, those thin scars like an entry stamp for some horrible concert. "All the shitty stuff people do to themselves . . . it can all be the same thing, you know? Just a way to drown out your own voice. To kill your memories without having to kill yourself."

There is a long silence. Her eyes roam the floor and mine stay on her face, waiting for her to come home. She takes a deep breath, looks at me, and gives a little shrug. "Shrug," she says in a small voice, and forces a smile.

Slowly, I stand up and go over to my record player. I pull out one of my favorite LPs, an obscure compilation of Sinatra songs from various albums. I don't know why I like this one so much. I once spent three full days motionless in front of it, just watching the vinyl spin. I know the grooves in this record better than the grooves in my palms. People used to say music was the great communicator; I wonder if this is still true in this posthuman, posthumous age. I put the record on and begin to move the needle as it plays, skipping measures, skipping songs, dancing through the spirals to find the words I want to fill the air. The phrases are off key, off tempo, punctuated by loud scratches like the ripping of fascia tissue, but the tone is flawless. Frank's buttery baritone says it better than my croaky vocals ever could had I the diction of a Kennedy. I stand over the record, cutting and pasting the contents of my heart into an airborne collage.

I don't care if you are called—scratch—*when people say you're*—scratch—*wicked witchcraft*—scratch—*don't change a hair for me, not if you*—scratch—*'cause you're sensational*—scratch—*you just the way you are*—scratch—*you're sensational . . . sensational . . . That's all . . .*

I leave the record to play out its normal repertoire and sit back down in front of Julie. She stares at me with damp, red-rimmed eyes. I press my hand against her chest, feeling the gentle thump inside. A tiny voice speaking in code.

Julie sniffs. She wipes a finger across her nose. "What *are* you?" she asks me for the second time.

I smile a little. Then I get up and exit the plane, leaving her question floating there, still unanswerable. In my palm I can feel the echo of her pulse, standing in for the absence of mine.

. . .

That night, lying on the floor of Gate 12, I fall asleep. The new sleep is different, of course. Our bodies aren't "tired," we aren't "resting." But every so often, after days or weeks of unrelenting consciousness, our minds simply can't carry the weight anymore, and we collapse. We allow ourselves to die, to shut down and have no thoughts at all for hours, days, weeks. However long it takes to regather the electrons of our ids, to keep ourselves intact a little longer. There's nothing peaceful or lovely about it; it's ugly and compulsory, an iron lung for the wheezing husks of our souls, but tonight . . . something different happens.

I dream.

Underdeveloped, murky, faded to sepia like centuries-old film, scenes from my former life flicker in the void of sleep. Amorphous figures walk through melting doorways into shadowy rooms. Voices crawl through my head, deep and slurring like drunken giants. I play ambiguous sports, I watch incoherent movies, I talk and laugh with anonymous blurs. Among these foggy snapshots of an unexamined life, I catch glimpses of a pastime, some passionate pursuit long ago sacrificed on the blood-soaked altar of pragmatism. Guitar? Dancing? Dirt bikes? Whatever it was, it fails to penetrate the thick smog choking my memory. Everything remains dark. Blank. Nameless.

I have begun to wonder where I came from. The person I am now, this fumbling, stumbling supplicant . . . was I built on the foundations of my old life, or did I rise from the grave a blank slate? How much of me is inherited, and how much is my own creation? Questions that were once just idle musings have begun to feel strangely urgent. Am I firmly rooted to what came before? Or can I choose to deviate?

I wake up staring at the distant ceiling. The memories, empty as they already were, evaporate completely. It's still night, and I can hear my wife having sex with her new lover behind the door of a nearby staff room. I try to ignore them. I already walked in on them once today. I heard noises, the door was wide open, so I walked in. There they were, naked, awkwardly slamming their bodies together, grunting and groping each other's pale flesh. He was limp. She was dry. They watched each other with puzzled expressions, as if some unknown force had shoved them together into this moist tangle of limbs. Their eyes seemed to ask each other, "Who the hell are you?" as they jiggled and jerked like meat marionettes.

They didn't stop when they noticed me. They just looked at me and kept grinding. I nodded, and walked back to Gate 12, and this was the final weight that broke my mind's kneecaps. I crumpled to the floor and slept.

I don't know why I'm awake already, after just a few feverish hours. I still feel the weight of my accumulated thoughts bearing down on my tender brain, but I don't think I can sleep anymore. A burr and a buzz tickle my mind, keeping me alert. I reach for the only thing that's ever helped in times like these. I reach into my pocket and pull out my last chunk of cerebrum.

As residual life energy fades from the brain, the useless clutter is first to go. The movie quotes, the radio jingles, the celebrity gossip and political slogans, they all melt away, leaving only the most potent and wrenching of the memories. As the brain dies, the life inside clarifies and distills. It ages like a fine wine.

The piece in my hand has shriveled somewhat, taking on a

brownish gray tint. I'll be lucky to get another few minutes of Perry's life out of this, but what blazing, urgent minutes these will be. Closing my eyes, I pop it into my mouth and chew, thinking, *Don't leave me yet, Perry. Just a little longer. Just a little more. Please.*

. . .

I erupt from the dark, crushing tunnel into a flash of light and noise. A new kind of air surrounds me, dry and cold as they wipe the last smears of home off my skin. I feel a sharp pain as they snip something, and suddenly I am less. I am no one but myself, tiny and feeble and utterly alone. I am lifted and swung through great heights across yawning distances and given to Her. She wraps around me, so much bigger and softer than I ever imagined from inside, and I strain my eyes open. I see Her. She is immense, cosmic. She is the world. The world smiles down on me, and when She speaks it's the voice of God, vast and resonant with meaning, but words unknowable, ringing gibberish in my blank white mind.

She says—

. . .

I am in a dark, crooked room, gathering medical supplies and loading them into boxes. A small crew of civilian recruits is with me on this salvage, all of them handpicked by Colonel Rosso except one. One of them picked herself. One of them saw a look in my eyes and worried. One of them wants to save me.

"Did you hear that?" Julie says, glancing around.

"No," I reply instantly, and keep loading.

"I did," Nora says, brushing her frizzy curls out of her eyes. "Pear, maybe we should—"

"We're fine. We scoped it out, we're secure. Just work."

They watch me constantly, tensed like hospital orderlies, ready to intervene. It changes nothing. I won't endanger them but I'll still find a way. When I'm alone, when no one's looking, I'll do it. I'll make it happen. They keep trying and trying but the beauty of their love only drives me deeper. Why can't they understand it's too late?

A noise. I hear it now. A rumble of footsteps up the staircase, a chorus of groans. Are Julie's ears so much more sensitive or have I stopped listening? I pick up my shotgun and turn—

No, I blurt into the middle of the vision. *Not this. This isn't what I want to see.*

To my surprise, everything halts. Perry looks up at me, the voice in the sky. "These are *my* memories, remember? You're the guest here. If you don't want to see it, you can spit it out."

This is a shock. The memory has come unscripted. Am I having a conversation with the very mind I'm digesting? I don't know how much of this is actually Perry and how much is just me, but I'm swept along.

We should be seeing your life! I shout down at him. *Not this! Why would you want your last thought to be a replay of your dirty, meaningless death?*

"You think death isn't meaningful?" he retorts, chambering a round in his shotgun. Julie and the others wait in their positions like background props, fidgeting impatiently. "Wouldn't you want to remember *yours* if you could? How else are you going to reverse-engineer yourself into something new?"

Something new?

"Of course, you dumb corpse." He puts his eye to the sight and makes a slow scan of the room, holding for a moment on Berg. "There are a thousand kinds of life and death across the whole metaphysical spectrum, not to mention the metaphorical. You don't want to stay dead for the rest of your life, do you?"

Well, no . . .

"Then relax, and let me do what I need to do."

I swallow the lump in my throat and say, *Okay . . .*

. . .

—pick up my shotgun and turn, just as the thundering footfalls reach our floor. The door blows open and they burst inside, roaring. We shoot them, we shoot them, we shoot them, but there are too many, and they're *fast*. I crouch over Julie, shielding her as best I can.

No. Oh God. This is not what I wanted.

A tall skinny one is suddenly behind me, grabbing my legs. I fall and hit the table and my vision flashes red. Everything is wrong, but as the red fades to black I still allow an exultant shout, one last selfish orgasm before I go to sleep forever:

Finally. Finally!

And then—

. . .

"Perry." A jab in my ribs. "Perry!"

"What?"

"Don't you go to sleep on me now."

I open my eyes. An hour of sun glaring through my closed lids has faded all the colors of the world to bluish gray, like an old movie poster in a dying local video store. I turn my head to look at her. She smiles wickedly and jabs me again. "Never mind. Go ahead and sleep."

Beyond her face I see the looming white posts of the stadium roof arches, and beyond that, the deep cerulean sky. I slowly alternate my focus between her and the sky, letting her face blur into a peach-and-gold cloud, then refocusing it.

"What?" she says.

"Tell me something hopeful."

"What kind of hopeful?"

I sit up, crossing my arms over my knees. I look out at the surrounding city, the crumbling buildings, the empty streets and lonely sky, clean and blue and deathly quiet without its white-sketching airplanes.

"Tell me this isn't the end of the world."

She lies there for a minute, looking up at the sky. Then she sits up and pulls one of her earbuds out of her tangled blond hair. She gently plugs it into my ear.

The warbled strumming of a broken guitar, the swelling of an orchestra, the oohs and ahhs of a studio choir, and John Lennon's weary, woozy voice, singing limitless undying love. Everyone playing this song is now bones in a grave, but here they are anyway, exciting and inviting me, calling me on and on. The final fadeout breaks something inside me, and tears squeeze out of my eyes. The brilliant truth and the inescapable lie, sitting side by side just like Julie and I. Can I have both? Can I survive in this doomed world and still love Julie, who dreams above it? For this moment at least, tied to her brain by the white wire between our ears, I feel like I can.

Nothing's gonna change my world, Lennon chants, over and over. *Nothing's gonna change my world.*

Julie sings a high harmony and I murmur a low. There on the hot white roof of humanity's last outpost, we look out over our rapidly, hopelessly, irretrievably changing world, and we sing:

Nothing's gonna change my world. Nothing's gonna change my world.

. . .

I am staring at the airport ceiling again. I drop the last chunk of Perry's brain into my mouth and chew, but nothing happens. I spit it out like gristle. The story is over. The life is gone.

I find my eyes burning again, craving tears that my ducts can't supply. I feel as if I've lost someone dear. A brother. A twin. Where is his soul now? Am I Perry Kelvin's afterlife?

I finally drift back to sleep. I'm in the darkness. The molecules of my mind are still scattered, and I float through oily black space, trying to swipe them up like fireflies. Every time I go to sleep, I know I may never wake up. How could anyone expect to? You drop your tiny, helpless mind into a bottomless well, crossing your fingers and hoping that when you pull it out on its flimsy fishing wire it hasn't been gnawed to bones by nameless beasts below. Hoping you pull up anything at all. Maybe this is why I sleep only a few hours a month. I don't want to die again. This has become clearer and clearer to me recently, a desire so sharp and focused I can hardly believe it's mine: I don't want to die. I don't want to disappear. I want to stay.

Semicircular canals.

Cochlea.

Opening of aqueductus vestibuli.

Bristle passed through foramen rotundum.

Opening of aqueductus cochleæ.

AWAKE to the sound of screaming.

My eyes snap open and I spit a few bugs out of my mouth. I lurch upright. The sound is far away but it's not from the school. It lacks the plaintive panic of the school's still-breathing cadavers. I recognize the defiant spark in these screams, the relentless hope in the face of undeniable hopelessness. I leap to my feet and run faster than any zombie has ever run.

Following the screams, I find Julie at the Departures gate. She is backed into a corner, surrounded by six drooling Dead. They close in on her, rearing back a little each time she swings her smoke-belching hedge trimmer but advancing steadily. I rush at them from behind and crash into their tight circle, scattering them like bowling pins. The one closest to Julie I punch so hard the bones of my hand shatter into seashell crumbs. His face cracks inward and he drops. The next closest I ram into the wall, then grab his head and smash it into the concrete until his brain pops and he goes down. One of them grabs me from behind and takes a bite out of my rib meat. I reach back, tear off his rotten arm, and swing it at him like Babe Ruth. His head spins a full three-sixty on his neck, then tilts, tears, and falls off. I stand there in front of Julie, brandishing the musclebound limb, and the Dead stop advancing.

"Julie!" I snarl at them while pointing at her. "Julie!"

They stare at me. They sway back and forth.

"Julie!" I say again, not sure how else to put it. I walk up to her and press my hand against her heart. I drop the arm-club and put my other hand on my own heart. "Julie."

The room is silent except for the low grumble of her hedge trimmer. The air is thick with the rotten-apricot smell of stabilized gasoline, and I notice several decapitated corpses I had nothing to do with lying at her feet. *Well done, Julie,* I think with a faint smile. *You are a lady and a scholar.*

"What . . . the *fuck!*" growls a deep voice behind me.

A tall, bulky form is picking itself up off the floor. It's the first one I attacked, the one I punched in the face. It's M. I didn't even recognize him in the heat of the moment. Now, with his cheekbone crushed into his head, he's even harder to identify. He glares at me and rubs his face. "What are . . . doing, you . . ." He trails off, at a loss for even simple words.

"Julie," I say yet again, as if this is an irrefutable argument. And in a way, it is. That one word, a fully fleshed *name.* It's having the effect of a glowing, chattering cell phone raised before a mob of primitives. All the remaining Dead stare at Julie in hushed silence, except M. He is baffled and enraged.

"Living!" he sputters. "Eat!"

I shake my head. "No."

"Eat!"

"No!"

"*Eat,* fucking—"

"*Hey!*"

M and I both turn. Julie has stepped out from behind me. She glares at M and revs the trimmer. "Fuck off," she says. She links an arm into my elbow, and I feel a tingle of warmth spreading out from her touch.

M looks at her, then at me, back to her, then back to me. His permanent grimace is tight. We appear to be in a standoff, but before it can escalate any further the stillness is pierced by a reverberating noise, an eerie, airless horn blast.

We all turn to the escalators. Yellowed skeletons are rising up one by one from the floors below. A small committee of Boneys emerges from the stairs and approaches me and Julie. They stop in front of us and fan out into a line. Julie backs away a little, her bravado flattening under their black, eyeless stares. Her grip on my arm tightens.

One of them steps forward and stops in front of me, inches from my face. No breath wafts from its hollow mouth, but I can feel a faint, low hum emanating from its bones. This hum is not found in me, nor in M, nor in any of the other fleshclad Dead, and I begin to wonder what exactly these dried-up creatures really are. I can no longer believe in any voodoo spell or laboratory virus. This is something deeper, darker. This comes from the cosmos, from the stars, or the unknown blackness behind them. The shadows in God's boarded-up basement.

The ghoul and I are locked in a stare-down, toe to toe, eye to eyesocket. I don't blink, and it can't. What seems like hours pass. Then it does something that slightly undermines the horror of its presence. It raises a stack of Polaroids in its pointy fingers and begins handing them to me, one by one. I'm reminded of a proud old man showing off his grandkids, but the skeleton's grin is far from grandfatherly, and the photos are far from heartwarming. Off-the-hip shots of some kind of battle. Organized ranks of soldiers firing rockets into our hives, rifles popping us off with precision, one two three. Private citizens with their machetes and chain saws hacking through us like blackberry vines, spattering our dark juices on the camera lens. Monumental stacks of freshly rekilled corpses, soaked in gasoline and lit.

Smoke. Blood. Family photos from our vacation in Hell.

But as unsettling as this slide show is, I've seen it before. I've witnessed the Boneys performing it dozens of times, usually for children. They drift around the airport with cameras dangling from their vertebrae, occasionally following us on feeding trips, lingering in the back to document the bloodshed, and I always wonder what it is they're after. Their subject matter follows a precise theme that never varies: Corpses. Battles. Newly converted zombies. And themselves. Their meeting rooms are wallpapered with these photos, floor to ceiling, and sometimes they drag in a young zombie and make him stand there for hours, even days, silently appreciating their work.

Now this skeleton, identical to the rest, hands me these Polaroids slowly and civilly, confident that the images speak for themselves. The message of today's sermon is clear: *inevitability*. The immutable, binary results of our interactions with the Living.

They die / we die.

A noise rises from where the skeleton's throat would be, a crowing sound full of pride and reproach and stiff, rigid righteousness. It says everything it and the rest of the Boneys have to say, their motto and mantra. It says, *I rest my case,* and *That's the way it is,* and *Because I said so.*

Looking straight into its eyesockets, I let the photos fall to the floor. I rub my fingers against each other as if trying to brush off some dirt.

The skeleton does not react. It just stares at me with that horrible, hollow stare, so utterly motionless it seems to have stopped time. The dark hum in its bones dominates everything, a low sine wave prickling with sour overtones. And then, so abruptly it makes me jump, the creature pivots away and rejoins its comrades. It barks out one last horn blast, and the Boneys descend the escalator. The rest of the Dead disperse, sneaking hungry glances at Julie. M is the last to go. He scowls at me, then lumbers away. Julie and I are alone.

I turn to face her. Now that the situation has settled and the blood on the floor is drying, I'm finally able to contemplate what's happening here, and somewhere deep in my chest, my heart wheezes. I gesture toward what I assume is the Departures sign and give Julie a questioning look, unable to hide the hurt behind it.

Julie looks at the floor. "It's been a few days," she mumbles. "You said a few days."

"Wanted to . . . take you home. Say good-bye."

"Why? What's the point? I have to leave. I mean I can't *stay* here. You realize that, right?"

Yes. Of course I realize that.

She's right, and I'm ridiculous.

And yet . . .

But what if . . .

I want to do something impossible. Something astounding and unheard of. I want to scrub the moss off the space shuttle and fly Julie to the moon and colonize it, or float a capsized cruise ship to some distant island where no one will protest us, or just harness the magic that brings me into the brains of the Living and use it to bring Julie into mine, because it's warm in here, it's quiet and lovely, and in here we aren't an absurd juxtaposition, we are perfect.

She finally meets my eyes. She looks like a lost child, confused and sad. "But thanks for, uh . . . saving me. Again."

With great effort, I pull out of my reverie and give her a smile. "Any . . . time."

She hugs me. It's tentative at first, a little scared, and yes, a little repulsed, but then she melts into it. She rests her head against my cold neck and embraces me. Unable to believe what's happening, I put my arms around her and just hold her.

I almost swear I can feel my heart thumping. But it must just be hers, pressed tight against my chest.

. . .

We walk back to the 747. Nothing has been resolved, but she's agreed to postpone her escape. After the messy scene we just caused, it seems prudent to lay low for a bit. I don't know exactly how much the Boneys will object to the irregularity Julie represents, because this is the first time anyone has challenged them. My case has no precedent.

We enter a connecting hallway suspended over a parking lot, and Julie's hair dances in the wind whistling through shattered windows. Decorative indoor shrub beds have been overrun with wild daisies. Julie sees them, smiles, picks a handful. I pluck one from her hands and clumsily stick it in her hair. It still has its leaves, and it protrudes awkwardly from the side of her head. But she leaves it in.

"Do you remember what it was like living with people?" she asks as we walk. "Before you died?"

I wave a hand in the air vaguely.

"Well, it's changed. I was ten when my hometown got overrun and we came here, so I remember what it used to be like. Things are so different now. Everything's gotten smaller and more cramped, noisier and colder." She pauses at the end of the overpass and looks out the empty windows at a pale sunset. "We're all corralled in the stadium with nothing to think about but surviving to the end of the day. No one writes, no one reads, no one really even talks." She spins the daisies in her hands, sniffs one. "We don't have flowers anymore. Just crops."

I look out the opposite windows, at the dark side of the sunset. "Because of *us*."

"No, not because of you. I mean, yeah, because of you, but not *just* you. Do you really not remember what it was like before? All the political and social breakdowns? The global flooding? Wars and riots and constant bombings? The world was pretty far gone before you guys even showed up. You were just the final judgment."

"But we're . . . what's killing you. Now."

She nods. "Sure, zombies are the most obvious threat now. The fact that almost everyone who dies comes back and kills two more

70

people . . . yeah, that's some grim math. But the root problem has to be bigger than that, or maybe smaller, more subtle, and killing a million zombies isn't going to fix it, because there's always going to be more."

Two Dead appear from around a corner and lunge at Julie. I crack their heads together and drop them, wondering if I might have studied martial arts in my old life. I seem to be a lot stronger than my lean frame suggests.

"My dad doesn't care about any of that," Julie continues as we walk down the loading tunnel and enter the plane. "He was an Army general back when the government was still going on, so that's how he thinks. Locate the threat, kill the threat, wait for orders from the big-picture people. But since the big picture is gone and the people who drew it are all dead, what are we supposed to do now? No one knows, so we do nothing. Just salvage supplies, kill zombies, and expand our walls farther out into the city. Basically Dad's idea of saving humanity is building a really big concrete box, putting everybody in it, and standing at the door with guns till we get old and die." She flops across a seat and takes a deep breath, lets it out again. She sounds so tired. "I mean obviously, staying alive is pretty fucking important . . . but there's got to be something beyond that, right?"

My mind drifts through the last few days, and I find myself thinking about my kids. The image of them in that hallway, making a toy out of a stapler, playing together and laughing. *Laughing.* Have I seen other Dead children laugh? I can't remember. But thinking about them, that look in their eyes as they hugged my legs, I feel strange emotions welling up in me. What *is* that look? Where does it come from? In that lovely film projected on their faces, what beautiful score is playing? What language is the dialogue? Can it be translated?

The jet cabin is silent for several minutes. Lying on her back, Julie cranes her head and looks out the window upside down. "You live in an airplane, R," she says. "That's pretty cool. I miss seeing airplanes in the sky. Have I told you about how I miss airplanes?"

I go to the record player. The Sinatra record is still going, skipping on a blank inner groove, so I nudge the needle to "Come Fly with Me."

Julie smiles. "Smooth."

I lie out on the floor and fold my hands over my chest, gazing up at the ceiling, haphazardly mouthing the song's words.

"Have I also told you," Julie says, twisting her head to look at me, "that in a weird way it's actually been kinda nice, being here? I mean aside from almost getting eaten like four times. It's been years since I've had this much time to just breathe and think and look out windows. And you have a pretty decent record collection."

She reaches down and sticks a daisy into my folded hands, then giggles. It takes me a moment to realize I look like the corpse in an old-fashioned funeral. I jolt upright as if struck by lightning, and Julie bursts out laughing. I can't help a little smile.

"And you know the craziest part, R?" she says. "Sometimes I barely believe you're a zombie. Sometimes I think you're just wearing stage makeup, because when you smile . . . it's pretty hard to believe."

I lie down again and fold my hands behind my head. Embarrassed, I keep my face mirthless until Julie falls asleep. Then I slowly let it creep back, smiling at the ceiling as the stars flicker to life outside.

• • •

Early the following afternoon, her soft snoring tapers off. Still lying on the floor, I wait for the sounds of her waking up. The shifting of weight, the tight inhale of breath, the small whimper.

"R," she says groggily.

"Yeah."

"They're right, you know."

"Who?"

"Those skeletons. I saw the pictures they showed you. They're right about what'll probably happen."

I say nothing.

"One of our people got away. When your group attacked us, my friend Nora hid under a desk. She saw you . . . capture me. It might take Security some time to track which hive you took me to, but they'll figure it out soon, and my dad will come here. He'll kill you."

"Already . . . dead," I reply.

"No you're not," she says, and sits up in her chair. "You're obviously not."

I think about what she's saying for a moment. "You want . . . to go back."

"No," she says, and then seems startled. "I mean, yeah, of course, but . . ." She lets out a flustered groan. "It doesn't matter either way, I *have* to. They're going to come here and wipe you out. *All* of you."

I fall silent again.

"I don't want to be responsible for that, okay?" She seems to be pondering something as she talks. Her voice is tight, conflicted. "I've always been taught that zombies are just walking corpses to be disposed of, but . . . look at you. You're more than that, right? So what if there are others like you?"

My face is stiff.

Julie sighs. "R . . . maybe you're sappy enough to find martyrdom romantic, but what about the rest of these people? Your kids? What about them?"

She is nudging my mind down streets it's rarely traveled. For however many months or years I've been here, I've never thought of these other creatures walking around me as people. Human, yes, but not *people*. We eat and sleep and shuffle through the fog, walking a marathon with no finish line, no medals, no cheering. None of the airport's citizens seemed much perturbed when I killed four of us today. We view ourselves the same way we view the Living: as meat. Nameless, faceless, disposable. But Julie's right. I have thoughts. I have some kind of a soul, shriveled and impotent as it may be. So maybe the others do, too. Maybe there's something there worth salvaging.

"Okay," I say. "You have . . . to leave."

She nods silently.

"But I'm . . . going with you."

She laughs. "To the stadium? Tell me that was a lame joke."

I shake my head.

"Well, let's think about that a moment, shall we? You? Are a zombie. As well preserved and kinda charming as you may be, you *are* a zombie, and guess what everyone in the stadium over the age of ten is training seven days a week to do?"

I say nothing.

"Exactly. To kill zombies. So, if I can make this any clearer—you can't come with me. Because they will *kill* you."

I clench my jaw. "So?"

She tilts her head and her sarcasm dissolves. Her voice becomes tentative. "What do you mean 'so'? Do you *want* to be dead? *Really* dead?"

My reflex is to shrug. The shrug has been my default response for so long. But as I lie there on the floor with her worried eyes looking down at me, I remember the feeling that jolted through me the moment I woke up yesterday, that feeling of *No!* and *Yes!* That feeling of *anti-shrug*.

"No," I say to the ceiling. "I don't want to die."

As I say it, I realize I've just broken my syllable record.

Julie nods. "Well, good."

I take a deep breath and stand up. "Need . . . to think," I tell her, avoiding eye contact. "Back . . . soon. Lock . . . door."

I leave the plane, and her eyes follow me out.

. . .

People are staring at me. I was always a bit of an outsider here in the airport, but now my mystique has thickened like port wine. When I enter a room, everyone stops moving and watches me. But the looks on their faces aren't entirely cold. There are notes of fascination buried in their reproach.

I find M studying his reflection in a lobby window, sticking his fingers in his mouth and prodding. I think he's trying to put his face back together.

"Hi," I say, standing a safe distance away.

He glares at me for a moment, then looks back at the window. He gives his upper jaw a firm push, and his cheekbone pops back into place with a loud snap. He turns to me and smiles. "How's . . . look?"

I wiggle my hand noncommittally. Half of his face looks relatively normal. The other half is still a bit concave.

He sighs and looks back at the window. "Bad . . . news . . . for the ladies."

I smile. As deeply different as we are, I have to give M some credit. He is the only zombie I've met who's managed to maintain a dangling scrap of humor. Also worthy of note . . . four syllables without pause. He has just matched my former record.

"Sorry," I say to him. "About . . . that."

He doesn't respond.

"Talk to you . . . a minute?"

He hesitates, then shrugs again. He follows me to the nearest set of chairs. We sit down in a dark, defunct Starbucks. Two cups of moldy espresso sit in front of us, abandoned long ago by two friends, two business partners, two people who just met in the terminal and bonded over a shared interest in brains.

"Really . . . sorry," I say. "Irrit . . . able. Lately."

M narrows his brow. "What . . . going on . . . with you?"

"Don't . . . know."

"Brought back . . . Living girl?"

"Yes."

"You . . . crazy?"

"Maybe."

"What's . . . feel like?"

"What?"

"Living . . . sex."

I give him a warning look.

"She's . . . hot. I would—"

"Shut up."

He chuckles. "Fucking . . . with you."

"It's not . . . that. Not . . . like that."

"Then . . . what?"

I hesitate, not sure how to answer. "More."

His face gets eerily serious. "What. Love?"

I think about this, and I find no response beyond a simple shrug. So I shrug, trying not to smile.

M throws back his head and does his best impression of laughter. He thumps me on the shoulder. "My . . . boy! Lover . . . boy!"

"Leaving . . . with her," I tell him.

"Where?"

"Taking . . . her home."

"Stadium?"

I nod. "Keep her . . . safe."

M considers this, watching me with concern clouding his bruised face.

"I . . . know," I sigh.

M folds his arms over his chest. "What . . . going on . . . with you?" he asks me again.

And again, I have no answer but a shrug.

"You . . . okay?"

"Changing."

He nods uncertainly, and I squirm under his probing eyes. I'm not used to having deep conversations with M. Or with any of the Dead, for that matter. I rotate the coffee cup in my fingers, intently studying its fuzzy green contents.

"When . . . figure out . . . ," M finally says, in a tone more earnest than I've ever heard from him, "tell me. Tell . . . *us*."

I wait for him to crack wise, turn it into a joke, but he doesn't. Rare for him or anyone else in this mordant era: he is actually sincere.

"I will," I say. I slap him on the shoulder and stand up. As I walk away, he gives me that same strange look I'm finding on the faces of all the Dead. That mixture of confusion, fear, and faint anticipation.

THE SCENE as Julie and I make our way out of the airport re-sembles either a wedding procession or a buffet line. The Dead are lined up in the halls to watch us pass. Every last one of them is here. They look restless, agitated, and would clearly love to devour Julie, but they don't move or make a sound. Over Julie's heated protests I asked M to escort us out. He follows a few paces behind, huge and vigilant, scanning the crowd like a Secret Service agent.

The unnatural silence of a room full of people who don't breathe is surreal. I swear I can hear Julie's heart pounding. She is trying to look cool and calm, but her darting eyes betray her.

"Are you sure about this?" she whispers.

"Yes."

"There's like . . . hundreds of them."

"Keep you safe."

"Right, right, I'm completely safe, how could I forget." Her voice grows very small. "Seriously, R . . . I mean I've seen you kick a few asses, but you know if they decide to ring the dinner bell right now I'm going to be sushi."

"They . . . won't," I tell her with a surprising degree of confidence. "We're . . . new thing. Haven't . . . seen before. Look at them."

She looks closer at the surrounding faces, and I hope she can see what I've been seeing. The strange array of their reactions to us, to the anomaly we represent. I know they will let us through, but Julie appears unconvinced. A tight wheeze creeps into her breathing. She fumbles in her messenger bag and pulls out an inhaler, takes a hit from it and holds it in, eyes still darting.

"You'll . . . be okay," M says in his low rumble.

She expels the breath and whips her head around to glare at him. "Who the fuck asked *you,* you fucking blood sausage? I should have hedge-trimmed you in half yesterday."

M chuckles and raises his eyebrows at me. "Got . . . a live one . . . 'R.'"

We continue unmolested all the way to the Departures gate. As we step out into the daylight, I feel a nervous buzz in my stomach. At first I think it's just the everpresent terror of the open sky, now looming over us in bruised shades of gray and purple, boiling with high-altitude thunderheads. But it's not the sky. It's the *sound.* That low, warbling tone, like baritone madmen humming nursery rhymes. I don't know if I've just gotten more attuned to it or if it's actually louder, but I hear it even before the Boneys make their appearance.

"Shit, oh shit," Julie whispers to herself.

They march around both corners of the loading zone and form a line in front of us. There are more of them than I've ever seen in one place. I had no idea there even *were* this many, at least not in our airport.

"Problem," M says. "They look . . . pissed."

He's right. There is something different in their demeanor. Their body language seems stiffer, if that's possible. Yesterday they were a jury stepping in to review our case. Today they are judges, announcing the sentence. Or perhaps executioners, executing it.

"Leaving!" I shout at them. "Taking her back! So they won't . . . come here!"

The skeletons don't move or respond. Their bones harmonize in some sour alien key.

"What . . . do you want?" I demand.

The entire front row raises its arms in unison and points at Julie. It strikes me how wrong this is, how fundamentally different these creatures are from the rest of us. The Dead are adrift on a foggy sea of ennui. They don't *do* things in unison.

"Taking her *back*!" I shout louder, faltering in my attempt at reasonable discourse. "If . . . kill her . . . they'll *come here*. Kill . . . *us*!"

There is no hesitation, no time for them to consider anything I've said; their response is predetermined and immediate. In unison, like demon monks chanting Hell's vespers, they emit that noise from their chest cavities, that proud crow of unyielding conviction, and although it's wordless, I understand exactly what it's saying:

> *No need to speak.*
> *No need to listen.*
> *Everything is already known.*
> *She will not leave.*
> *We will kill her.*
> *That is how things are done.*
> *Always has been.*
> *Always will be.*

I look at Julie. She is trembling. I grip her hand and look at M. He nods.

With the pulse-warmth of Julie's hand flooding through my icy fingers, I run.

We bolt left, trying to dodge around the edge of the Boneys' platoon. As they clatter forward to block my path, M surges out in front of me and rams his bulk into the nearest row, knocking them into a pile of hooked limbs and interlocked rib cages. A fierce blast of their invisible horn stabs the air.

"What are you *doing*?" Julie gasps as I drag her behind me. I am actually running *faster* than her.

"Keep you sa—"

"Don't you even *think* about saying 'Keep you safe'!" she shrieks. "This is about as far from safe as I've ever—"

She screams as a skinless hand pinches down on her shoulder and digs in. The creature's jaw opens to sink its filed fangs into her neck, but I grab it by the spine and wrench it off of her. I fling it to the concrete as hard as I can, but there is no impact and no shattering of bones. The thing almost seems to float in defiance of gravity, its rib cage barely touching the ground before it springs upright again, lurching toward my face like some hideous, unkillable insect.

"M!" I croak as it grapples for my throat. "Help!"

M is busy trying to peel skeletons off his arms, legs, and back, but he seems to be standing his ground thanks to his superior size and mass. As I struggle to keep the skeleton's fingers out of my eyes, M lumbers toward me, pulls the thing off me, and flings it into three others about to jump on him from behind.

"Go!" he yells, and shoves me forward, then turns to face our pursuers. I grab Julie's hand and dash toward our target. Finally, she sees it. The Mercedes. "Oh!" she pants. "Okay!"

We jump in the car and I bring the engine to life. "Oh Mercey . . . ," Julie says, stroking the dashboard like it's a beloved pet. "So happy to see you right now." I put the car in gear and release the clutch, gunning us forward. Somehow, it seems easy now.

M has given up trying to fight and is now just running for his life with a mob of skeletons trailing behind him. Hundreds of zombies stand outside the Departures entry area, watching everything in silence. What are they thinking? *Are* they thinking? Is there any chance they're forming a reaction to this event unfolding in front of them? This sudden explosion of anarchy in the state-approved program of their lives?

M cuts across the street, directly across our exit route, and I floor the accelerator. M crosses in front of us, then the Boneys cross in front of us, then four thousand pounds of German engineering smash into their brittle, ossified bodies. They shatter. Bits of anatomy fly everywhere. Two thigh bones, three hands, and half a cranium land inside the car, where they vibrate and twitch on the seats, releasing dry gasps and insectile buzzes. Julie hurls them out of the car and frantically wipes her hands on her sweatshirt, shuddering in revulsion and whimpering, "Oh my God oh my God."

But we are safe. Julie is safe. We roar past the Arrivals gate, onto the freeway, and out into the wider world while the stormclouds churn overhead. I look at Julie. She looks at me. We both smile as the first raindrops begin to fall.

TEN MINUTES LATER, the storm has launched into its big opening movement, and we are getting soaked. The convertible was a poor choice for a day like this. Neither of us can figure out how to put the top up, so we drive in silence with heavy sheets of rain beating down on our heads. We don't complain, though. We try to stay positive.

"Do you know where you're going?" Julie asks after about twenty minutes. Her hair is matted flat on her face.

"Yes," I say, looking down the road at the dark gray horizon.

"Are you sure? 'Cause I have no idea."

"Very . . . sure."

I prefer not to explain *why* I know the route between the airport and the city so well. Our hunting route. Yes, she knows what I am and what I do, but do I have to remind her? Can we just have a nice drive and forget certain things for a while? In the sunny fields of my imagination we are not a teenager and a walking corpse driving in a rainstorm. We are Frank and Ava cruising treelined country lanes while a scratchy vinyl orchestra swoons our soundtrack.

"Maybe we should stop and ask directions."

I look at her. I look around at the crumbling districts surrounding us, nearly black in the evening gloom.

"Kidding," she says, her eyes peeking out between plastered wet clumps of hair. She leans back in the seat and folds her arms behind her head. "Let me know when you need a break. You kinda drive like an old lady."

. . .

As the rain pools into standing water at our feet, I notice Julie shivering a little. It's a warm spring night, but she's saturated, and the cab of the old convertible is a cyclone of freeway wind. I take the next exit and we ease down into a silent graveyard of suburban grid homes. Julie looks at me with questioning eyes. I can hear her teeth chattering.

I drive slowly past the houses, looking for a good place to stop for the night. Eventually I pull into a weedy cul-de-sac and park next to a rusted Plymouth Voyager. I take Julie's hand and pull her toward the nearest house. The door is locked, but the dry-rotted wood gives way with a light kick. We step into the relative warmth of some long-dead family's cozy little nest. There are old Coleman lanterns placed throughout the house, and once Julie lights them they provide a flickering campsite glow that feels oddly comforting. She ambles around the kitchen and living room, looking at toys, dishes, stacks of old magazines. She picks up a stuffed koala bear and looks it in the eyes. "Home sweet home," she mumbles.

She reaches into her messenger bag, pulls out a Polaroid camera, points it at me and snaps a shot. The flash is shocking in this dark place. She grins at my startled expression and holds up the camera. "Look familiar? I stole it from the skeletons' meeting room yesterday morning." She hands me the developing photo. "It's important to capture things, you know? Especially now, since the world is on its way out." She puts the viewfinder to her eye and turns in a slow circle, taking in the whole room. "Everything you see, you might be seeing for the last time."

I wave the picture in my hand. A ghostly image begins to take shape. It's me, R, the corpse that thinks it's alive, staring back at me with those wide, pewter-gray eyes. Julie hands the camera to me.

"You should always be taking pictures, if not with a camera then with your mind. Memories you capture on purpose are always more vivid than the ones you pick up by accident." She strikes a pose and grins. "Cheese!"

I take her picture. When it rolls out of the camera she reaches for it, but I pull it away and hide it behind my back. I hand her mine. She rolls her eyes, takes the photo and studies it, tilting her head. "Not bad. I think the rain cleaned you up a little."

She lowers the photo and squints at me for a moment. "Why are your eyes like that?"

I look at her warily. "Like . . . what?"

"That weird gray. It's nothing like how corpse eyes look. Not clouded over or anything. Why are they like that?"

I give this some thought. "Don't know. Happens at . . . conversion."

She's looking at me so hard I start to squirm. "It's creepy," she says. "Looks . . . supernatural, almost. Do they ever change color? Like when you kill people or something?"

I try not to sigh. "I think . . . you're thinking . . . of vampires."

"Oh, right, right." She chuckles and gives a rueful shake of her head. "At least *those* aren't real yet. Too many monsters to keep track of these days."

Before I can take offense, she looks up at me and smiles. "Anyway . . . I like them. Your eyes. They're actually kinda pretty. Creepy . . . but pretty."

It's probably the best compliment I've received in my entire Dead life. Ignoring my idiot stare, Julie wanders off into the house, humming to herself.

. . .

The storm is raging outside, with occasional thunderclaps. I'm grateful that our house happens to have all its windows intact. Most of the others' were smashed long ago by looters or feeders. I glimpse a few debrained corpses on our neighbors' green lawns, but I'd like to imagine our hosts got out alive. Made it to one of the stadiums, maybe even some walled-off paradise in the mountains, angelic choirs singing behind pearl-studded titanium gates . . .

I sit in the living room listening to the rain fall while Julie putters around the house. After a while she comes back with an armful of dry clothes and dumps them on the love seat. She holds up a pair of jeans about ten sizes too big. "What do you think?" she says, wrapping the waist around her entire body. "Do these make me look fat?" She drops them and digs around in the pile, pulls out a mass of cloth that appears to be a dress. "I can use this for a tent if we get lost in the woods tomorrow. God, these folks must have made a fancy feast for some lucky zombie."

I shake my head, making a gag face.

"What, you don't eat fat people?"

"Fat . . . not alive. Waste product. Need . . . meat."

She laughs. "Oh, so you're an audiophile *and* a food snob! Jesus." She tosses the clothes aside and lets out a deep breath. "Well, all right. I'm exhausted. The bed in there isn't too rotten. I'm going to sleep."

I lie back on the cramped love seat, settling in for a long night alone with my thoughts. But Julie doesn't leave. Standing there in the bedroom doorway, she looks at me for a long minute. I've seen this look before, and I brace myself for whatever's coming.

"R . . . ," she says. "Do you . . . *have* to eat people?"

I sigh inside, so exhausted by these ugly questions, but when did a monster ever deserve its privacy?

"Yes."

"Or you'll die?"

"Yes."

"But you didn't eat me."

I hesitate.

"You *rescued* me. Like three times."

I nod slowly.

"And you haven't eaten anyone since then, right?"

I frown in concentration, thinking back. She's right. Not counting the few bites of leftover brains here and there, I've been gastronomically celibate since the day I met her.

A peculiar little half smile twitches on her face. "You're kind of . . . changing, aren't you?"

As usual, I am speechless.

"Well, good night," she says, and shuts the bedroom door.

I lie there on the couch, gazing up at the water-stained cottage-cheese ceiling.

"What's going on with you?" M asks me over a cup of moldy coffee in the airport Starbucks. "Are you okay?"

"Yeah, I'm okay. Just changing."

"How can you change? If we all start from the same blank slate, what makes you diverge?"

"Maybe we're not blank. Maybe the debris of our old lives still shapes us."

"But we don't remember those lives. We can't read our diaries."

"It doesn't matter. We are where we are, however we got here. What matters is where we go next."

"But can we choose that?"

"I don't know."

"We're Dead. Can we really choose anything?"

"Maybe. If we want to bad enough."

The rain drumming on the roof. The creak of weary timbers. The prickle of the old couch cushions through the holes in my shirt. I'm busy searching my post-death memory for the last time I went this long without food when I notice Julie standing in the doorway again. Her arms are folded on her chest and her hip is pressed against the door frame. Her foot taps an anxious rhythm on the floor.

"What?" I ask.

"Well . . . ," she says. "I was just thinking. The bed's a king-size. So I guess, if you wanted to . . . I wouldn't care if you joined me in there." I raise my eyebrows a little. Her face reddens. "Look, all I'm saying—*all* I'm saying—is I don't mind giving you a side of the bed. These rooms are kinda spooky, you know? I don't want the ghost of Mrs. Sprat crushing me in my sleep. And considering I haven't showered in over a week, you really don't smell much worse than I do; maybe we'll cancel each other out." She shrugs one shoulder, *whatever,* and disappears into the bedroom.

I wait a few minutes. Then, with great uncertainty, I get up and follow her in. She is already in the bed, curled into the fetal position with the blankets pulled tight around her. I slowly ease myself onto the far opposite edge. The blankets are all on her side, but I don't need their warmth. I am perpetually room-temperature.

Despite the pile of luxurious down comforters wrapped around her, Julie is still shivering. "These clothes are . . . ," she mutters, and sits up in bed. "Fuck." She glances over at me. "I'm going to lay my clothes out to dry. Just . . . relax, okay?" With her back to me, she wriggles out of her wet jeans and peels her shirt over her head. The skin of her back is blue-white from the cold. Almost the same hue as mine. In her polka-dot bra and plaid panties, she gets out of bed and drapes her clothes over the dresser, then quickly crawls back under the covers and curls up. "Good night," she says.

I lay my head on my folded arms, staring up at the ceiling. We are both on the very edges of the mattress, about four feet of space between us. I get the feeling that it's not just my ghoulish nature that makes her so wary. Living or Dead, virile or impotent, I still appear to be a man, and maybe she thinks I'll act the same as any other man would, lying so close to a beautiful woman. Maybe she thinks I'll try to take things from her. That I'll slither over and try to consume her. But then why am I even in this bed? Is it a test? For me, or for her? What strange hopes are compelling her to take this risk?

I listen to her breaths slow as she falls asleep. After a few hours, with her fear safely tucked away in dreams, she rolls over, removing most of the gap between us. She's facing me now. Her faint breath tickles my ear. If she were to wake up right now, would she scream? Could I ever make her understand how safe she really is? I won't deny that this proximity ignites more urges in me than the instinct to kill and eat. But although these new urges are there, some of them startling in their intensity, all I really *want* to do is lie next to her. In this moment, the most I'd ever hope for would be for her to lay her head on my chest, let out a warm, contented breath, and sleep.

Now here is an oddity. A question for the zombie philosophers. What does it mean that my past is a fog but my present is brilliant, bursting with sound and color? Since I became Dead I've recorded new memories with the fidelity of an old cassette deck, faint and muffled and ultimately forgettable. But I can recall every hour of the last few days in vivid detail, and the thought of losing a single one horrifies me. Where am I getting this focus? This clarity? I can trace a solid line from the moment I met Julie all the way to now, lying next to her in this sepulchral bedroom, and despite the millions of past moments I've lost or tossed away like highway trash, I know with a lockjawed certainty I'll remember this one for the rest of my life.

. . .

Sometime in the predawn, as I lie there on my back with no real need to rest, a dream flickers on like a film reel behind my eyes. Except it's not a dream, it's a vision, far too crisp and bright for my lifeless brain to have rendered. Usually these secondhand memories are preceded by the taste of blood and neurons, but not tonight. Tonight I close my eyes and it just *happens,* a surprise midnight showing.

We open on a dinner scene. A long metal table laid out with a minimalist spread. Bowl of rice. Bowl of beans. Rectangle of flax bread.

"Thank you, Lord, for this food," says the man at the head of the table, hands folded in front of him but eyes wide open. "Bless it to our bodies. Amen."

Julie nudges the boy sitting next to her. He squeezes her thigh under the table. The boy is Perry Kelvin. I'm in Perry's mind again. His brain is gone, his life evaporated and inhaled . . . yet he's still here. Is this a chemical flashback? A trace of his brain still dissolving somewhere in my body? Or is it actually *him*? Still holding on somewhere, somehow, somewhy?

"So, Perry," Julie's dad says to him—to me. "Julie tells me you're working for Agriculture now."

I swallow my rice. "Yes, sir, General Grigio, I'm a—"

"This isn't the mess hall, Perry, this is dinner. *Mr.* Grigio will be fine."

"Okay. Yes, sir."

There are four chairs at the table. Julie's father sits at the head, and she and I sit next to each other on his right. The chair at the other end of the table is empty. What Julie tells me about her mother is this: "She left when I was twelve." And though I've gently probed, she has never offered me more, not even while we're lying naked in my twin bed, exhausted and happy and as vulnerable as any two people can be.

"I'm a planter right now," I tell her father, "but I think I'm on track for a promotion. I'm shooting for harvest supervisor."

"I see," he says, nodding thoughtfully. "That isn't a *bad* job . . . but I wonder why you don't join your father in Construction. I'm sure he could use more young men working on that all-important corridor."

"He's asked me to, but, ah . . . I don't know, I just don't think Construction is the place for me right now. I really like working with plants."

"Plants," he repeats.

"I just feel like in this day and age there's something meaningful about *growing* things. The soil's so depleted it's hard to get much out of it, but it's pretty satisfying when you finally do see some green coming through that gray crust."

Mr. Grigio stops chewing, blank-faced. Julie looks uneasy. "Remember that little shrub we had in our living room back east?" she says. "The one that looked like a skinny little tree?"

"Yes . . . ," her dad says. "What about it?"

"You loved that thing. Don't act like you don't get gardening."

"That was your mother's plant."

"But you're the one who loved it." She turns to me. "So Dad used to be quite the interior designer, believe it or not; he had our old house decked out like an IKEA showroom, all this modern glass and metal stuff, which my mom couldn't *stand*—she wanted everything earthy and natural, all hemp fiber and sustainable hardwoods . . ."

Mr. Grigio's face looks tight. Julie either doesn't notice or doesn't care.

". . . so to fight back, she buys this lush, bright green shrub, puts it in a huge wicker pot, and sticks it right in the middle of Dad's perfect white and silver living room."

"It wasn't *my* living room, Julie," he interjects. "As I recall we took a vote on every piece of furniture, and you always sided with me."

"I was like eight, Dad, I probably liked pretending I lived in a spaceship. Anyway, Mom buys this plant and they argue about it for a week—Dad says it's 'incongruous,' Mom says either the plant stays or she goes—" She hesitates momentarily. Her father's face gets tighter. "That, um, that went on for a while," she continues, "but then Mom being Mom, she got obsessed with something else and quit watering the plant. So when it started dying, guess who adopted the poor thing?"

"I wasn't going to have a dead shrub as our living room's centerpiece. Someone had to take care of it."

"You watered it every day, Dad. You gave it plant food and pruned it."

"Yes, Julie, that's how you keep a plant alive."

"Why can't you say you loved the stupid plant, Dad?" She regards him with a mixture of amazement and frustration. "I don't get it, what is so wrong with that?"

"Because it's absurd," he snaps, and the mood of the room suddenly shifts. "You can water and prune a plant but you cannot 'love' a plant."

Julie opens her mouth to speak, then shuts it.

"It's a meaningless decoration. It sits there consuming time and resources, and then one day it decides to die, no matter how much you watered it. It's absurd to attach an emotion to something so brief and pointless."

There are a few long seconds of silence. Julie breaks away from her father's stare and pokes at her rice. "Anyway," she mumbles, "my point was, Perry . . . that Dad used to be a gardener. So you should share gardening stories."

"I'm interested in a lot more than gardening," I offer, racing to change the subject.

"Oh?" Mr. Grigio says.

"Yeah, ah . . . motorcycles? I salvaged a BMW R 1200 a while ago and I've been working on bulletproofing it, getting it combat-ready just in case."

"You have mechanical experience, then. That's good. We have a shortage of mechanics in the Armory right now."

Julie rolls her eyes and shovels beans into her mouth.

"I'm also spending a lot of time on my marksmanship. I've been requesting extra assignments from school and I've gotten pretty good with the M40."

"Hey Perry," Julie says, "why don't you tell Dad about your other plans? Like how you've always wanted to—"

I step on her foot. She glares at me.

"Always wanted to what?" her father asks.

"I don't—I'm not really . . ." I take a drink of water. "I'm not really sure yet, sir, to be honest. I'm not sure what I want to do with my life. But I'm almost sixteen; I know I'll have it figured out soon."

What were you going to say? R wonders aloud, interrupting the scene again, and I feel a lurch as we swap places. Perry glances up at him—at *me*—frowning.

"Come on, corpse, not now. This is the first time I met Julie's father and it's not going well. I need to focus."

"It's going fine," Julie tells Perry. "This is my dad these days; I warned you about him."

"You better pay attention," Perry says to me. "You might have to meet him someday, too, and you're going to have a much harder time winning his approval than I did."

Julie runs a hand through Perry's hair. "Aw, babe, don't talk about the present. It makes me feel left out."

He sighs. "Yeah, okay. These were better times anyway. I turned into a real neutron star when I grew up."

I'm sorry I killed you, Perry. It's not that I wanted to, it's just—

"Forget it, corpse, I understand. Seems by that point I wanted out anyway."

"I bet I'll always miss you when I think back to these days," Julie says wistfully. "You were pretty cool before Dad got his claws into you."

"Take care of her, will you?" Perry whispers up to me. "She's been through some hard stuff. Keep her safe."

I will.

Mr. Grigio clears his throat. "I would start planning now if I were you, Perry. With your skill set, you should really consider training for Security. Green shoots coming through the dirt are all well and good but we don't strictly *need* all these fruits and vegetables. You can live on nothing but Carbtein for almost a year before cell fatigue is even measurable. The most important thing is keeping us all alive."

Julie tugs on Perry's arm. "Come on, do we have to sit through this again?"

"Nah," Perry says. "This isn't worth reliving. Let's go somewhere nice."

• • •

We're on a beach. Not a real beach, carved over the millennia by the master craft of the ocean—those are all underwater now. We're on the young shore of a recently flooded city port. Small patches of sand appear between broken slabs of sidewalk. Barnacled streetlamps rise out of the surf, a few of them still flickering on in the evening gloom, casting circles of orange light on the waves.

"Okay guys," Julie says, throwing a stick into the water. "Quiz time. What do you want to do with your life?"

"Oh hi Mr. Grigio," I mutter, sitting next to Julie on a driftwood log that was once a telephone pole.

She ignores me. "Nora, you go first. And I don't mean what do you think you *will* end up doing, I mean what do you *want* to do."

Nora is sitting in the sand in front of the log, playing with some pebbles and pinching a smoldering joint between her middle finger and half a ring finger, missing past the first knuckle. Her eyes are earth brown; her skin is creamy coffee. "Maybe nursing?" she says. "Healing people, saving lives . . . maybe working on a cure? I could get into that."

"Nurse Nora," Julie says with a smile. "Sounds like a kids' TV show."

"Why a nurse?" I ask. "Why not go for doctor?"

Nora scoffs. "Oh, yeah, seven years of college? I doubt civilization's gonna last that long."

"Yes it will," Julie says. "Don't talk like that. But there's nothing wrong with being a nurse. Nurses are sexy!"

Nora smiles and pulls idly at her thick black curls. She looks at me. "Why a doctor, Pear? Is that your target?"

I shake my head emphatically. "I've already seen enough blood and viscera for one lifetime, thanks."

"Then what?"

"I like writing," I say like a confession. "So . . . I guess I want to be a writer."

Julie smiles. Nora tilts her head. "Really? Do people still *do* that?"

"What? Write?"

"I mean is there still like . . . a book industry?"

I shrug. "Well . . . no. Not really. Good point, Nora."

"Sorry, I was just—"

"No, I know, but you're right, it's dumb even for a fantasy. Colonel Rosso says only about thirty percent of the world's cities are still functioning, so unless the zombies are learning how to read . . . not a great time to get into the literary arts. I'll probably just end up in Security."

"Shut the fuck up, Perry," Julie says, punching me in the shoulder. "People still read."

"Do they?" Nora asks.

"Well *I* do. Who cares if there's an industry behind it? If everyone's too busy building things and shooting things to bother feeding their souls, screw them. Just write it on a notepad and give it to me. *I'll* read it."

"A whole book for just one person," Nora says, looking at me. "Could that ever be worth it?"

Julie answers for me. "At least his thoughts would get out of his head, right? At least *someone* would get to see them. I think it'd be beautiful. It'd be like owning a little piece of his brain." She looks at me intently. "Give me a piece of your brain, Perry. I want to taste it."

"Oh my," Nora laughs. "Should I leave you two alone?"

I put my arm around Julie and smile the worldweary smile I've recently perfected. "Oh my little girl," I say, and squeeze her. She frowns.

"What about you, Jules?" Nora says. "What's your pipe dream?"

"I want to be a teacher." She takes a deep breath. "And a painter, and a singer, and a poet. And a pilot."

Nora smiles. I secretly roll my eyes. Nora passes the joint to Julie, who takes a small puff and offers it to me. I shake my head, older than Julie and wiser than Nora. We all gaze out at the glittering water, three kids on the same log watching the same sunset, thinking very different thoughts while white gulls fill the air with mournful calls.

You're going to do those things, R murmurs down to Julie, and he and I swap places again. Julie looks up at me, the corpse in the clouds, floating over the ocean like a restless spirit. She gives me a radiant smile, and I know it's not really her, I know nothing I say here will ever escape the confines of my own skull, but I say it anyway. *You're going to be strong and beautiful and brilliant, and you're going to live forever. You're going to change the world.*

"Thanks, R," she says. "You're so sweet. Do you think you'll be able to let me go when the time comes? Do you think you'll be able to say good-bye?"

I swallow hard. *Will I really have to?*

Julie shrugs, smiling innocently, and whispers, "Shrug."

. . .

In the morning the storm has passed. I am lying on my back in a bed next to Julie. A sharp beam of sunlight cuts through the dust in the air and makes a hot white pool on her huddled form. She is still wrapped tightly in the blankets. I get up and step out onto the front porch. The spring sun bleaches the neighborhood white, and the only sound is rusty backyard swing sets creaking in the breeze. The dream's cold question echoes in my head. I don't want to face it, but I realize that very soon this will be over. I will return her to her daddy's porch by nine, and that will be it. The door will boom shut, and I'll skulk away home. *Will I be able to let her go?* I've never asked a harder question. A month ago there was nothing on Earth I missed, enjoyed, or longed for. I knew I could lose everything and not feel anything, and I rested easy in that knowledge. But I'm growing tired of easy things.

. . .

When I go back inside, Julie is sitting on the edge of the bed. She looks groggy, still half-asleep. Her hair is a natural disaster, post-hurricane palm trees.

"Good morning," I say.

She groans. I try valiantly not to stare at her as she arches her back and stretches, adjusting her bra strap and letting out a little whimper. I can see every muscle and vertebra, and since she's already half-naked I imagine her without skin. I know from grim experience that there is a beauty to her inner layers, too. Marvels of symmetry and craftsmanship sealed away inside her like the jeweled movements of a timepiece, fine works of art never meant to be seen.

"What are we doing for breakfast," she mutters. "I'm starving."

I hesitate. "Can probably . . . get to . . . stadium . . . in hour. Going to . . . need gas . . . though. For Mercey."

She rubs her eyes. She begins to pull her still-damp clothes back on. Once again I try not to stare. Her body wiggles and bounces in ways Dead flesh doesn't.

Her eyes suddenly flash alert. "Shit. You know what? I need to call my dad."

She picks up the corded phone, and I'm surprised to hear a dial tone. I guess her people would have made it a priority to keep the phone lines running. Anything digital or satellite based probably died long ago, but the physical lines, real connections between real objects that need no fragile magic to exist . . . those might endure a little longer.

Julie dials. She waits, tensed. Then relief floods her face. "Dad! It's Julie."

There is a loud burst of exclamations from the other end. Julie pulls the phone away from her ear and gives me a look that says, *Here we go.* "Yeah Dad, I'm okay, I'm okay. Alive and intact. Nora told you what happened, right?" More noise from the other end. "Yeah, I knew you'd be looking, but you were way off. It was that small hive at Oran Airport. They put me in this room with all these dead people, like a food locker or something, but after a few days . . . I guess they just *forgot* about me. I walked right out, found a car and drove off. I'm on my way back now, I just stopped to call you." A pause. She glances at me. "No, um, don't send anyone, okay? I'm in the suburbs down south, I'm almost—" She waits. "I don't know, somewhere close to the freeway, but Dad—" She freezes, and her face changes. "What?" She takes a deep breath. "Dad, why are you talking about Mom right now? No, why are you talking about her, this is *nothing* like that. I'm on my way *back,* I just—Dad! Wait, will you *listen* to me? *Don't send* anyone, I'm coming home, okay? I have a car, I'm on my way, just—Dad!" There is silence from the earpiece. "Dad?" Silence. She bites her lip and looks at the floor. She hangs up.

I raise my eyebrows, full of questions that I'm afraid to ask.

She massages her forehead and lets out a slow breath. "Can you go find the gas by yourself, R? I need . . . to think for a minute." She doesn't look at me as she speaks. Tentatively, I reach out and put a hand on her shoulder. She flinches, then softens, then suddenly turns and embraces me hard, burying her face in my shirt.

"I just need a minute," she says, pulling away and recovering herself.

So I leave her there. I find an empty gas can in the garage and begin working my way around the block, looking for a vehicle with a full tank to drain. As I kneel beside a recently crashed Chevy Tahoe with the siphon tube gurgling in my hand, I hear the sound of an engine starting in the distance. I ignore it. I focus on the taste of gasoline, still harsh and astringent in my mouth. When the can is full I walk back to the cul-de-sac, closing my eyes and letting the sun flood through my eyelids. Then I open them, and just stand there for a while, holding the red plastic can like a belated birthday gift. The Mercedes is gone.

. . .

Inside the house, on the dining room table, I find a note. Something is written on it, letters I can't assemble into words, but next to it are two Polaroids. Both pictures are of Julie, taken by Julie, with the camera extended at arm's length and pointed at herself. In one of them, she is waving. The gesture looks limp, halfhearted. In the other one, she is holding that hand against her chest. Her face is stoic, but her eyes are damp.

Good-bye, R, the picture whispers to me. *It's that time now. It's time to say it. Can you say it?*

I hold the picture in front of me, staring at it. I rub my fingers on it, smearing its fresh emulsion into rainbow blurs. I consider taking it with me, but no. I'm not ready to make Julie a souvenir.

Say it, R. Just say it.

I set the picture back on the table and leave the house. I don't say it.

. . .

I begin walking back to the airport. I'm not sure what's waiting for me. Full-death? Quite possibly. After the commotion I caused, the Boneys might simply dispose of me like infectious waste. But I'm alone again. My world is small, my options are few. I don't know where else to go.

The journey of forty minutes by car will be a daylong trip on foot. As I walk, the wind seems to reverse direction, and yesterday's thunderheads creep back onto the horizon for an encore. They spiral over me, slowly shrinking the circle of blue sky like an immense camera aperture. I walk fast and stiff, almost marching.

The blue above me darkens to gray, then indigo, then the clouds finally snap it shut. The rain comes. It blasts down in torrents that make last night's shower seem like a gentle produce-aisle mist. To my utter confusion I find myself *cold*. As the water pounds its way through my clothes and into every pore, I actually shiver. And despite the obscene gluttony of sleep I've indulged in lately, I feel the pull again. This is nearly three nights in a row.

I walk off the freeway at the next exit and climb into a triangle of landscaping between the road and the off-ramp. I crash through the brush and duck into the little cluster of trees, a miniforest of ten or twelve cedars arranged in a pleasing pattern for overstressed commuter ghosts.

I curl into a ball at the base of one of these trees, achieving some degree of shelter under its scrawny branches, and close my eyes. As lightning flickers on the horizon like flashbulbs and thunder rumbles in my bones, I drift into darkness.

. . .

I am with Julie on the 747. I realize it's a dream. A *real* dream, not just another rerun of Perry Kelvin's syndicated life. This is coming purely from me. The clarity has improved since the blurry sludge of my brain's first attempt back in the airport, but there's still an awkward, shaky quality to everything, like amateur video to Perry's slick feature films.

Julie and I sit cross-legged, facing each other, floating above the clouds on the plane's bright white wing. The wind ruffles our hair, but no more than a leisurely ride in a convertible.

"So you dream now?" Julie says.

I smile nervously. "I guess I do."

Julie doesn't smile. Her eyes are cold. "Guess you had nothing to dream about till you got some girl problems. You're like a grade school kid trying to keep a diary."

Now we're on the ground, sitting on a sunny green suburban lawn. A morbidly obese couple barbecues human limbs in the background. I try to keep Julie in focus.

"I'm changing," I tell her.

"I don't care," she replies. "I'm home now. I'm back in the real world, where you don't exist. Summer camp is over."

A winged Mercedes rumbles past in the distant sky and vanishes in a muffled sonic boom.

"I'm gone," she says, staring me hard in the eyes. "It was fun, but it's over now. This is how things go."

I shake my head, avoiding her gaze. "I'm not ready."

"What did you think was going to happen?"

"I don't know. I was just hoping for something. A miracle."

"Miracles don't exist. There is cause and effect, dreams and reality, Living and Dead. Your hope is absurd. Your romanticism, embarrassing."

I look at her uneasily.

"It's time for you to grow up. Julie has gone back to her position, and you will go back to your position, and that is the way it is. Always has been. Always will be."

She grins, and her teeth are jagged yellow fangs. She kisses me, gnawing through my lips, biting out my teeth, gnashing up toward my brain and screaming like a dying child. I gag on my hot red blood.

• • •

My eyes flash open and I stand up, pushing dripping branches out of my face. It's still night. The rain is still pummeling the earth. I step out of the trees and climb up onto the overpass. I lean against the railing, looking out at the empty freeway and the dark horizon beyond it. One thought pounds in my head like a migraine of rage: *You're wrong. You fucking monsters are wrong. About everything.*

Out of the corner of my eye, I glimpse a silhouette on the other side of the overpass. The dark form moves toward me with steady, lumbering steps. I hunch my muscles together, preparing for a fight. After wandering alone for too long, the unincorporated Dead will sometimes lose the ability to distinguish their own kind from the Living. And some are so far gone, so deep into this way of life, they just don't care either way. They will eat anyone, anything, anywhere, because they can't fathom any other way to interact. I imagine one of these creatures surprising Julie as she stops the Mercedes to get her bearings, wrapping filthy hands around her face and biting down on her slender neck, and as that image ferments in my head, I prepare to rip this thing in front of me into unrecognizable chunks. The primordial rage that fills me every time I think of someone harming her is frightening. The violence of killing and eating people feels like friendly teasing compared to this consuming bloodlust.

The towering shadow staggers closer. A flash of lightning illuminates its face, and I drop my arms to my sides.

"M?"

I almost fail to recognize him at first. His face has been torn and clawed, and there are countless small pieces bitten out of his body.

"Hey," he grunts. The rain streaks down his face and pools in his wounds. "Let's . . . get out of . . . rain." He walks past my leaky trees and climbs down the slope to the freeway below. I follow him to the dry space under the overpass. We huddle there in the dirt, surrounded by old beer cans and syringes.

"What . . . doing . . . he . . . out . . . out here?" I ask him, fighting for the words. I've been silent less than a day and I'm already rusty.

"Take . . . guess," M says, pointing at his wounds. "Boneys. Drove me out."

"Sorry."

M grunts. "Fuck . . . it." He kicks a sun-faded beer can. "But guess . . . what?" Something like a smile illuminates his mangled face. "Some . . . came with me."

He points down the freeway, and I see about nine other figures moving slowly toward us.

I look at M, confused. "Came . . . with? Why?"

He shrugs. "Things . . . crazy . . . back home. Things . . . shaken." He jabs a finger at me. "You."

"Me?"

"You and . . . her. Something . . . in air. Movement."

The nine zombies stop under the overpass and stand there, looking at us blankly.

"Hi," I say.

They sway and groan a little. One of them nods.

"Where's . . . girl?" M asks me.

"Her name is Julie." This comes off my tongue fluidly, like a swish of warm chamomile.

"Ju . . . lie," M repeats with some effort. "Okay. Where's . . . she?"

"Left. Went home."

M studies my face. He drops a hand onto my shoulder. "You . . . okay?"

I close my eyes and take a slow breath. "No." I look out at the freeway, toward the city, and something blooms in my head. First a feeling, then a thought, then a choice. "I'm going after her."

Six syllables. I have broken my record again.

"To . . . stadium?"

I nod.

"Why?"

"To . . . save her."

"From . . . what?"

"Ev . . . rything."

M just looks at me for a long time. Among the Dead, a piercing look can last several minutes. I wonder if he can possibly have any idea what I'm talking about, when I'm not even sure I do. Just a gut feeling. The soft pink zygote of a plan.

He gazes up at the sky, and a faraway look comes into his eyes. "Had . . . dream . . . last night. *Real* dream. *Memories*."

I stare at him.

"Remembered . . . when young. Summer. Cream . . . of Wheat. A girl." His eyes refocus on me. "What . . . is it like?"

"What?"

"You've . . . felt. Do you know . . . what it is?"

"What are . . . talking about?"

"My dream," he says, his face full of wonder like a child's at a telescope. "Those things . . . love?"

A tingle runs up my spine. What is happening? To what distant reaches of space is our planet hurtling? M is dreaming, reclaiming memories, asking astonishing questions. I am breaking my syllable records every day. Nine unknown Dead are with us under this overpass, miles from the airport and the hissing commands of the skeletons, standing here awaiting . . . *something*.

A fresh canvas is unfurling in front of me. What do I paint on it? What's the first hue to splash on this blank field of gray?

"I'll . . . go with," M says. "Help you . . . get in. Save her." He turns to the waiting Dead. "Help us?" he asks, not raising his voice above its easy rumble. "Help save . . . girl? Save . . ." He closes his eyes and concentrates. "*Ju . . . lie?*"

The Dead quicken at the sound of the name, fingers twitching and eyes darting. M looks pleased. "Help find . . . something lost?" he asks in a voice more solid than I've ever heard from his tattered throat. "Help . . . exhume?"

The zombies look at M. They look at me. They look at each other. One of them shrugs. Another nods. "Help," one of them groans, and they all wheeze in agreement.

I find a grin spreading across my face. I don't know what I'm doing, how I'm doing it, or what will happen when it's done, but at the very bottom of this rising siege ladder, I at least know I'm going to see Julie again. I know I'm not going to say good-bye. And if these staggering refugees want to help, if they think they see something bigger here than a boy chasing a girl, then they can help, and we'll see what happens when we say *yes* while this rigor mortis world screams *no*.

We start lumbering north on the southbound freeway, and the thunder drifts away toward the mountains like it's scared of us.

Here we are on the road. We must be going somewhere.

taking

I AM YOUNG. I am a teenage boy aflame with health, strong and virile and pounding with energy. But I get older. Every second ages me. My cells spread themselves thinner, stiffening, cooling, darkening. I am fifteen, but each death around me adds a decade. Each atrocity, each tragedy, each small moment of sadness. Soon I will be ancient.

Here I am, Perry Kelvin in the stadium. I hear birds in the walls. The bovine moans of pigeons, the musical chirps of starlings. I look up and breathe deep. The air is so much cleaner lately, even here. I wonder if this is what the world smelled like when it was new, centuries before smokestacks. It frustrates and fascinates me that we'll never know for sure, that despite the best efforts of historians and scientists and poets, there are some things we'll just never know. What the first song sounded like. How it felt to see the first photograph. Who kissed the first kiss, and if it was any good.

"Perry!"

I smile and wave at my little admirer as he and his dozen foster siblings cross the street in a line, hand in hand. "Hey . . . buddy," I call to him. I can never remember his name.

"We're going to the gardens!"

"Cool!"

Julie Grigio grins at me, leading their line like a mother swan. In a city of thousands I run into her almost every day, sometimes near the schools, where it seems probable, sometimes in the outermost corners of the stadium, where the odds are slim. Is she stalking me or am I stalking her? Either way, I feel a pulse of stress hormones shoot through me every time I see her, rushing to my palms to make them sweat and to my face to make it pimply. Last time we met, she took me up on the roof. We listened to music for hours, and when the sun went down, I'm pretty sure we almost kissed.

"Want to come with us, Perry?" she says. "It's a field trip!"

"Oh, fun . . . a field trip to where I just spent eight hours working."

"Hey, there aren't a lot of options in this place."

"So I've noticed."

She waves for me to come over and I immediately comply, while trying my best to look reluctant. "Don't they ever get to go outside?" I wonder, watching the kids march in clumsy lockstep.

"Mrs. Grau would say we *are* outside."

"I mean *outside*. Trees, rivers, etc."

"Not till they're twelve."

"Awful."

"Yeah . . ."

We walk in silence except for the burble of child-speak behind us. The stadium walls loom protectively like the parents these kids will never know. My excitement at seeing Julie darkens under a sudden cloud of melancholy.

"How do you stand it here," I say, barely a question.

Julie frowns at me. "*We* get to go out. Twice a month."

"I know, but . . ."

She waits. "What, Perry?"

"Do you ever wonder if it's even worth it?" I gesture vaguely at the walls. "All this?"

Her expression sharpens.

"I mean, are we really that much better off in here?"

"Perry," she snaps with unexpected vehemence. "Don't you start talking like that, don't you fucking start."

She notices the abrupt silence behind us and cringes. "Sorry," she says to the kids in a confidential whisper. "*Bad words.*"

"Fuck!" my little friend yells, and the whole line explodes with laughter.

Julie rolls her eyes. "Great."

"Tsk tsk."

"You shut your mouth. I meant what I said to you. That's evil talk."

I look at her uncertainly.

"We get to go outside twice a month. More if we're on salvage. And we get to stay alive." She sounds like she's reciting a Bible verse. An old proverb. As if sensing her own lack of conviction, she glances at me, then snaps her eyes forward. Her voice goes quiet. "No more evil talk if you want to come on our field trip."

"Sorry."

"You haven't been here long enough. You grew up in a safe place. You don't understand the dangers."

Dark feelings flood my belly at this, but I manage to hold my tongue. I don't know the pain she's speaking from, but I know it's deep. It makes her hard and yet so terribly soft. It's her thorns and it's her hand reaching out from the thicket.

"Sorry," I say again, and fumble for that hand, nudging it out of her jeans pocket. It's warm. My cold fingers wrap around hers, and my mind conjures an unwelcome image of tentacles. I blink it away. "No more evil talk."

The kids gaze at me eagerly, huge eyes, spotless cheeks. I

wonder what they are and what they mean and what's going to happen to them.

. . .

"Dad."

"Yeah?"

"I think I have a girlfriend."

My dad lowers his clipboard, adjusts his hard hat. A smile creeps into the deep creases of his face. "Really."

"I think so."

"Who?"

"Julie Grigio?"

He nods. "I've met her. She's—hey! Doug!" He leans over the edge of the bulwark and yells at a worker carrying a steel pylon. "That's forty-gauge, Doug, we're using fifty for the arterial sections." He looks back at me. "She's cute. Watch out though; seems like a firecracker."

"I like firecrackers."

My dad smiles. His eyes drift. "Me too, kid."

His walkie-talkie crackles and he pulls it out, starts giving instructions. I look out at the ugly concrete vista under construction. We are standing on the terminating end of a wall, fifteen feet high, currently a few blocks long. Another wall runs parallel to it, making Main Street into an enclosed corridor that cuts through the heart of the city. Workers swarm below, laying concrete pour-forms, erecting framework.

"Dad?"

"Yeah."

"Do you think it's stupid?"

"What?"

"To fall in love."

He pauses, then puts his walkie away. "What do you mean, Pear."

"Like . . . now. The way things are now. I mean everything's so uncertain . . . is it stupid to waste time on stuff like that in a world like this? When everything might fall apart any minute?"

My dad looks at me for a long time. "When I met your mom," he says, "I asked myself that. And all we had going on back then was a few wars and recessions." His walkie starts crackling again. He ignores it. "I got *nineteen years* with your mom. But do you think I would've turned down the idea if I'd known I'd only get one year? Or one month?" He surveys the construction, shaking his head slowly. "There's no benchmark for how life's 'supposed' to happen, Perry. There is no ideal world for you to wait around for. The world is always just what it is *now*, and it's up to you how you respond to it."

I look into the dark window holes of ruined office buildings. I imagine the skeletons of their occupants still sitting at their desks, working toward quotas they will never meet.

"What if you'd only gotten a week with her?"

"Perry . . . ," my dad says, slightly amazed. "The world isn't ending tomorrow, buddy. Okay? We're working on fixing it. Look." He points at the work crews below. "We're building roads. We're going to connect to the other stadiums and hideouts, bring the enclaves together, pool our research and resources, maybe start looking for a cure again." My dad claps me on the shoulder. "You and me, everyone . . . we're going to make it. Don't give up on us yet. Okay?"

I relent with a small release of breath. "Okay."

"Promise?"

"Promise."

My dad smiles. "I'll hold you to that."

• • •

Do you know what happened next, corpse? Perry whispers from the deep shadows of my awareness. *Can you guess?*

"Why are you showing me all this?" I ask the darkness.

Because it's what's left of me, and I want you to feel it. I'm not ready to disappear.

"Neither am I."

I sense a cold smile in his voice.

Good.

. . .

"There you are."

Julie heaves herself up the ladder and stands on the roof of my new home, watching me. I glance at her, then put my face back in my hands.

She makes her way over, cautious steps on the flimsy sheet metal, and sits next to me on the roof edge. Our legs dangle, swinging slowly in the cold autumn air.

"Perry?"

I don't answer. She studies the side of my face. She reaches out and brushes two fingers through my shaggy brown hair. Her eyes pull on me like gravity, but I resist. I stare down at the muddy street.

"I can't believe I'm here," I mumble. "This stupid house. With all these discards."

She doesn't respond immediately. When she does, it's quiet. "They're not discards. They were loved."

"For a while."

"Their parents didn't *leave*. They were taken."

"Is there a difference?"

She looks at me so hard I have no choice but to meet her gaze. "Your mom loved you, Perry. You've never had to doubt that. And so did your dad."

I can't hold the weight. I give in and let it fall on me. I twist my head away from Julie as the tears come.

"Believe that God discarded you if you want to, fate or destiny or whatever, but at least you know *they* loved you."

"What does it even matter," I croak, avoiding her eyes. "Who gives a shit. They're dead. That's the present. That's what matters now."

We don't speak for a few minutes. The cold breeze pricks tiny bumps on our arms. Bright leaves find their way in from the outer forests, spinning down into the stadium's vast mouth and landing on the house's roof.

"You know what, Perry?" Julie says. Her voice is shaky with hurts all her own. "Everything dies eventually. We all know that. People, cities, whole civilizations. Nothing lasts. So if existence was just binary, dead or alive, here or not here, what would be the fucking point in anything?" She looks up at some falling leaves and puts out her hand to catch one, a flaming red maple. "My mom used to say that's why we have memory. And the opposite of memory— hope. So things that are gone can still matter. So we can build off our pasts and make futures." She twirls the leaf in front of her face, back and forth. "Mom said life only makes any sense if we can see time how God does. Past, present, and future all at once."

I allow myself to look at Julie. She sees my tears and tries to wipe one away. "So what's the future?" I ask, not flinching as her fingers brush my eye. "I can see the past and the present, but what's the future?"

"Well . . . ," she says with a broken laugh. "I guess that's the tricky part. The past is made out of facts . . . I guess the future is just hope."

"Or fear."

"No." She shakes her head firmly and sticks the leaf in my hair. "Hope."

• • •

The stadium rises on the horizon as the Dead stumble forward. It looms above most of the surrounding buildings and consumes several city blocks, a gaudy monument to an era of excess, a world of waste and want and misguided dreams that is now profoundly over.

Our cadaverous cadre has been walking for a little over a day, roaming the open roads like Kerouac beats with no gas money. The others are hungry, and there's a brief, mostly wordless debate between M and the rest before they stop at an old boarded-up town house to feed. I wait outside. It's been more days than I can remember since my last meal, but I find myself strangely content. There's a neutral feeling in my veins, balanced precisely between hungry and sated. The screams of the people in the house pierce me more sharply than in all my days of hands-on killing, and I'm not even anywhere near them. I'm standing far out in the street, pushing my palms into my ears and waiting for it to be over.

When they emerge, M avoids my gaze. He wipes the blood off his mouth with the back of his hand and shoots me just one guilty glance before brushing past. The others are not quite there yet, not even to M's level of conscience, but there is something a little different about them, too. They take no leftovers. They dry their bloody hands on their pants and walk in uneasy silence. It's a start.

As we get close enough to the stadium to catch the first whiffs of the Living, I go over the plan in my head. It's not much of a plan, really. It's cartoonishly simple, but here's why it might work: it's never been tried before. There has never been enough will to make a way.

A few blocks from the entry gate, we stop in an abandoned house. I go into the bathroom and study myself in the mirror like the former resident must have done a thousand times. In my head I jog through the maddening repetitions of the morning routine, getting into character. Alarm—shower—clothes—breakfast. Do I look my best? Am I putting my best foot forward? Am I stepping out the door prepared for everything this world has to throw at me?

I run some gel through my hair and straighten my tie. I adjust my shirt to hide a few black wounds. I splash on some cologne.

"Ready," I tell the others.

M sizes me up. "Close . . . enough."

We head for the gates.

• • •

Within a few blocks, the smell of the Living is nearly overpowering. It's as if the stadium is a massive Tesla coil crackling with storms of fragrant pink life-lightning. Everyone in our group stares at it in awe. Some of them drool freely. If they hadn't just eaten, our loosely constructed strategy would collapse in an instant.

Before we get within sight of the gate, we take a side street and stop at an intersection, hiding behind a UPS truck. I step out slightly and look around the corner. Less than two blocks away, four guards stand in front of the stadium's main entrance doors, dangling shot-guns over their shoulders and chatting among themselves. Their gruff, military sentences use even fewer syllables than ours.

I look at M. "Thanks. For . . . doing this."

"Sure," M says.

"Don't . . . die."

"Never do. Are . . . ready?"

I nod.

"Look . . . alive . . . out there."

I smile. I brush my hair back one more time, take a deep breath, and run for it.

"Help!" I scream, waving my arms. "Help, they're . . . right be-hind me!"

With my best possible balance and poise, I run toward the doors. M and the others lumber after me, groaning theatrically.

The guards react on instinct: they raise their guns and open fire on the zombies. An arm flies off. A leg. One of the anonymous nine loses a head and goes down. But not a single weapon points in my direction. Painting Julie's face on the air in front of me, I sprint with Olympian focus. My stride is good, I can feel it; I look normal, *alive,* and so I snap neatly into a category: "human." Two more guards emerge with guns drawn, but they barely even look at me. They squint, they take aim at their targets, and they shout, "Go! Get in there, man!"

Two more zombies hit the ground behind me. As I slip in through the doors, I see M and the remaining Dead veer off and retreat. Their gait suddenly changes. They lose their stumble and run like living things. Not as fast as me, not as graceful, but with purpose. The guards hesitate, the gunfire falters. "What the fuck . . . ?" one of them mutters.

Inside the entrance is a man with a clipboard and a notebook. An immigration officer, ready to take my name and have me fill out a stack of request forms before most likely tossing me out. The Dead have depended on this man for years to provide us with the defenseless stragglers we eat in the ruins outside. He comes toward me, flipping through his notebook, making no eye contact. "Close call, eh, friend? I'm going to need you to—"

"Ted! Look at this shit!"

Ted looks up, looks through the open doors, sees his fellow soldiers standing dumbstruck. He glances at me. "Wait right here."

Ted jogs out and stops next to the guards, staring at the eerily animate zombies dashing off into the distant streets like real people. I imagine the look on the men's faces, their stomachs bubbling with the queasy sensation that the earth under their feet is moving.

Momentarily forgotten, I turn and run. I run through the dark entry corridor toward the light on the other end, wondering if this is a birth canal or the tunnel to Heaven. Am I coming or going? Either way, it's too late to reverse. Hidden in the gloom under a red evening sky, I step into the world of the Living.

Pigmentary layer.

Jacob's membrane.

Membrana limitans

Outer nuclear layer.

Outer molecular layer.

Inner nuclear layer.

Fibre of Müller.

Inner molecular layer.

Vesicular layer.

Fibrous layer.

Membrana limitans inh

THE SPORTS ARENA Julie calls home is unaccountably large, perhaps one of those dual-event "super-venues" built for an era when the greatest quandary facing the world was where to put all the parties. From the outside there is nothing to see but a mammoth oval of featureless walls, a concrete ark that not even God could make float. But the interior reveals the stadium's soul: chaotic yet grasping for order, like the sprawling slums of Brazil designed by a modern architect.

All the bleachers have been torn out to make room for an expansive grid of miniature skyscrapers, rickety houses built unnaturally tall and skinny to conserve the limited real estate. Their walls are a hodgepodge of salvaged materials—one of the taller towers begins as concrete and grows flimsier as it rises, from steel to plastic to a precarious ninth floor of soggy particleboard. Most of the buildings look like they should collapse in the first breeze, but the whole city is supported by rigid webs of cable running from tower to tower, cinching the grid tight. The stadium's inner walls loom high over everything, bristling with severed pipes, wires, and spikes of rebar that sprout from the concrete like beard stubble. Underpowered streetlamps provide dim orange illumination, leaving this snow globe city smothered in shadows.

The moment I step out of the entry tunnel my sinuses inflame with an overwhelming rush of life-smell. It's all around me, so sweet and potent it's almost painful; I feel like I'm drowning in a perfume bottle. But in the midst of this thick haze, I can sense Julie. Her signature scent peeks out of the noise, calling out like a voice underwater. I follow it.

The streets are the width of sidewalks, narrow strips of asphalt poured over the old Astroturf, which peeks through any unpaved gaps like bright green moss. There are no names on the street signs. Instead of listing off states or presidents or varieties of trees, they display simple white graphics—apple, ball, cat, dog—a child's guide to the alphabet. There is mud everywhere, slicking the asphalt and piling up in corners along with the detritus of daily life: pop cans, cigarette butts, used condoms and bullet shells.

I am trying not to gawk at the city like the rube tourist I am, but something beyond curiosity is gluing my attention to every curb and rooftop. As foreign as it all is to me, I feel a ghostly sense of recognition, even nostalgia, and as I make my way down what must be Eye Street, some of my stolen memories begin to stir.

This is where we started. This is where they sent us when the coasts disappeared. When the bombs fell. When our friends died and rose as strangers, unfamiliar and cold.

It's not Perry's voice—it's everyone's, a murmuring chorus of all the lives I've consumed, gathering in the dark lounge of my subconscious to reminisce.

Flag Avenue, where they planted our nation's colors, back when there were still nations and their colors mattered. Gun Street, where they set up the war camps, planned attacks and defenses against our endless enemies, Living as often as Dead.

I walk with my head down, keeping as close to the walls as I can. When I meet someone coming the other way I keep my eyes straight ahead until the last possible moment, then I allow fleeting contact. We pass briskly with awkward nods.

It didn't take much to bring down the card house of civilization. Just a few gusts and it was done, the balance tipped, the spell broken. Good citizens realized the lines that had shaped their lives were imaginary and easily crossed. They had wants and needs and the power to satisfy them, so they did. The moment the lights went out, everyone stopped pretending.

I begin to worry about my clothes. Everyone I encounter is wearing thick gray denim, a waterproof coat, mud-caked work boots. What world am I still living in where people dress for aesthetics? If no one realizes I'm a zombie, they may still call in a report on the stylish lunatic roaming the streets in a fitted shirt and tie. I quicken my pace, sniffing desperately for Julie's trail.

Island Avenue, where they built the courtyard for the community meetings, where "they" became "we," or so we believed. We cast our votes and raised our leaders, charming men and women with white teeth and silver tongues, and we shoved our many hopes and fears into their hands, believing those hands were strong because they had firm handshakes. They failed us, always. There was no way they could not fail us—they were human, and more importantly, so were we.

I veer off Eye Street and start working my way toward the center of the grid. Julie's scent grows more distinct, but its exact direction remains vague. I keep hoping some clue will emerge from the chanting in my head, but these ancient ghosts have no interest in my insignificant search.

Jewel Street, where we built the schools once we finally accepted that this was reality, that this was the world our children would inherit. We taught them how to shoot, how to pour concrete, how to kill and how to survive, and if they made it that far, if they mastered those skills and had time to spare, then we taught them how to read and write, to reason and relate and understand their world. We tried hard at first, there was much hope and faith, but it was a steep hill to climb in the rain, and many slid to the base.

I notice the maps in these memories are slightly outdated; the street they're calling Jewel has been renamed. The sign is newer, a fresh primary green, and instead of a visual icon it has an actual word printed on it. Intrigued, I turn at this intersection and approach an atypically wide metal building. Julie's scent is still distant, so I know I shouldn't stop, but the pale light coming through the windows seems to prick some new anguish in my inner voices. As I press my nose against the glass, they go quiet.

A large, wide-open room. Row upon row of white metal tables under fluorescent lights. Dozens of children, all younger than ten, divided by row into project groups: a row repairing generators, a row treating gasoline, a row cleaning rifles, sharpening knives, stitching wounds. And at the edge, very near the window I'm staring through: a row dissecting cadavers. Except of course they aren't cadavers. As an eight-year-old girl in blond pigtails peels the flesh away from her subject's mouth, revealing the crooked grin underneath, its eyes flick open and it looks around, struggles briefly against its restraints, then relaxes, looking weary and bored. It glances toward my window and we make brief eye contact, just before the girl cuts out its eyes.

We tried to make a beautiful world here, the voices mumble. *There were those who saw the end of civilization as an opportunity to start over, to undo the errors of history—to relive mankind's awkward adolescence with all the wisdom of our modern age. But everything was happening so fast.*

I hear the noise of a violent scuffle from the other end of the building, shoes scraping against concrete, elbows banging sheet metal. Then a low, wet groan. I traverse the building, searching for a better viewpoint.

Outside our walls were hordes of men and monsters eager to steal what we had, and inside was our own mad stew, so many cultures and languages and incompatible values packed into one tiny box. Our world was too small to share peacefully; consensus never came, harmony was impossible. So we adjusted our goals.

Through another window I see a big open space like a warehouse, dimly lit and scattered with broken cars and chunks of debris as if simulating the outer city landscape. A crowd of older kids surrounds a corral of chain-link fencing and concrete freeway barriers. It resembles the "free speech zones" once used to contain protesters outside political rallies, but instead of being crammed full of sign-waving dissidents, this cage is occupied by just four figures: a teenage boy armored head to toe in police riot gear, and three badly desiccated Dead.

Can the Dark Ages' doctors be blamed for their methods? The bloodletting, the leeches, the holes in skulls? They were feeling their way blind, grasping at mysteries in a world without science, but the plague was upon them; they had to do something. When our turn came, it was no different. Despite all our technology and enlightenment, our laser scalpels and social services, it was no different. We were just as blind and just as desperate.

I can tell by the way they stagger that the Dead in this arena are starving. They must know where they are and what's going to happen to them, but they are far beyond what little self-control they ever had. They lunge for the boy and he aims his shotgun.

The outside world had already sunk under a sea of blood, and now those waves were lapping over our last stronghold—we had to shore up the walls. We realized that the closest we'd ever get to objective truth was the belief of the majority, so we enthroned the majority and ignored all other voices. We appointed generals and contractors, police and engineers; we discarded every inessential ornament. We smelted our ideals under great heat and pressure until the soft parts burned away, and what emerged was a tempered frame rigid enough to endure the cruel world we'd created.

"Wrong!" the instructor shouts at the boy in the cage as the boy fires into the advancing Dead, blowing holes in their chests and blasting off fingers and feet. "Get the head! Forget the rest is even there!" The boy fires two more rounds that miss entirely, thudding into the heavy plywood ceiling. The quickest of the three zombies seizes his arms and wrenches the gun out of his hands, struggles with the pulse-checking safety trigger for a moment, then throws the gun aside and tackles the boy into the fence, biting wildly against the helmet's face guard. The instructor storms into the cage and jabs his pistol into the zombie's head, fires a round and holsters the gun. "Remember," he announces to the whole room, "the recoil on an automatic shotgun will drive the barrel upward, especially on these old Mossbergs, so aim low or you'll be shooting blue sky." He scoops up the weapon and shoves it into the boy's trembling hands. "Continue."

The boy hesitates, then raises the barrel and fires twice. Bits of gore slap against his face guard, spattering it black. He rips the helmet off and stares at the corpses at his feet, breathing hard and struggling not to cry.

"Good," the instructor says. "Beautiful."

We knew it was all wrong. We knew we were diminishing ourselves in ways we couldn't even name, and we wept sometimes at memories of better days, but we no longer saw a choice. We were doing our best to survive. The equations at the roots of our problems were complex, and we were far too tired to solve them.

A snuffling noise at my feet finally tears me away from the scene in the window. I look down to see a German shepherd puppy studying my leg with flaring wet nostrils. It looks up at me. I look down at it. It pants happily for a moment, then starts eating my calf.

"Trina, *no!*"

A little boy rushes up and grabs the dog's collar, pulls her off me and drags her back toward the open doorway of a house. "*Bad* dog."

Trina twists her head around to gaze at me longingly.

"Sorry!" the boy calls from across the street.

I give him an easy wave, *No problem*.

A young girl emerges from the doorway and stands next to him, sticking out her belly and watching me with big dark eyes. Her hair is black; the boy's is curly blond. They are both around six.

"Don't tell our mom?" she asks.

I shake my head, swallowing back a sudden reflux of emotions. The sound of these kids' voices, their perfect, childish diction . . .

"Do you . . . know Julie?" I ask them.

"Julie Cabernet?" the boy says.

"Julie Gri . . . gio."

"We like Julie Cabernet a lot. She reads to us every Wednesday."

"*Stories!*" the girl adds.

I don't recognize this name, but some scrap of memory perks at the sound of it. "Do you know . . . where she lives?"

"Daisy Street," the boy says.

"No, Flower Street! It's a flower!"

"A daisy *is* a flower."

"Oh."

"She lives on a corner. It's Daisy Street and Devil Avenue."

"Cow Avenue!"

"It's not a cow, it's the Devil. Cows and the Devil both have horns."

"Oh."

"Thanks," I tell the kids, and turn to leave.

"Are you a zombie?" the girl asks in a shy squeak.

I freeze. She waits for my answer, twisting left and right on her heels. I relax, smile at the girl, and shrug. "Julie . . . doesn't think so."

An angry voice from a fifth-floor window yells something about curfew and shutting the door and not talking to strangers, so I wave to the kids and hurry off toward Daisy and Devil. The sun is down and the sky is rust. A distant loudspeaker blares out a sequence of numbers, and most of the windows around me go dark. I loosen my tie and start to run.

. . .

The intensity of Julie's scent doubles with each block. As the first few stars appear in the stadium's oval sky, I turn a corner and halt below a solitary edifice of white aluminum siding. Most of the buildings seem to be multifamily apartment complexes, but this one is smaller, narrower, and separated from its tightly packed neighbors by an awkward distance. Four stories tall but barely two rooms wide, it looks like a cross between a town house and a prison watchtower. The windows are all dark except for a third-floor balcony jutting out from the side of the house. The balcony seems incongruously romantic on this austere structure, until I notice the swivel-mounted sniper rifles on each corner.

Lurking behind a stack of crates in the Astroturf backyard, I hear voices inside the house. I close my eyes, luxuriating in their sweet rhythms and tart timbres. I hear Julie. Julie and another girl, discussing something in tones that jitter and syncopate like jazz. I find myself swaying slightly, dancing to their conversational beat.

Eventually the talk trails off, and Julie emerges onto the balcony. It's been only one day since she left, but the sense of reunion that surges in me is decades strong. She rests her elbows on the railing, looking cold in just a loose black T-shirt over bare legs. "Well, here I am again," she says, apparently to no one but the air. "Dad clapped me on the back when I walked in the door. Actually clapped me on the back, like a fucking football coach. All he said was, 'So glad you're okay,' then he ran off to some project meeting or something. I can't believe how much he's . . . I mean, he was never exactly *cuddly,* but . . ." I hear a tiny click and she doesn't speak for a moment. Then another click. "Until I called him he had to have assumed I was dead, right? Yeah, he sent out the search parties, but how often do people really come back from stuff like this? So to him . . . I was dead. And maybe I'm being too harsh but I absolutely can't picture him crying over it. Whoever told him the news, they probably both clapped each other on the back and said

'Soldier on, soldier,' and then went back to work." She stares at the ground as if she's seeing through it, down into the hellish core of the earth. "What's wrong with people?" she says, almost too quiet for me to hear. "Were they born with parts missing or did it all fall out somewhere along the way?"

She is silent for a while, and I'm about to show myself when she suddenly laughs, closing her eyes and shaking her head. "I actually miss that stupid . . . I miss R! I know that's crazy, but is it really *that* crazy? Just because he's . . . whatever he is? I mean, isn't 'zombie' just a silly name we came up with for a state of being we don't understand? What's in a name, right? If we were . . . If there was some kind of . . ." She trails off, then stops and raises a mini cassette recorder to eye level, glaring at it. "Fuck this thing," she mumbles to herself. "Tape journaling . . . not for me." She fast-pitches it off the balcony. It bounces off a supply crate and lands at my feet. I pick it up, tuck it into my shirt pocket, and press my hand against it, feeling its corners dig into my chest. If I ever return to my 747, this memento will go in the stack closest to where I sleep.

Julie hops onto the balcony railing and sits with her back to me, scribbling in her battered old Moleskine.

Journal or poetry?

Both, silly.

Am I in it?

I step out from the shadows. "Julie," I whisper.

She doesn't startle. She turns slowly, and a smile melts across her face like a slow spring thaw. "Oh . . . my God," she half-giggles, then hops off the railing and spins around to face me. "R! You're *here*! Oh my *God*!"

I grin. "Hello."

"What are you *doing* here?" she hisses, trying to keep her voice down.

I shrug, deciding that this gesture, while easy to abuse, does have its place. It may even be vital vocabulary in a world as unspeakable as ours.

"Came to . . . see you."

"But I had to go home, remember? You were supposed to say good-bye."

"Don't know why you . . . say good-bye. I say . . . hello."

Her lip quivers between reactions, but she ends up with a reluctant smile. "God you're a cheeseball. But seriously, R—"

"Jules!" a voice calls from inside the house. "Come here, I wanna show you something."

"One sec, Nora," Julie calls back. She looks down at me. "This is crazy, okay? You're going to get killed. It doesn't matter how changed you are, the people in here won't care, they won't listen, they'll just *shoot* you. Do you understand?"

I nod. "Yes."

I start climbing up the drainpipe.

"Jesus, R! Are you listening to me?"

I get about three feet off the ground before I realize that although I'm now capable of running, speaking, and maybe falling in love, *climbing* is still a ways down the road for me. I lose my grip on the pipe and fall flat on my back. Julie covers her mouth, but some laughter slips through.

"Hey Cabernet!" Nora calls again. "What's going on, are you talking to somebody?"

"Hang *on*, okay? I'm just doing a tape journal."

I stand up and dust myself off. I look up at Julie. Her brows are tight and she bites her lip. "R . . . ," she says miserably. "You can't . . ."

The balcony door swings open and Nora appears, her curls just as thick and wild as they were in my visions, all those years ago. I've never seen her standing, and she's surprisingly tall, at least half a foot above Julie, long brown legs bare under a camouflage skirt. I had assumed she and Julie were classmates, but now I realize Nora is a few years older, maybe in her mid-twenties.

"What are you—" she starts to say, then she notices me, and her eyebrows go up. "Oh my holy Lord. Is that *him*?"

Julie sighs. "Nora, this is R. R . . . Nora."

Nora stares at me like I'm Sasquatch, the Chupacabra, maybe a unicorn. "Um . . . nice to meet you . . . R."

"Likewise," I reply, and Nora slaps a hand over her mouth to stifle a delighted squeak, looks at Julie, then back at me.

"What should we do?" Julie asks Nora, trying to ignore her giddiness. "He just showed up. I'm trying to tell him he's going to get killed."

"Well he needs to get up here, first of all," Nora says, still staring at me.

"Into the house? Are you stupid?"

"Come on, your dad's not back for another two days. Safer for him in the house than on the street."

Julie thinks for a minute. "Okay. Hold on, R, I'll come down."

I go around to the front of the house and stand at the door, waiting nervously in my dress shirt and tie. She opens it, grinning shyly. Prom night at the end of the world.

"Hi, Julie," I say, as if none of the previous conversation happened.

She hesitates, then steps forward and hugs me. "I actually missed you," she says into my shirt.

"I . . . heard that."

She pulls back to look at me, and something wild glints in her eyes. "Hey R," she says. "If I kissed you, would I get . . . you know . . . converted?"

My thoughts skip like a record in an earthquake. As far as I know, only a bite, a violent transfer of blood and essences, has the power to make the Living join the Dead before actually dying. To expedite the inevitable. But then again, I'm fairly sure Julie's question has never, *ever* been asked before.

"Don't . . . think so," I say, "but—"

A spotlight flashes at the end of the street. The sound of two guards barking commands breaks the night quiet.

"Shit, the patrol," Julie whispers, and yanks me inside the house.

"We should get the lights out, it's after curfew. Come on." She runs up the stairs and I follow her, relief and disappointment mixing in my chest like unstable chemicals.

Julie's home feels eerily unoccupied. In the kitchen, the den, the short halls and steep staircases, the walls are white and unadorned. The few pieces of furniture are plastic, and rows of fluorescent lights glare down on stainproof beige carpets. It feels like the vacated office of a bankrupt company, empty echoing rooms and the lingering scent of desperation.

Julie turns lights off as she goes, darkening the house until we reach her bedroom. She switches off the overhead bulb and flicks on a Tiffany lamp by her bed. I step inside and turn in slow circles, greedily absorbing Julie's private world.

If her mind were a room, it would look like this.

Each wall is a different color. One red, one white, one yellow, one black, and a sky-blue ceiling strung with model airplanes. Each wall seems designated for a theme. The red is nearly covered with movie ticket stubs and concert posters, all browned and faded with age. The white is crowded with paintings, starting near the floor with a row of amateur acrylics and leading up to three stunning oil canvases: a sleeping girl about to be devoured by tigers, a nightmarish Christ on a geometric cross, and a surreal landscape draped with melting clocks.

"Recognize those?" Julie says with a grin she can barely contain. "Salvador Dalí. Originals, of course."

Nora comes in from the balcony, sees me with my face inches from the canvases, and laughs. "Nice decor, right? Me and Perry wanted to get Julie the *Mona Lisa* for her birthday because it reminded us of that little smirk she's always—there! Right there!—but, yeah, it's a long way to Paris on foot. We make do with the local exhibitions."

"Nora has a whole wall of Picassos in her room," Julie adds. "We'd be legendary art thieves if anyone still cared."

I crouch down to get a closer look at the bottom row of acrylics.

"Those are Julie's," Nora says. "Aren't they great?"

Julie averts her eyes in disgust. "Nora made me put those up."

I study them intently, searching for Julie's secrets in their clumsy brushstrokes. Two are just bright colors and thick, tortured texture. The third is a crude portrait of a blond woman. I glance over at the black wall, which bears only one ornament: a thumbtacked Polaroid of what must be the same woman. Julie plus twenty hard years.

Julie follows my gaze and she and Nora exchange a glance. "That's my mom," Julie says. "She left when I was twelve." She clears her throat and looks out the window.

I turn to the yellow wall, which is notably unadorned. I point at it and raise my eyebrows.

"That's, um . . . my hope wall," she says. Her voice contains an embarrassed pride that makes her sound younger. Almost innocent. "I'm leaving it open for something in the future."

"Like . . . what?"

"I don't know yet. Depends on what happens in the future. Hopefully something happy."

She shrugs this off and sits on the corner of her bed, tapping her fingers on her thigh and watching me. Nora settles down next to her. There are no chairs, so I sit on the floor. The carpet is a mystery under ancient strata of wrinkled clothes.

"So . . . R," Nora says, leaning toward me. "You're a zombie. What's that feel like?"

"Uh . . ."

"How did it happen? How'd you get converted?"

"Don't . . . remember."

"I'm not seeing any old bites or gunshot wounds or anything. Must've been natural causes. No one was around to debrain you?"

I shrug.

"How old are you?"

I shrug.

"You look twentysomething, but you could be thirtysomething.

You have one of those faces. How come you're not all rotten? I barely even smell you."

"I don't . . . um . . ."

"Do your body functions still work? They don't, right? I mean can you actually still, you know—?"

"Jesus, Nora," Julie cuts in, elbowing her in the hip. "Will you back off? He didn't come here for an interrogation."

I shoot Julie a grateful look.

"I do have one question, though," she says. "How the hell did you get *in* here? Into the stadium?"

I shrug. "Walked . . . in."

"How'd you get past the guards?"

"Played . . . Living."

She stares at me. "They *let* you in? *Ted* let you in?"

"Distrac . . . ted."

She puts a hand to her forehead. "Wow. That's . . ." She pauses, and an incredulous smile breaks through. "You look . . . less gross. Did you comb your hair, R?"

"He's in drag!" Nora laughs. "He's in Living drag!"

"I can't believe that worked on the guards."

"Do you think he could pass?" Nora wonders. "Out on the streets with real people?"

Julie studies me dubiously, like a photographer forced to consider a chubby model. "Well," she allows. "I guess . . . it's *possible*."

I squirm under their scrutiny. Finally Julie takes a deep breath and stands up. "Anyway, you'll have to stay here at least for tonight, till we can figure out what to do with you. I'm going to go heat up some rice. You want some, Nora?"

"Nah, I just had Carbtein nine hours ago." She looks at me cautiously. "Are you, uh . . . hungry, R?"

I shake my head. "I'm . . . fine."

"'Cause I don't know what we're supposed to do about your dietary restrictions. I mean, I know you can't help it, Julie explained all about you, but we don't—"

"Really." I stop her. "I'm . . . fine."

She looks uncertain. I can imagine the footage rolling behind her eyes. A dark room filling with blood. Her friends dying on the floor. Me, crawling toward Julie with red hands outstretched. Julie may have convinced her that I'm a special case, but I shouldn't be surprised to get a few nervous looks. Nora watches me in silence for a few minutes. Then she breaks away and starts rolling a joint.

When Julie comes back with the food, I borrow her spoon and take a small bite of rice, smiling as I chew. As usual it goes down like Styrofoam, but I do manage to swallow it. Julie and Nora look at each other, then at me.

"How's it taste?" Julie asks tentatively.

I grimace.

"Okay, but still, you haven't eaten any people in a long time. And you're still walking. Do you think you could ever wean yourself off . . . live foods?"

I give her a wry smile. "I guess . . . it's *possible*."

Julie grins at this. Half at my unexpected use of sarcasm, half at the implied hope behind it. Her whole face lights up in a way I've never seen before, so I hope I'm right. I hope it's true. I hope I haven't just learned how to lie.

. . .

Around one AM, the girls start to yawn. There are canvas cots in the den, but no one feels like venturing out of Julie's room. This gaudily painted little cube is like a warm bunker in the frozen emptiness of Antarctica. Nora takes the bed. Julie and I take the floor. Nora scribbles homework notes for about an hour, then clicks off the lamp and starts snoring like a small, delicate chain saw. Julie and I lie on our backs under a thick blanket, using piles of her clothes for a mattress on the rock-hard floor. It's a strange feeling, being so utterly surrounded by her. Her life scent is on everything. She's on me and under me and next to me. It's as if the entire room is made out of her.

"R," she whispers, looking up at the ceiling. There are words and doodles smeared up there in glow-in-the-dark paint.

"Yeah."

"I hate this place."

"I know."

"Take me somewhere else."

I pause, looking up at the ceiling. I wish I could read what she's written there. Instead, I pretend the letters are stars. The words, constellations.

"Where do . . . want to go?"

"I don't know. Somewhere far away. Some distant continent where none of this is happening. Where people just live in peace."

I fall silent.

"One of Perry's older friends used to be a pilot . . . we could take your housejet! It'd be like a flying Winnebago, we could go anywhere!" She rolls onto her side and grins at me. "What do you think, R? We could go to the other side of the world."

The excitement in her voice makes me wince. I hope she can't see the grim light in my eyes. I don't know for sure, but there is something in the air lately, a deathly stillness as I walk through the city and its outskirts, that tells me the days of running away from problems are over. There will be no more vacations, no road trips, no tropical getaways. The plague has covered the world.

"You said . . . ," I begin, psyching myself up to express a complex thought. "You said . . . the . . ."

"Come on," she encourages. "Use your words."

"You said . . . the plane's not . . . its own world."

Her grin falters. "What?"

"Can't . . . float above . . . the mess."

She frowns. "I said that?"

"Your dad . . . concrete box . . . walls and guns . . . Running away . . . no better . . . than hiding. Maybe worse."

She thinks for a moment. "I know," she says, and I feel guilty for crashing her brief flight of fancy. "I know this. It's what I've been telling myself for years, that there's still hope, that we can turn things around somehow, blah fucking blah. It's just . . . getting a lot harder to believe lately."

"I know," I say, trying to hide the cracks in my sincerity. "But can't . . . give up."

Her voice darkens. She calls my bluff. "Why are you so hopeful all of a sudden? What are you really thinking?"

I say nothing, but she reads my face like a front-page headline, the kind that announced the atomic bomb and the *Titanic* and all the World Wars in progressively smaller type.

"There's nowhere left, is there," she says.

Almost imperceptibly, I shake my head.

"The whole world," she says. "You think it's all exed? All overrun?"

"Yes."

"How could you know that?"

"I don't. But . . . I feel."

She lets out a long breath, staring at the model planes dangling above us. "So what are we supposed to do?"

"Have to . . . fix it."

"Fix what?"

"Don't know. Ev . . . rything."

She props herself up on one elbow. "What are you talking about?" Her voice is no longer quiet. Nora stirs and stops snoring. "Fix everything?" Julie says, her eyes sparking in the dark. "How exactly are we supposed to do that? If you have some big revelation, please share, 'cause it's not like I don't think about this literally *all* the time. It's not like this hasn't been burning my brain every morning and night since my mom left. How do we fix everything? It's *so* broken. Everyone is *dying*, over and over again, in deeper and darker ways. What are we supposed to do? Do you know what's causing it? This plague?"

I hesitate. "No."

"Then how can you do anything about it? I want to know, R. How are we supposed to 'fix it'?"

I'm staring up at the ceiling. I'm staring at the verbal constellations, glimmering green in distant space. As I lie there, letting my mind rise into those imaginary heavens, two of the stars begin to change. They rotate, and focus, and their shapes clarify. They become . . . *letters*.

T

R

"Ter—" I whisper.

"What?"

"Truh—" I say, trying to pronounce it. It's a sound. It's a syllable. The blurry constellation is becoming a word. "What is . . . that?" I ask, pointing at the ceiling.

"What? The quotes?"

I stand up and indicate the general area of the sentence. "This one."

"It's a line from 'Imagine.' The John Lennon song."

"Which . . . line?"

"'It's easy if you try.'"

I stand there for a minute, gazing up like an intrepid explorer of the cosmos. Then I lie down and fold my arms behind my head, eyes wide open. I don't have the answers she's asking for, but I can feel their existence. Faint points of light in the distant dark.

SLOW STEPS. Mud under boots. Look nowhere else. Strange mantras loop through my head. Old bearded mutterings from dark alleys. *Where are you going, Perry? Foolish child. Brainless boy. Where?* Every day the universe grows larger, darker, colder. I stop in front of a black door. A girl lives here in this metal house. Do I love her? Hard to say anymore. But she is all that's left. The final red sun in an ever-expanding emptiness.

I walk into the house and find her sitting on the staircase, arms crossed over her knees. She puts a finger to her lips. "Dad," she whispers to me.

I glance up the staircase toward the general's bedroom. I hear his voice slurring in the dimness.

"This picture, Julie. The water park, remember the water park? Had to haul ten buckets up for just one slide. Twenty minutes of work for ten seconds of fun. Seemed worth it back then, didn't it? I liked watching your face when you flew out of the tube. You looked just like her, even back then."

Julie stands up quietly, moves toward the front door.

"You're all her, Julie. You aren't me, you're *her*. How could she do it?"

I open the door and back out. Julie follows me, soft steps, no sound.

"How could she be so weak?" the man says in a voice like steel melting. "How could she leave us here?"

We walk in silence. The drizzling rain beads in our hair and we shake it out like dogs. We come to Colonel Rosso's house. Rosso's wife opens the door, looks at Julie's face, and hugs her. We walk inside into the warmth.

I find Rosso in the living room, sipping coffee, peering through his glasses at a water-stained old book. While Julie and Mrs. Rosso murmur in the kitchen, I sit down across from the colonel.

"Perry," he says.

"Colonel."

"How are you holding up?"

"I'm alive."

"A good start. How are you settling into the home?"

"I despise it."

Rosso is quiet for a moment. "What's on your mind?"

I search for words. I seem to have forgotten most of them. Finally, quietly, I say, "He lied to me."

"How so?"

"He said we were fixing things, and if we didn't give up everything might turn out okay."

"He believed that. I think I do, too."

"But then he *died*." My voice trembles and I fight to squeeze it tight. "And it was *senseless*. No battle, no noble sacrifice, just a stupid work accident that could have happened to anyone anywhere, any time in history."

"Perry . . ."

"I don't understand it, sir. What's the point of trying to fix a world we're in so briefly? Where's the meaning in all that work if it's just going to disappear? Without any warning? A fucking brick on the head?"

Rosso says nothing. The low voices in the kitchen become audible in our silence, so they drop to whispers, trying to hide from the colonel what I'm sure he already knows. Our little world is far too tired to care about the crimes of its leaders.

"I want to join Security," I announce. My voice is solid now. My face is hard.

Rosso lets out a slow breath and sets his book down. "Why, Perry?"

"Because it's the only thing left worth doing."

"I thought you wanted to write."

"That's pointless."

"Why?"

"We have bigger concerns now. General Grigio says these are the last days. I don't want to waste my last days scratching letters on paper."

"Writing isn't letters on paper. It's communication. It's memory."

"None of that matters anymore. It's too late."

He studies me. He picks up the book again and holds the cover out. "Do you know this story?"

"It's Gilgamesh."

"Yes. *The Epic of Gilgamesh*, one of the earliest known works of literature. Humanity's debut novel, you could say." Rosso flips through the brittle yellow pages. "Love, sex, blood, and tears. A journey to find eternal life. To escape death." He reaches across the table and hands the book to me. "It was written over four thousand years ago on clay tablets by people who tilled the mud and rarely lived past forty. It's survived countless wars, disasters, and plagues, and continues to fascinate to this day, because here I am, in the midst of modern ruin, reading it."

I look at Rosso. I don't look at the book. My fingers dig into the leather cover.

"The world that birthed that story is long gone, all its people are dead, but it continues to touch the present and future because someone cared enough about that world to keep it. To put it in words. To remember it."

I split the book open to the middle. The pages are riddled with ellipses, marking words and lines missing from the tablets, rotted out and lost to history. I stare at these marks and let their black dots fill my vision. "I don't want to remember," I say, and I shut the book. "I want to join Security. I want to do dangerous stuff. I want to forget."

"What are you saying, Perry?"

"I'm not saying anything."

"It sounds like you are."

"No." The shadows in the room pool in the lines of our faces, draining our eyes of hue. "There's nothing left worth saying."

• • •

I am numb. Adrift in the blackness of Perry's thoughts, I reverberate with his grief like a low church bell.

"Are you working, Perry?" I whisper into the emptiness. "Are you reverse-engineering your life?"

Shhhhh, Perry says. *Don't break the mood. I need this to cut through.*

I float there in his unshed tears, waiting in the salty dark.

• • •

Morning sun streams through the balcony window of Julie's bedroom. The green constellations have faded back into the blue-sky ceiling. The girls are still asleep, but I've been lying here awake for all but a few uneasy hours. Unable to stay motionless any longer, I slip out of the blankets and stretch my creaky joints, letting the sun baste one side of my face, then the other. Nora sleep-mumbles a bit of nursing jargon, "mitosis" or "meiosis," possibly "necrosis," and I notice the dog-eared textbook resting open on her stomach. Curious, I hover over her for a moment, then carefully lift up the book.

I can't read the title. But I immediately recognize the cover. A serenely sleeping face offering its throat of exposed veins to the viewer. The medical reference book *Gray's Anatomy.*

Looking nervously over my shoulder, I whisk the heavy tome out into the hallway and start flipping through its pages. Intricate drawings of human architecture, organs and bones all too familiar to me, although here the filleted bodies are shown clean and perfect, their details unblurred by filth or fluids. I pore over the illustrations as the minutes tick by, wracked by guilt and fascination like a pubescent Catholic with a *Playboy.* I can't read the captions, of course, but a few Latin words pop into my head as I study the images, perhaps distant recalls from my old life, a college lecture or TV documentary I absorbed somewhere. The knowledge feels grotesque in my mind but I grasp it and hold it tight, etching it deep into my memory. Why am I doing this? Why do I want to know the names and functions of all the beautiful structures I've spent my years violating? Because I don't deserve to keep them anonymous. I want the pain of knowing them, and by extension myself: who and what I really am. Maybe with that scalpel, red-hot and sterilized in tears, I can begin to carve out the rot inside me.

Hours pass. When I've seen every page and wrung every syllable from my memory, I gently replace the book on Nora's belly and tiptoe out onto the balcony, hoping the warm sun will grant some relief from the moral nausea churning inside me.

I lean against the railing and take in the cramped vistas of Julie's city. As dark and lifeless as it was last night, now it bustles and roars like Times Square. What is everyone doing? The undead airport has its crowds but no real activity. We don't do things; we wait for things to happen. The collective volition bubbling up from the Living is intoxicating, and I have a sudden urge to be down in those masses, rubbing shoulders and elbowing for space in all that sweat and breath. If my questions have answers, they must certainly be down there, under the pounding soles of those filthy feet.

I hear the girls chatting quietly in the bedroom, finally waking up. I go back inside and crawl under the blankets next to Julie.

"Good morning, *R*," Nora says, not quite sincerely. I think addressing me like a human is still a novelty for her; she looks like she wants to titter every time she acknowledges my presence. It's aggravating, but I understand. I'm an absurdity that takes some getting used to.

"Morning," Julie croaks, watching me from across the pillow. She looks about as unpretty as I've ever seen her, eyes puffy and hair insane. I wonder how well she sleeps at night and what kind of dreams she has. I wish I could step into them like she steps into mine.

She rolls onto her side and props her head on her elbow. She clears her throat. "So," she says. "Here you are. What now?"

"Want to . . . see your city."

Her eyes search my face. "Why?"

"Want to . . . see how you live. Living people."

Her lips tighten. "Too risky. Someone would notice you."

"Come on, Julie," Nora says. "He walked all the way here, let's give him a tour! We can fix him up, disguise him. He already got past Ted, I'm sure he'll be okay strolling around a little if we're careful. You'll be careful, right, R?"

I nod, still looking at Julie. She allows a long silence. Then she rolls onto her back and closes her eyes, releasing a slow breath that sounds like consent.

"Yay!" Nora says.

"We can *try* it. But R, if you don't look convincing after we fix you up, no tour. And if I see anyone staring at you too hard, tour's over. Deal?"

I nod.

"No nodding. Say it."

"Deal."

She crawls out of the blankets and climbs onto the side of the bed. She looks me up and down. "Okay," she says, her hair sticking out in every direction. "Let's get you presentable."

. . .

I would like my life to be a movie so I could cut to a montage. A quick sequence of shots set to some trite pop song would be much easier to endure than the two grueling hours the girls spend trying to convert me, to change me back into what's widely considered human. They wash my hair. They wear out a fresh toothbrush on my teeth, although for my smile anything above a coffee-addicted Brit is not in the cards. They attempt to dress me in some of Julie's more boyish clothes, but Julie is a pixie and I rip through T-shirts and snap buttons like a bodybuilder. Finally they give up, and I wait naked in the bathroom while they run my old business wear through the wash.

While I wait, I decide to take a shower. This is an experience I had long forgotten, and I savor it like a first sip of wine, a first kiss. The steaming water cascades over my battered body, washing away months or years of dirt and blood, some of it mine, much of it others'. All this filth spirals down the drain and into the underworld where it belongs. My true skin emerges, pale gray, marked by cuts and scrapes and grazing bulletwounds, but clean.

This is the first time I have seen my body.

When my clothes are dry and Julie has sewn up the most noticeable holes, I dress myself, relishing the unfamiliar feeling of cleanness. My shirt no longer sticks to me. My slacks no longer chafe.

"You should at least lose the tie," Nora says. "You're about ten wars behind the fashion curve in that fancy getup."

"No, leave it," Julie pleads, regarding the little strip of cloth with a whimsical smile. "I like that tie. It's the only thing keeping you from being completely gray."

"It sure won't help him blend in, Jules. Remember all the stares we got when we started wearing sneakers instead of work boots?"

"Exactly. People already know you and me don't wear the uniform; as long as R stays with us he could wear spandex shorts and a top hat and no one would mention it."

Nora smiles. "I like *that* idea."

So the tie remains, in all its red silk incongruity. Julie helps me knot it. She brushes my hair and runs some goo through it. Nora thoroughly fumigates me with men's body spray.

"Ugh, Nora," Julie objects. "I hate that stuff. And he doesn't even stink."

"He stinks a little bit."

"Yeah, *now* he does."

"Better he smell like a chemical plant than a corpse, right? It'll keep the dogs away from him."

There is some debate about whether or not to make me wear sunglasses to hide my eyes, but they eventually decide this would be more conspicuous than just letting that ethereal gray show itself.

"It's actually not that noticeable," Julie says. "Just don't have a staring contest with anyone."

"You'll be fine," Nora adds. "No one in this place really looks at each other anyway."

The final step in their remodeling plan is makeup. As I sit in front of the mirror like a Hollywood starlet getting ready for her close-up, they powder me, they rouge me, they colorize my black-and-white skin. When they're done, I stare at the mirror in amazement.

I am alive.

I am a handsome young professional, happy, successful, in the bloom of health, just emerging from a meeting and on my way to the gym. I laugh out loud. I look at myself in the mirror and the joyful absurdity of it just bubbles out.

Laughter. Another first for me.

"Oh my . . . ," Nora says, standing back to look at me, and Julie says, "Huh." She tilts her head. "You look . . ."

"You look *hot!*" Nora blurts. "Can I have him, Julie? Just for one night?"

"Shut your dirty mouth," Julie chuckles, still inspecting me. She touches my forehead, the narrow, bloodless slot where she once threw a knife. "Should probably cover that. Sorry, R." She sticks a Band-Aid over the wound and presses it down with gentle strokes. "There." She steps back again and studies me like a perfectionist painter, pleased but cautious.

"Con . . . vincing?" I ask.

"Hmm," she says.

I offer her my best attempt at a winning smile, stretching my lips wide.

"Oh, God. Definitely don't do that."

"Just be natural," Nora says. "Pretend you're home at the airport surrounded by friends, if you people have those."

I think back to the moment Julie named me, that warm feeling that crept into my face for the first time as we shared a beer and a plate of Thai food.

"There you go, that's better," Nora says.

Julie nods, pressing her knuckles against her smiling lips as if to hold back some outburst of emotion. A giddy cocktail of amusement, pride, and affection. "You clean up nice, R."

"Thank . . . you."

She takes a deep, decisive breath. "Okay then." She pulls a wool beanie over her wild hair and zips up her sweatshirt. "Ready to see what humanity's been up to since you left it?"

Triangle
of Petit

In my old days of scavenging the city I often gazed up at the stadium walls and imagined a paradise inside. I assumed it was perfect, that everyone was happy and beautiful and wanted for nothing, and in my numb, limited way I felt envy and wanted to eat them all the more. But look at this place. The corrugated sheet metal glaring in the sun. The fly-buzzing pens of moaning, hormone-pumped cattle. The hopelessly stained laundry hanging from support cables between buildings, flapping in the wind like surrender flags.

"Welcome to Citi Stadium," Julie says, spreading her arms wide. "The largest human habitation in what used to be America."

Why did we stay? the voices mutter deep inside me as Julie calls out landmarks and points of interest. *What is a city and why do we keep building them? Take away the culture, the commerce, the business and pleasure; is there anything left? Just a grid of nameless streets filled with nameless people?*

"There are over twenty thousand of us crammed into this fishbowl," Julie says as we push through the dense crowds in the central square. "Pretty soon it'll be so tight we'll all just squish together. The human race will be one big mindless amoeba."

Why didn't we scatter? Head for high ground and plant our roots where the air and water were clean? What is it we needed from each other in this sweaty crush of bodies?

As much as possible I keep my eyes to the ground, trying to blend in and avoid notice. I sneak glances at guard towers, water tanks, new buildings rising under the bright strobe of arc welders, but mostly my view is of my feet. The asphalt. Mud and dog shit softening the sharp angles.

"We're growing less than half what we need to survive," Julie says as we pass the gardens, just a blurry dream of green behind the translucent walls of the hothouses. "So all the real food gets rationed out in tiny servings, and we fill the gaps in our diet with Carbtein." A trio of teenage boys in yellow jumpsuits haul a cart of oranges past us, and I notice one of them has strange sores running down the side of his face, sunken brown patches like the bruises on an apple, as if the cells have simply collapsed. "Not to mention we're burning through a pharmacy worth of medicine every month. Salvage teams can barely keep up. It's only a matter of time before we go to war with the other enclaves over the last bottle of Prozac."

Was it just fear? the voices wonder. *We were fearful in the best of times; how could we cope with the worst? So we found the tallest walls and poured ourselves behind them. We kept pouring until we were the biggest and strongest, elected the greatest generals and found the most weapons, thinking all this maximalism would somehow generate happiness. But nothing so obvious could ever work.*

"What's amazing to me," Nora says, squeezing past the strained belly of a morbidly pregnant woman, "is that despite all these needs and shortages we have, people keep pumping out kids. Flooding the world with copies of themselves just because that's tradition, that's what's done."

Julie glances at Nora and opens her mouth, then closes it.

"And even though we're about to starve to death under a mountain of poopy diapers, no one's brave enough to even *suggest* that people keep their seed in their nuts for a while."

"Yeah, but . . . ," Julie says, her voice uncharacteristically timid. "I don't know . . . there's something kind of beautiful about it, don't you think? That we keep living and growing even though our world is a corpse? That we keep coming back no matter how many of us die?"

"Why is it beautiful that humanity keeps coming back? So does herpes."

"Oh shut up, Nora, you love people. Being a misanthrope was Perry's thing."

Nora laughs and shrugs.

"It's not about keeping up the population, it's about passing on who we are and what we've learned, so things keep *going*. So we don't just *end*. Sure it's selfish, in a way, but how else do our short lives mean anything?"

"I guess that's true," Nora allows. "It's not like we have any other legacies to leave in this post-everything era."

"Right. It's all fading. I heard the world's last country collapsed in January."

"Oh, really? Which one was it?"

"Can't remember. Sweden, maybe?"

"So the globe is officially blank. That's depressing."

"At least you have some heritage you can hold on to. Your dad was Ethiopian, right?"

"Yeah, but what's that mean to me? He didn't remember his country, I never went there, and now it doesn't exist. All that leaves me with is brown skin, and who pays any attention to color anymore?" She waves a hand toward my face. "In a year or two we're all gonna be gray anyway."

I fall behind as they continue to banter. I watch them talk and gesticulate, listening to their voices without hearing the words.

What is left of us? the ghosts moan, drifting back into the shadows of my subconscious. *No countries, no cultures, no wars but still no peace. What's at our core, then? What's still squirming in our bones when everything else is stripped?*

. . .

By late afternoon, we've come to the road once known as Jewel Street. The school buildings wait for us ahead, squat and self-satisfied, and I feel my stomach knotting. Julie hesitates at the intersection, looking pensively toward their glowing windows. "Those are the training facilities," she says. "But you don't want to see in there. Let's move on."

I gladly follow her away from that dark boulevard, but I stare hard at the fresh green sign as we pass. I'm fairly sure the first letter is a "J."

"What's . . . that street called?" I ask, pointing to the sign.

Julie smiles. "Why, that's Julie Street."

"It used to be a graphic of a diamond or something," Nora says, "but her dad renamed it when they built the schools. Isn't that sweet?"

"It *was* sweet," Julie admits. "That's the type of gesture Dad can manage sometimes."

She takes us around the perimeter of the walls to a wide, dark tunnel directly across from the main gate. I realize these tunnels must be where sports teams once made their triumphal entries onto the field, back when thousands of people could still cheer for things so trivial. And since the tunnel on the other end is the passage into the world of the Living, it seems fitting that this one leads to a graveyard.

Julie flashes an ID badge at the guards and they wave us through the back gate. We step out onto a hilly field surrounded by hundreds of feet of chain-link fencing. Black hawthorn trees curl toward the mottled gray and gold sky, standing guard over classical tombstones, complete with crosses and statues of saints. I suspect these were reappropriated from some forgotten funeral home, as the engraved names and dates have been covered over with crude letters stenciled in white paint. The epitaphs resemble graffiti tags.

"This is where we bury . . . what's left of us," Julie says. She walks a few steps ahead as Nora and I stand in the entry. Out here, with the door shut behind us, the pulsing noise of human affairs is gone, replaced by the stoic silence of the truly dead. Each body resting here is either headless, brainless, or nothing but scraps of half-eaten flesh and bones piled in a box. I can see why they chose to build the cemetery outside the stadium walls: not only does it take up more land than all the indoor farmlands combined, it also can't be very good for morale. This is a reminder far more grim than the old world's sunny yards of peaceful passings and *requiem eternum*. This is a glimpse of our future. Not as individuals, whose deaths we can accept, but as a species, a civilization, a world.

"Are you sure you want to go in here today?" Nora asks Julie softly.

Julie looks out at the hills of patchy brown grass. "I go every day. Today's a day. Today's Tuesday."

"Yeah, but . . . do you want us to wait here?"

She glances back at me and considers for a moment. Then she shakes her head. "No. Come on." She starts walking and I follow her. Nora trails an awkward distance behind me, a look of muted surprise on her face.

There are no paths in this cemetery. Julie walks in a straight line, stepping over headstones and across grave mounds, many still soft and muddy. Her eyes are focused on a tall spire topped by a marble angel. We stop in front of it, Julie and I side by side, Nora still lingering behind. I strain to read the name on the grave, but it doesn't reveal itself. Even the first few letters remain out of reach.

"This is . . . my mom," Julie says. The cool evening wind blows her hair into her eyes, but she doesn't brush it away. "She left when I was twelve."

Nora squirms behind us, then wanders away and pretends to browse the epitaphs.

"She went crazy, I guess," Julie says. "Ran out into the city by herself one night and that was that. They found a few pieces of her but . . . there's nothing in this grave." Her voice is casual. I'm reminded of her trying to imitate the Dead back in the airport, the overacting, the paper-thin mask. "I guess it was too much for her, all of this." She waves a hand vaguely at the graveyard and the stadium behind us. "She was a real free spirit, you know? This wild bohemian goddess full of fire. She met my dad when she was nineteen; he swept her off her feet. Hard to believe it, but he was a musician back then, played keys in a rock band, was actually pretty good. They got married really young, and then . . . I don't know . . . the world went to shit, and Dad changed. Everything changed."

I try to read her eyes but her hair obscures them. I hear a tremor in her voice. "Mom tried. She really did try. She did her part to keep everything together, she did her daily work, and then it was all me. She poured everything into me. Dad was hardly around, so it was always just her and the little brat. I remember having so much fun; she used to take me to this water park back in—" A tiny sob catches her by surprise, choking off the words, and she covers her mouth with her hand. Her eyes plead with me through strands of dirty hair. "She just wasn't built for this fucking place," she says, her voice warbling in falsetto. "What was she supposed to do here? Everything that made her alive was gone. All she had left was this stupid twelve-year-old with ugly teeth who kept waking her up every night wanting to snuggle away a nightmare. No wonder she wanted out."

"Stop," I say firmly, and turn her to face me. "Stop." Tears are running down her face, salty secretions shooting through ducts and tubes, past bright pulsating cells and angry red tissues. I wipe them away and pull her into me. "You're . . . alive," I mumble into her hair. "You're . . . worth living for."

I feel her shudder against my chest, clinging to my shirt as my arms surround her. The air is silent except for the light whistle of the breeze. Nora is looking our way now, twisting a finger through her curls. She catches my eye and gives me a sad smile, as if to apologize for not warning me. But I'm not afraid of the skeletons in Julie's closet. I look forward to meeting the rest of them, looking them hard in the eye, giving them firm, bone-crunching handshakes.

As she dampens my shirt with sadness and snot, I realize I'm about to do another thing I've never done before. I suck in air and attempt to sing. "You're . . . sensational . . . ," I croak, struggling for a trace of Frank's melody. "Sensational . . . that's all."

There's a pause, and then something shifts in Julie's demeanor. I realize she's laughing.

"Oh wow," she giggles, and looks up at me, her eyes still glistening above a grin. "That was beautiful, R, really. You and Zombie Sinatra should record *Duets III*."

I cough. "Didn't get . . . warm-up."

She brushes some stray hairs out of my face. She looks at the grave. She reaches into her back pocket and pulls out a wilted airport daisy with four petals remaining. She sets it on the bare dirt in front of the headstone. "Sorry, Mom," she says softly. "Best I could find." She grabs my hand. "Mom, this is R. He's really nice, you'd love him. The flower is from him too."

Even though the grave is empty, I half expect her mother's hand to burst out of the earth and grip my ankle. After all, I'm a cell in the cancer that killed her. But if Julie is any indication, I suspect her mother might forgive me. These people, these beautiful Living women, they don't seem to make the connection between me and the creatures that keep killing everything they love. They allow me to be an exception, and I feel humbled by this gift. I want to pay it back somehow, *earn* their forgiveness. I want to repair the world I've helped destroy.

Nora rejoins us as we leave Mrs. Grigio's grave. She rubs Julie's shoulder and kisses the side of her head. "You okay?"

Julie nods. "As much as ever."

"Want to hear something nice?"

"So badly."

"I saw a patch of wildflowers by my house. They're growing in a ditch."

Julie smiles. She rubs the last few tears out of her eyes and doesn't say anything more.

I peruse the headstones as we walk. They are crooked and haphazardly placed, making the cemetery look ancient despite the dozens of freshly dug graves. I am thinking about death. I'm thinking how brief life is compared to it. I'm wondering how deep this graveyard goes, how many layers of coffins are stacked on top of each other, and what portion of Earth's soil is made from our decay.

Then something interrupts my morbid reflections. I feel a lurch in my stomach, a queer sensation like what I imagine a baby kicking in the womb might feel like. I stop midstep and turn around. A featureless rectangular headstone is watching me from a nearby hill.

"Hold on," I say to the girls, and begin climbing the hill.

"What's he doing?" I hear Nora ask under her breath. "Isn't that . . . ?"

I stand in front of the grave, staring at the name on the stone. A queasy sensation of vertigo rises through my legs, as if a vast pit is opening up in front of me, drawing me toward its edge with some dark, inexorable force. My stomach lurches again, I feel a sharp tug on my brain stem . . . I fall in.

I AM PERRY KELVIN, and this is my last day alive.

What a strange feeling, waking up to that awareness. All my life I have battled the alarm clock, pummeling the snooze button over and over with mounting self-loathing until the shame is finally strong enough to lever me upright. It was only on the brightest of mornings, those rare days of verve and purpose and clear reasons to live, that I ever sprang awake easily. How strange, then, that I do today.

Julie whimpers as I extract myself from her goose-bumped arms and slip out of bed. She gathers my half of the blankets around her and curls up against the wall. She will sleep for hours more, dreaming endless landscapes and novas of color both gorgeous and frightening. If I stayed she would wake up and describe them to me. All the mad plot twists and surrealist imagery, so vivid to her while so meaningless to me. There was a time when I treasured listening to her, when I found the commotion in her soul bittersweet and lovely, but I can no longer bear it. I lean over to kiss her good-bye, but my lips stiffen and I cringe away from her. I can't. I can't. I'll collapse. I pull back and leave without touching her.

Two years ago today my father was crushed under the wall he was building, and I became an orphan. I have missed him for seven hundred and thirty days, my mother for even longer, but tomorrow I will not miss anyone. I think about this as I descend the winding stairs of my foster home, this wretched house of discards, and emerge into the city. Dad, Mom, Grandpa, my friends . . . tomorrow I won't miss anyone.

It's early and the sun is barely over the mountains, but the city is already wide awake. The streets are crawling with laborers, repair crews, moms pushing knobby-tired strollers and foster moms herding lines of kids like cattle. Somewhere in the distance someone is playing a clarinet; its quavery notes drift through the morning air like birdsong, and I try to shut it out. I don't want to hear music, I don't want the sunrise to be pink. The world is a liar. Its ugliness is overwhelming; the scraps of beauty make it worse.

I make my way to the Island Street administrative building and tell the receptionist I'm here for my seven o'clock with General Grigio. She walks me back to his office and shuts the door behind me. The general doesn't look up from the paperwork on his desk. He raises one finger at me. I stand and wait, letting my eyes roam the contents of his walls. A picture of Julie. A picture of Julie's mother. A faded picture of himself and a younger Colonel Rosso in proper U.S. Army uniforms, smoking cigarettes in front of a flooded New York skyline. Next to this, another shot of the two men smoking cigarettes, this time overlooking a crumbled London. Then bombed-out Paris. Then smoldering Rome.

The general finally sets down his paperwork. He takes off his glasses and looks me over. "Mr. Kelvin," he says.

"Sir."

"Your very first salvage as team manager."

"Yes, sir."

"Do you feel ready?"

My tongue stalls for an instant as images of horses and cellists and red lips on a wineglass flicker through my mind, trying to knock me off course. I burn them like old film. "Yes, sir."

"Good. Here is your exit pass. See Colonel Rosso at the community center for your team assignments."

"Thank you, sir." I take the paperwork and turn to leave. But I pause on the doorway threshold. "Sir?" My voice cracks a little even though I swore I wouldn't let it.

"Yes, Perry?"

"Permission to speak freely, sir?"

"Go ahead."

I moisten my dry lips. "Is there a reason for all this?"

"Pardon me?"

"Is there a reason for us to keep doing all these things? The salvages and . . . everything?"

"I'm afraid I don't understand your question, Perry. The supplies we salvage are keeping us alive."

"Are we trying to stay alive because we think the world will get better someday? Is that what we're working toward?"

His expression is flat. "I suppose."

My voice becomes shaky and very undignified, but I can no longer control it. "What about right now? Is there anything right now that you love enough to keep living for?"

"Perry—"

"Will you tell me what it is, sir? Please?"

His eyes are marbles. A noise like the beginning of a word forms in his throat, then it stops. His mouth tightens. "This conversation is inappropriate." He lays his hands flat on his desk. "You should be on your way now. You have work to do."

I swallow hard. "Yes, sir. Sorry, sir."

"See Colonel Rosso at the community center for your team assignments."

"Yes, sir."

I step through the door and shut it behind me.

In Colonel Rosso's office I conduct myself with utmost professionalism. I request my team assignments and he gives them to me, handing over the manila envelope with warmth and pride in his squinty, failing eyes. He wishes me luck and I thank him; he invites me to dinner and I politely decline. My voice does not crack. I lose no composure.

Marching back through the community center lobby I glance toward the gym and see Nora staring at me through the tall windows. She's wearing snug black shorts and a white tank top, as are all the preteens on the volleyball court behind her. Nora's "team," her sad attempt to distract a few kids from reality for two hours a week. I walk past her without so much as a nod, and as I start to push the front doors open I hear her sneakers slapping the tile floor behind me.

"Perry!"

I stop and let the doors swing shut. I turn around and face her. "Hey."

She stands in front of me with her arms crossed, her eyes stony. "So today's the big day, huh?"

"I guess so."

"What area are you hitting? You got it all planned out?"

"The old Pfizer building on Eighth Ave."

She nods rapidly. "Good, that sounds like a good plan, Perry. And you'll be all done and home by six, right? 'Cause remember we're taking you to the Orchard tonight. We're not letting you spend today moping alone like you did last year."

I watch the kids in the gym, bumping-setting-spiking, laughing and cursing. "I don't know if I'll make it. This salvage might go a little later than usual."

She keeps nodding. "Oh. Oh okay. Because that building is crooked and full of cracks and dead ends and you have to be extra careful, right?"

"Right."

"Yeah." She nods toward the envelope in my hand. "You checked that yet?"

"Not yet."

"Well you should probably check it, Perry." Her foot taps the floor; her body vibrates with restrained anger. "You need to make sure you know everyone's profiles, strengths and weaknesses and all that. Mine, for instance, because I'm on there."

My face goes blank. "What?"

"Sure, I'm going, Rosso put me on yesterday. Do you know my strengths and weaknesses? Is there anything on your agenda you think might be an issue for me? 'Cause I'd hate to jeopardize your very first salvage as team manager."

I rip the top off the envelope and start scanning the names.

"Julie signed up, too, did she mention that?"

My eyes flash up from the page.

"That's right, fucker, will that be a problem for you?" Her voice is strained to breaking. There are tears in her eyes. "Is that a conflict at all?"

I shove open the front doors and burst out into the cold morning air. Birds overhead. Those blank-eyed pigeons, those shrieking gulls, all the flies and beetles that eat their shit—the gift of flight dumped on Earth's most worthless creatures. What if it were mine instead? That perfect, weightless freedom. No fences, no walls, no borders; I would fly everywhere, over oceans and continents, mountains and jungles and endless open plains, and somewhere in the world, somewhere in all that distant untouched beauty, I would find a reason.

· · ·

I am floating in Perry's darkness. I am deep in the earth, buried upside down. Somewhere beyond my feet are roots and worms and an inverted graveyard where the coffins are the markers and the headstones are beneath, piercing down into that airy blue emptiness, hiding all the names and pretty epitaphs and leaving me with the rot.

I feel a stirring in the dirt that surrounds me. A hand burrows through and grabs my shoulder.

"Hello, corpse."

• • •

We are in the 747. My piles of souvenirs are sorted and arranged in neat stacks. The aisle is softened with layers of oriental throw rugs. Dean Martin croons on the record player.

"Perry?"

He's in the cockpit, in the pilot's chair with his hands on the controls. He's wearing a pilot's uniform, the white shirt stained with blood. He smiles at me, then gestures at the windows, where streaks of clouds flicker past. "We are now approaching cruising altitude. You're free to move about the cabin."

With slow, cautious movements, I get up and join him in the cockpit. I look at him uneasily. He grins. I rub a finger through the familiar layers of dust on the controls. "This isn't one of your memories, is it?"

"No. This is yours. I wanted you to be comfortable."

"Is it your grave I'm standing on right now?"

He shrugs. "I suppose. I think it's just my empty skull in there, though. You and your friends took most of me home for snacks, remember?"

I open my mouth to apologize again, but he shuts his eyes and waves it away. "Don't, please. We're past all that. Besides, that wasn't really *me* you killed, that was older, wiser Perry. I think this is mostly junior-high Perry you're talking to, young and optimistic and writing a novel called *Ghosts vs. Werewolves*. I'd rather not think about being dead right now."

I eye him uncertainly. "You're a lot more cheerful here than in your memories."

"I have perspective here. It's hard to take your life so seriously when you can see it all at once."

I peer at him. His reality is very convincing, pimples and all. "Are you . . . really you?" I ask.

"What does that mean?"

"All this time I've been talking to you, are you just . . . leftovers from your brain? Or are you really actually you?"

He chuckles. "Does it really actually matter?"

"Are you Perry's soul?"

"Maybe. Kind of. Whatever you want to call it."

"Are you . . . in Heaven?"

He laughs and tugs his blood-soaked shirt. "Yeah, not exactly. Whatever I am, 'R,' I'm in *you*." He laughs again at the look on my face. "Fucked up, isn't it? But Older Wiser went out of this life pretty darkly. Maybe this is our chance to catch up with him and work some things out before . . . you know. Whatever's next."

I look out the window. No glimpse of land or sea, just the silky mountains of Cloud World spread out below us and piled high above. "Where are we headed?"

"Toward whatever's next." He lifts his eyes to the heavens with mock solemnity, then grins. "You're going to help me get there, and I'm going to help you."

I feel my guts twist as the plane surges and drops on erratic air currents. "Why would you help me? I'm the reason you're dead."

"Come on, R, don't you get this yet?" He seems upset by my question. He locks eyes with me and there's a feverish intensity in them. "You and I are victims of the same disease. We're fighting the same war, just different battles in different theaters, and it's way too late for me to hate you for anything, because we're the same damn thing. My soul, your conscience, whatever's left of me woven into whatever's left of you, all tangled up and conjoined." He gives me a hearty clap on the shoulder that almost hurts. "We're in this together, corpse."

A low tremor rumbles through the plane. The control stick

wobbles in front of Perry, but he ignores it. I don't know what to say, so I just say, "Okay."

He nods. "Okay."

Another faint vibration in the floor, like the concussions of distant bombs.

"So," he says. "God has made us study partners. We need to talk about our project." He takes a deep breath and looks at me, tapping his chin. "I've been hearing a lot of inspirational thoughts prancing around in our head lately. But I'm not sure you really understand the storm we're flying into."

A few red lights blink on in the cabin. There is a scraping noise somewhere outside the plane.

"What am I missing?" I ask.

"How about a strategy? We're wandering around this city like a kitten in a dog kennel. You keep talking about changing the world, but you're sitting here licking your paws while all the pit bulls circle in on us. What's the plan, pussycat?"

Outside, the cotton clouds darken to steel wool. The lights flicker, my souvenirs rattle.

"I don't . . . have one yet."

"So when? You know things are moving. You're changing, your fellow Dead are changing, the world is ready for something miraculous. What are we waiting for?"

The plane shudders and begins to dive. I stumble into the co-pilot chair, feeling my stomach rise into my throat. "I'm not waiting. I'm doing it right now."

"Doing what? What are you doing?"

"I'm trying." I hold Perry's gaze and grip the sides of my seat as the plane shakes and groans. "I'm wanting it. I'm making myself care."

Perry's eyes narrow and his lips tighten, but he doesn't say anything.

"That's step one, isn't it?" I yell over the noise of wind and roaring engines. "That's where it has to start."

The plane lurches and my souvenir stacks collapse, scattering paintings, movies, dishes, dolls and love notes all over the cabin. More lights flare in the cockpit, and a voice crackles on the radio.

R? Helloooo? Are you okay?

Perry's face has gone cold, all playfulness gone. "Bad stuff is coming, R. Some of it's waiting for you right outside this graveyard. You're right, wanting change is step one, but step two is taking it. When the flood comes, I don't want to see you dreaming your way through it. You've got my little girl with you now."

Okay, you're creeping me out. Wake up!

"I know I didn't deserve her," Perry says, his quiet murmur somehow rising above the noise. "She offered me everything and I pissed on it. So now it's your turn, R. Go keep her safe. She's a lot softer than she seems."

God damn it you asshole! Wake up or I'll fucking shoot you!

I nod. Perry nods. Then he turns to face the window and folds his arms across his chest while the controls shake wildly. The storm clouds peel apart and we are diving to earth, hurtling directly toward the stadium, and there they are, the infamous R and J, sitting on a blanket on the rainsoaked roof. R looks up and sees us, his eyes open wide just as we—

. . .

My eyes open wide and I blink reality into focus. I am standing in front of a small grave in an amateur cemetery. Julie's hand is on my shoulder.

"Are you back?" she asks. "What the hell was that about?"

I clear my throat and look around. "Sorry. Daydreaming."

"God you're weird. Come on, I don't want to be here anymore." She strides briskly toward the exit.

Nora and I follow her. Nora keeps pace with me, eyeing me sideways. "Daydreaming?" she asks.

I nod.

"You were talking to yourself a little."

I look at her.

"Some pretty big words, too. I think I heard 'miraculous.'"

I shrug.

The waterfall noise of the city rushes into our ears as the guards open the doors and we step back into the stadium proper. The doors have barely slammed shut behind us when I feel that baby kick in my stomach again. A voice whispers, *Here it comes, R. Are you ready?*

"Oh this is lovely," Julie says under her breath.

There he is, marching around the street corner in front of us: Julie's dad, General Grigio. He strides directly toward us, trailed by three officers of some kind, although none of them wear traditional military attire. Their uniforms are light gray shirts and work pants, no decorations or rank insignias, just pockets and tool loops and laminated ID badges. High-caliber sidearms gleam softly in their belt holsters.

"Be cool, R," Julie whispers. "Don't say anything, just, um . . . pretend you're shy."

"Julie!" the general calls out from an awkward distance.

"Hi, Dad," Julie says.

He and his retinue stop in front of us. He gives Julie's shoulder a quick squeeze. "How are you?"

"Fine. Just went to see Mom."

His jaw muscle twitches, but he doesn't respond. He looks at Nora, gives her a nod, then looks at me. He looks at me very hard. He pulls out a walkie-talkie. "Ted. The individual who slipped past you yesterday. You said it was a young man in a red tie? Tall, thin, poorly complected?"

"Dad," Julie says.

The walkie squawks. The general puts it away and pulls a pair of thumb cuffs from his belt. "You are being detained for unauthorized entry," he recites. "You will be held in—"

"Jesus Christ, Dad." Julie steps forward to push his hands away. "What is wrong with you? He's not an *intruder,* he's visiting from

Goldman Dome. And he almost died on the way here, so cut him some slack on the legalities, will you?"

"Who is he?" the general demands.

Julie edges in front of me as if to block me from responding. "His name is . . . Archie—it was Archie, right?" She glances at me and I nod. "He's Nora's new boyfriend. I just met him today."

Nora grins and squeezes my arm. "Can you believe what a nice dresser he is? I didn't think anyone knew what a tie *was* anymore."

The general hesitates, then puts the cuffs away and forces a thin smile. "Pleased to meet you, Archie. You're aware of course that if you want to stay any longer than three days you'll need to register with our immigration officer."

I nod and try to avoid eye contact, but I can't seem to look away from his face. Although that tense dinner I witnessed in my visions couldn't have been more than a few years ago, he looks a decade older. His skin is thin and papery. His cheekbones protrude. His veins are blue in his forehead.

One of the officers with him clears his throat. "So sorry to hear about Perry, Miss Cabernet. We'll miss him very much." I know this man as well. Colonel Rosso is older than Grigio but has aged more gracefully. He is short and thick, with strong arms and a muscular chest above the inevitable old-man paunch. His hair is wispy and white, blue eyes big and watery behind thick glasses. Julie gives him a smile that seems genuine.

"Thanks, Rosy. So will I."

Their exchange sounds proper but rings false, as if paddling above deep undercurrents. I suspect they have already shared a less professional moment of grief somewhere away from Grigio's officious gaze. "We appreciate your condolences, Colonel Rosso," he says. "However I'll thank you not to replace our surname when addressing my daughter, whatever such 'revisions' she may have embraced."

The older man straightens. "Apologies, sir. I meant nothing by it."

"It's just a nickname," Nora says. "Me and Perry thought she was more of a cab than a . . ."

She trails off under Grigio's stare. He pans slowly over to me. I avoid eye contact until he dismisses me. "We have to be going," he says to no one in particular. "Good to meet you, Archie. Julie, I'll be in meetings all night tonight and then heading over to Goldman in the morning to discuss the merger. I expect to be back at the house in a few days."

Julie nods. Without another word, the general and his men depart. Julie examines the ground, seeming far away. After a moment, Nora breaks the silence. "Well that was scary."

"Let's go to the Orchard," Julie mutters. "I need a drink."

I'm still looking down the street, watching her father shrink into the distance. Just before rounding a corner he glances back at me, and my skin prickles. Will Perry's flood be of water, gentle and cleansing, or will it be a flood of a different kind? I feel movement under my feet. A faint vibration, as if the bones of every man and woman ever buried are rattling deep in the earth. Cracking the bedrock. Stirring the magma.

THE ORCHARD, as it turns out, is not part of the stadium's farming system. It's their one and only pub, or at least the closest thing they have to a pub in this new bastion of prohibition. Reaching its entrance requires an arduous vertical journey through the stadium's Escheresque cityscape. First, we climb four flights of stairs in a ramshackle housing tower while the residents glare at us through cracks in their doors. This is followed by a vertiginous crossing to a neighboring building—boys on the ground try to look up Nora's skirt as we wobble over a wire-mesh catwalk strung between the towers' support cables. Once inside the other building, we plod up three more flights of stairs before finally emerging onto a breezy patio high above the streets. The noise of crowds rumbles through the door at the other end: a wide slab of oak painted with a yellow tree.

I push awkwardly ahead of Julie to open the door for her. Nora grins at her and Julie rolls her eyes. They step inside and I follow them.

The place is packed, but the mood is eerily subdued. No shouting, no high-fiving, no woozy requests for phone numbers. Despite the speakeasy secrecy of its obscure location, the Orchard doesn't serve alcohol.

"I ask you," Julie says as we push our way through the well-behaved crowds, "is there anything sillier than a bunch of ex-marines and construction workers drowning their sorrows at a fucking juice bar? At least it's flask-friendly."

The Orchard is the first building in this city to have some trace of character. All the usual drinking accoutrements are here: dart-boards, pool tables, flat-screen TVs with football games. At first I'm amazed to see these broadcasts—does entertainment still exist? Are there still people out there engaging in frivolity despite the times? But then, ten minutes into the third quarter, the images warp like VHS tape and switch to a different game, the teams and scores changing in the middle of a tackle. Five minutes later they switch again, with just a quick stutter to mark the splice. None of the sports fans seem to notice. They watch these abbreviated, eternally looping contests with blank eyes and sip their drinks like players in a historical reenactment.

A few of the patrons notice me staring at them and I look away. But then I look back. Something about this scene is burrowing into my mind. A thought is developing like a ghost on a Polaroid.

"Three grapefruits," Julie tells the bartender, who looks vaguely embarrassed as he prepares the drinks. We settle in on bar stools and the two girls start talking. The music of their voices replaces the jangling classic rock on the jukebox, but then even this fades to a muffled drone. I'm staring at the TVs. I'm staring at the people. I can see the outline of their bones under their muscles. The edges of joints poking up under tight skin. I see their skeletons, and the idea taking shape in my head is something I hadn't expected: a blueprint of the Boneys. A glimpse into their twisted, dried-up minds.

The universe is compressing. All memory and all possibility squeezing down to the smallest of points as the last of their flesh falls away. To exist in that singularity, trapped in one static state for eternity—this is the Boneys' world. They are dead-eyed ID photos, frozen at the precise moment they gave up their humanity. That hopeless instant when they snipped the last thread and dropped into the abyss. Now there's nothing left. No thought, no feeling, no past, no future. Nothing exists but the desperate need to keep things *as they are,* as they *always have been.* They must stay on the rails of their loop or be overwhelmed, set ablaze and consumed by the colors, the sounds, the wide-open sky.

And so the thought hums in my head, whispering through my nerves like voices through phone lines: *What if we could derail them?* We've already disrupted their structure enough to incite a blind rage. What if we could create a change so deep, so new and astonishing, they would simply *break?* Surrender? Crumble into dust and ride out of town on the wind?

"R," Julie says, poking me in the arm. "Where are you? Daydreaming again?"

I smile and shrug. Once again my vocabulary fails me. I'm going to need to find a way to let her into my head soon. Whatever this thing is I'm trying to do, I know it can't be done alone.

The bartender returns with our drinks. Julie grins at me and Nora as we appraise the three tumblers of pale yellow nectar. "Remember how when we were kids, pure grapefruit juice was the toughguy drink? Like the whiskey of kiddie beverages?"

"Right," Nora laughs. "Apple juice, Capri Sun, that stuff was for bitches."

Julie raises her glass. "To our new friend, Archie."

I start to lift my glass off the bar and the girls clang theirs down against it. We drink. I don't exactly taste it, but the juice stings my mouth, finding its way into old cuts in my cheeks, bites I don't remember biting.

Julie orders another round, and when it arrives she hefts her messenger bag onto her shoulder and picks up all three glasses. She leans in close and gives me and Nora a wink. "Be right back." With the drinks in hand, she disappears into the bathroom.

"What's . . . she doing?" I ask Nora.

"Dunno. Stealing our drinks?"

We sit there in awkward silence, third-party friends lacking the connective tissue of Julie's presence. After a few minutes, Nora leans in and lowers her voice. "You know why she said you were my boyfriend, right?"

I shrug one shoulder. "Sure."

"It didn't mean anything, she was just trying to deflect attention away from you. If she said you were *her* boyfriend, or her friend, or anything to do with *her,* Grigio would've grilled the fuck out of you. And obviously if he really *looks* at you . . . the makeup's not perfect."

"I under . . . stand."

"And by the way, just so you know? That was a pretty big deal that she took you to see her mom today."

I raise my eyebrows.

"She doesn't tell people that stuff, ever. She didn't even tell *Perry* the whole story for like three years. I can't say exactly what that means for her, but . . . it's new."

I study the bar top, embarrassed. A strangely fond smile spreads across Nora's face. "You know you remind me a little of Perry?"

I tense. I begin to feel the hot remorse boiling up in my throat again.

"I don't know what it is, I mean you're sure not the blowhard he was, but you have some of that same , . . *sparkle* he had when he was younger."

I should stitch my mouth shut. Honesty is a compulsion that's damned me more than once. But I just can't hold it in anymore. The words build and explode out of me like an uncontainable sneeze. "I killed him. Ate . . . his brain."

Nora purses her lips and nods slowly. "Yeah . . . I thought you might have."

My face goes blank. "What?"

"I didn't see it happen, but I've been putting two and two together. It makes sense."

I look at her, stunned. "Julie . . . knows?"

"I don't think so. But if she did, I'm pretty sure she'd be okay." She touches my hand where it rests on the bar. "You could tell her, R. I think she'd forgive you."

"Why?"

"Same reason I forgive you."

"*Why?*"

"Because it wasn't you. It was the plague."

I wait for more. She watches the TV above the bar, pale green light flickering over her dark face. "Did Julie ever tell you about when Perry cheated on her with that orphan girl?"

I hesitate, then nod.

"Yeah, well . . . that was me."

My eyes dart toward the bathroom, but Nora doesn't seem to be hiding anything. "I'd only been here a week," she says. "Didn't know Julie yet. That's how I met her, actually. I fucked her boyfriend, and she hated me, and then time passed and a lot happened, and somehow we came out the other side as friends. Crazy, right?" She upends her empty glass over her tongue to catch the last drops, then pushes it aside. "What I'm trying to say is, it's a shitty world and shit happens, but we don't have to bathe in shit. Sixteen years old, R—my meth-head parents dumped me in the middle of a Dead-infested slum because they couldn't feed me anymore. I wandered on my own for *years* before I found Citi Stadium, and I don't have enough fingers to count all the times I almost died." She holds up her left hand and wiggles the half-gone finger like a bride-to-be showing off her diamond. "What I'm saying is, when you have weight like that in your life, you have to start looking for the bigger picture or you are gonna *sink*."

I peer into her eyes, failing to read her meaning like the illiterate I am. "What's . . . the bigger picture . . . of me killing Perry?"

"R, come on," she says, mock-slapping the side of my head. "You're a zombie. You have the plague. Or at least you did when you killed Perry. Maybe you're different now—I sure *hope* you are— but back then you didn't know you had choices. This isn't 'crime,' it's not 'murder,' it's something way deeper and more inevitable." She taps her temple. "Me and Julie get that, okay? There's a Zen saying, 'No praise, no blame, just so.' We don't care about assigning blame for the human condition, we just want to cure it."

Julie emerges from the bathroom and sets the drinks on the bar with a sly grin. "Even grapefruit juice can use a little kick sometimes."

Nora takes a test sip and turns away, covering her mouth. "Holy . . . Lord!" she coughs. "How much did you put in here?"

"Just a few minis of vodka," Julie whispers with girlish innocence. "Courtesy of our friend Archie, and Undead Airlines."

"Way to go *Archie*."

I shake my head. "Can please . . . stop calling me . . ."

"Right, right," Julie says. "No more Archie. But what do we toast to this time? It's your booze, R, you decide."

I hold the glass in front of me. I sniff it, insisting to myself that I can still smell things besides death and potential death, that I'm still human, still whole. A citrus tang pricks my nostrils. Glowing Florida orchards in summer. The toast that enters my head seems unbearably corny, but it comes out anyway. "To . . . life."

Nora stifles a laugh. "Really?"

Julie shrugs. "Corny, but what the hell." She raises her glass and clinks it against mine. "To life, Mr. Zombie."

"*L'chaim!*" Nora bellows, and drains her glass.

Julie drains her glass.

I drain my glass.

The vodka slams into my brain like a round of buckshot. This time it's no placebo. The drink is strong and I *feel* it. I am *feeling it*. How is that possible?

Julie orders another round of grapefruits, then promptly converts them into greyhounds, and she is generous with the pours. I expect the girls to be as lightweight as I am since alcohol is contraband here, but I realize it's probably quite routine to visit the liquor store while out salvaging the city. They quickly outpace me as I sip my second drink, marveling at the sensations that swirl through my body. The noise of the bar fades and I just watch Julie, the focal point in my blurry composition. She is laughing. A free, unreserved kind of laugh that I don't think I've heard before, throwing her head back and letting it just cascade out of her. She and Nora are recounting some shared memory. She turns to me and says something, inviting me into the joke with a word and a flash of white teeth, but I don't respond. I just look at her, resting my chin in my hand, my elbow on the bar, smiling.

Contentment. Is this what it might feel like?

After finishing my drink I feel a pressure in my lower regions, and I realize I have to piss. Since the Dead don't drink, urination is a rare event. I hope I can remember how to do it.

I wobble into the bathroom and lean my forehead against the wall in front of the urinal. I unzip, and I look down, and there it is. That mythical instrument of life and death and first-date backseat fucking. It hangs limp, useless now, silently judging me for all the ways I've misused it over the years. I think of my wife and her new lover, slapping their cold bodies together like poultry in a packing plant. I think of the anonymous blurs in my past life, probably all dead or Dead by now. Then I think of Julie curled next to me in that king-size bed. I think of her body in that comically mismatched underwear, her breath against my eyes as I study every line in her face, wondering what mysteries lie in the glowing nuclei of her cells.

There in the bathroom, surrounded by the stench of piss and shit, I wonder: Is it too late for me? Can I somehow snatch another chance from the skymouth's grinding teeth? I want a new past, new memories, a new first handshake with love. I want to start over, in every possible way.

When I come out of the bathroom the floor is spinning. Voices are muffled. Julie and Nora are deep in conversation, leaning close and laughing. A man in his early thirties approaches the bar and makes some kind of leering comment to Julie. Nora glares at him, says something that looks sarcastic, and Julie shoos him away. The man shrugs and retreats to the pool table, where his friend is waiting. Julie calls out something insulting and the friend laughs, but the man just grins coldly and calls back a retort. Julie looks frozen for a moment, then she and Nora turn their backs to the pool table and Nora starts whispering in Julie's ear.

"What's . . . wrong?" I ask, approaching the bar. I can sense both men at the pool table watching me.

"Nothing," Julie says, but she sounds shaken. "It's fine."

"R, could you give us a quick minute?" Nora says.

I look back and forth between them. They wait. I turn and walk out of the bar, feeling too many things at once. On the patio I slump against the railing, the streets a dizzying seven floors down. Most of the city's lights are out, but the streetlamps flicker and pulse like bioluminescence. Julie's mini cassette player is an insistent weight in my shirt pocket. I pull it out and stare at it. I know I shouldn't but I'm . . . I feel like I just need—

Closing my eyes, swaying gently with one arm on the railing, I rewind the tape for a moment and press play.

"—really that crazy? Just because he's . . . whatever he is? I mean, isn't 'zombie' just a silly name we—"

I press rewind again, and it occurs to me that the gap between the beginning of this entry and the end of the previous one comprises the entire time I've known Julie. Every meaningful moment of my life fits inside a few seconds of tape hiss.

I press stop, then play.

"—thinks no one knows but everyone knows, they're just afraid to do anything. He's getting worse, too. He said he loved me tonight. Actually said those words. Said I was beautiful and I was everything he loved about Mom and if anything ever happened to me he'd lose his mind. And I know *he meant it, I know all of that's really there inside him . . . but the fact that he had to be raging shitfaced drunk to let any of it out . . . it just made the whole thing seem sick. I fucking hated it."*

There is a long pause on the tape. I glance over my shoulder at the bar door, ashamed but desperate. I know these are confidences I should have to earn through months of slow intimacy, but I can't help myself. I just want to listen to her.

"I've thought about making a report," she continues. *"March into the community center and make Rosy go arrest him. I mean, I'm all for drinking, I love it, but with Dad it's . . . different. It's not a celebration for him, it seems like it's painful and scary, like he's numbing himself for some horrible medieval surgery. And yeah . . . I know why, and it's not like I haven't done worse stuff for the same reasons, but it's just . . . it's so . . ."* Her voice wavers and breaks off, and she sniffles hard like a self-rebuke. *"God,"* she whispers away from the microphone. *"Shit."*

Several seconds of tape hiss. I listen closer. Then the door flies open and I whirl around, tossing the player out into the dark. But it's not Julie. It's the two men from the pool table. They stumble out the door, jostling each other and laughing through the sides of their mouths as they light up cigarettes.

"Hey," the one who was talking to Julie calls to me, and he and his friend start ambling in my direction. He's tall, good-looking, his muscular arms sleeved in tattoos: snakes and skeletons and the logos of extinct rock bands. "What's up, man? You Nora's new guy?"

I hesitate, then shrug. They both laugh like I've made a dirty joke.

"Yeah, who ever knows with that chick, right?" He punches his friend in the chest while continuing to saunter toward me. "So you know Julie? You Julie's friend?"

I nod.

"Known her long?"

I shrug, but I feel a coil inside me tensing.

He stops a few feet away from me and leans against the wall, taking a slow drag on his cigarette. "That one used to be pretty wild too, a few years back. I was her firearms teacher."

I need to leave. I need to turn around right now and leave.

"She got all 'pure' after she started dating that Kelvin kid, but man, for a year or so she was ripe fruit." His exhalations form a haze of smoke that stings my dry eyes. "A hundred bucks won't even buy a pack of cigarettes anymore, but it sure went a long way with that bitch."

I lunge forward and crack his head into the wall. It's easy, I just palm his face and thrust forward like a shot putter, punching the wall with the back of his skull. I don't know if I've killed him and I don't care. When his friend tries to grab me I do the exact same to him, two big dents in the Orchard's aluminum siding. Both men slump to the ground. I wobble my way down the stairs and out onto the catwalk. Some kids leaning on the support cables smoking joints stare at me as I shove past them. *Excuse me,* I try to say, but I can't seem to find the syllables. I slide down the four apartment floors and lurch out onto Fairy Street or Tinkerbell Street or whatever the fuck it's called. I just need to get away from all these people for a minute, collect my thoughts. I'm so hungry. God, I'm starving.

After a few minutes of wandering, I'm completely lost and disoriented. A light rain is falling and I'm alone on some dark narrow street. The asphalt glitters black and wet under the crooked streetlamps. Up ahead, two guards converse in a rain-flecked cone of light, grunting to each other with the affected toughness of scared boys straining to be men.

". . . out in Corridor 2 all last week, pouring foundations. We're less than a mile away from Goldman Dome but we've barely got a fuckin' crew anymore. Grigio keeps pulling guys off Construction and dumping 'em into Security."

"What about the Goldman crew? How's their end coming?"

"Goldman is shit. They're barely out their front door. I've been hearing the merger's in bad shape anyway, thanks to Grigio's bad diplomacy. Starting to wonder if he even *wants* the mergers any-more, the way he handled Corridor 1. Wouldn't surprise me if he arranged the collapse himself."

"You know that's bullshit. Don't be spreading that story around."

"Yeah, well, either way, Construction's gone to shit since Kelvin got squished. We're just digging holes and filling 'em in."

"I'd still rather be out building something than playing rent-a-cop in here all night. You get any action out there?"

"Just a couple of Fleshies wandering out of the woods. Pop, pop, game over."

"No Boneys?"

"Haven't seen one of them in at least a year. They stick to their hives nowadays. Fuckin' bullshit."

"What, you *like* running into those things?"

"Hell of a lot more fun than Fleshies. Fuckers can *move*."

"Fun? Are you shitting me? Those things are *wrong;* I don't even like touching 'em with my bullets."

"Is that why your hit rate's one in twenty?"

"Doesn't even seem like they're human remains anymore, you know? They're like aliens or something. Creeps the shit out of me."

"Yeah well that's probably 'cause you're a pussy."

"Fuck you. I'm going to take a leak."

The guard disappears into the dark. His partner stands in the spotlight, pulling his parka tighter as the rain comes down. I'm still walking. I'm not interested in these men; I'm looking for a quiet corner where I can close my eyes and gather myself. But as I approach the light, the guard notices me, and I realize there's a problem. I'm *drunk*. My carefully studied gait has been replaced by an unsteady stagger. I lumber forward, my head lolling from side to side.

I look like . . . exactly what I am.

"Halt!" the guard shouts.

I halt.

He moves toward me a little. "Step into the light, please, sir."

I step into the light, standing on the very edge of the yellow circle. I try to stand as straight as I can, as motionless as I can. Then I realize something else. The rain is dripping off my hair. The rain is running down my face. The rain is washing away my makeup, revealing the pale gray flesh underneath. I stumble back a step, slightly out of the lamplight.

The guard is about five feet away from me. His hand is on his gun. He moves closer and peers at me through slitted eyes. "Have you been drinking alcohol tonight, sir?"

I open my mouth to say, *No, sir, absolutely not, just a few glasses of delicious and heart-healthy grapefruit juice with my good friend Julie Cabernet.* But the words evade me. My tongue is thick and dead in my mouth, and all that comes out is, "Uhhhnnn . . ."

"What the fuck—" The guard's eyes flash wide, he whips out his flashlight and shines it into my gray-streaked face, and I have no choice. I leap out of the shadows and pounce on him, knocking his gun aside and biting down on his throat. His life force rushes into my starved body and brain, soothing the agony of my hideous cravings. I start to tear into him, chewing deltoids and tender abdominals while the blood still pulses through them—but then I stop.

Julie stands in the bedroom doorway, watching me with a tentative smile.

I shut my eyes and grit my teeth.

No.

I drop the body to the ground and back away from it. I can no longer hide behind my ignorance. I know now that I have a choice, and I choose to change no matter what the cost. If I'm a thriving branch on the Tree of Death, I'll drop my leaves. If I have to starve myself to kill its twisted roots, I will.

The fetus in my stomach kicks, and I hear Perry's voice, gentle and reassuring. *You won't starve, R. In my short life I made so many choices just because I thought they were required, but my dad was right: there's no rule book for the world. It's in our heads, our collective human hive-mind. If there are rules, we're the ones making them. We can change them whenever we want to.*

I spit out the meat in my mouth and wipe the blood off my face. Perry kicks me in the gut again and I vomit. I lean over and purge myself of everything. The meat, the blood, the vodka. As soon as I straighten up and wipe my mouth, I'm sober. The fuzz is gone. My head is clear as a glossy new record.

The guard's body begins to twitch back to life. His shoulders slowly rise, dragging the rest of his limp parts with them, as if he's being pinched and pulled upward by unseen fingers. I need to kill him. I know I need to kill him, but I can't do it. After the vow I've just made, the thought of tearing into this man again and tasting his still-warm blood leaves me paralyzed with horror. He shudders and retches, choking and clawing the dirt, straining and dry-heaving, his eyes bulging wide as the gray sludge of new death slithers into them. A wet, wretched groan escapes his mouth, and it's too much for me. I turn and run. Even in my bravest moment, I am a coward.

· · ·

The rain is in full force. My feet splash in the streets and spatter mud on my freshly washed clothes. My hair hangs in my face like seaweed. In front of a big aluminum building with a plywood cross on the roof, I kneel in a puddle and splash water on my face. I wash my mouth out with dirty gutter runoff and spit until I can't taste anything. That holy wooden "t" looms overhead, and I wonder if the Lord might ever find cause to approve of me, wherever and whatever he is.

Have you met him yet, Perry? Is he alive and well? Tell me he's not just the mouth of the sky. Tell me there's more looking down on us than that empty blue skull.

Perry doesn't answer. I accept the silence. I get off my knees and I keep running.

Avoiding streetlights, I make my way back to Julie's house. I curl up against the wall, finding some shelter from the balcony overhead, and I wait there while the rain pounds the house's metal roof. After what seems like hours, I hear the girls' voices in the distance, but this time their rhythms stir no joy in me. The dance is a dirge, the music is minor.

They run toward the front door, Nora with her denim jacket pulled over her head, Julie with the hood of her red sweatshirt cinched tight on her face. Nora reaches the door first and rushes inside. Julie stops. I don't know if she sees me in the dark or just smells the fruity stench of my body spray, but something draws her to look around the corner of the house. She sees me huddled in the dark like a lost puppy. She ambles over slowly, her hands stuffed into her sweatshirt pockets. She crouches down and peeks out at me through the narrow opening of her hood. "You okay?" she says.

I nod dishonestly.

She sits next to me on the small patch of dry ground and leans against the house. She takes off her hood and lifts the wool beanie underneath to brush wet hair out of her eyes, then pulls it back down. "You scared me. You just disappeared."

I look at her miserably, but I don't say anything.

"Do you want to tell me what happened?"

I shake my head.

"Did you, um . . . did you knock out Tim and Matt?"

I nod.

A smile of embarrassed pleasure creeps onto her face, as if I've just given her an overlarge bouquet of roses or written her a bad love song. "That was . . . sweet," she says, holding back a giggle. A minute passes. She touches my knee. "We had fun today, didn't we? Despite a few sticky moments?"

I can't smile, but I nod.

"I'm a little buzzed. You?"

I shake my head.

"Too bad. It's fun." Her smile deepens and her eyes become faraway. "You know I had my first drink when I was eight?" There is just a faint slur in her voice. "My dad was a big wine buff and him and Mom used to throw tasting parties whenever Dad was between wars. They'd bring all their friends over and pop a prized vintage and get pretty well toasted. I'd sit there in the middle of the couch taking little sips off the half glass I was allowed and just laugh at all the silly grownups getting sillier. Rosy would get so flushed! One glass and he looked like Santa Claus. He and Dad arm-wrestled on the coffee table once and broke a lamp. It was . . . so great."

She starts doodling in the dirt with one finger. Her smile is wistful, aimed at no one. "Things weren't always so grim, you know? Dad has his moments, and even when the world fell apart we still had some fun. We'd take little family salvage trips and pick up the most crazy wines you can imagine. Thousand-dollar bottles of '97 Dom Romanée-Conti just rolling around on the floors of abandoned cellars." She chuckles to herself. "Dad would have absolutely lost his shit over those back in the day. By the time we moved here he was kinda . . . muted. But God, we drank some outrageous stuff."

I'm watching her talk. Watching her jaw move and collecting her words one by one as they spill from her lips. I don't deserve them. Her warm memories. I'd like to paint them over the bare plaster walls of my soul, but everything I paint seems to peel.

"And then Mom ran off." She pulls her finger out of the dirt, inspecting her work. She has drawn a house. A quaint little cottage with a smoke cloud in the chimney, a benevolent sun smiling down on the roof. "Dad thought she must have been drunk, hence the booze ban, but I saw her, and she wasn't. She was very sober."

She is still smiling, as if this is all just easy nostalgia, but the smile is cold now, lifeless.

"She came into my room that night and just looked at me for a while. I pretended I was asleep. Then right as I was about to pop up and yell 'boo' . . . she walked out. I didn't get to say anything."

She reaches a hand down to wipe away her drawing, but I touch her wrist. I look at her and shake my head. She regards me silently for a moment. Then she scoots around to face me and grins, inches from my face.

"R," she says, "if I kiss you, will I die?"

Her eyes are steady. She's *barely* drunk.

"You said I won't, right? I won't get infected? Because I really feel like kissing you." She fidgets. "And even if you do pass something to me, maybe it wouldn't be all bad. I mean, you're different now, right? You're *not* a zombie. You're . . . something new." Her face is very close. Her smile turns serious. "Well, R?"

I look into her eyes, splashing in their icy waters like a ship-wrecked sailor grasping for the raft. But there is no raft.

"Julie," I say. "I need . . . to show you something."

She cocks her head with gentle curiosity. "What?"

I stand up. I take her hand and start walking.

The night is still except for the primeval hiss of the rain. It drenches the dirt and slicks the asphalt, liquefying the shadows into shiny black ink. I stick to the narrow backstreets and unlit alleys. Julie follows slightly behind me, staring at the side of my face.

"Where are we going?" she asks.

I pause at an intersection to retrace the maps of my stolen memories, calling up images of places I've never been, people I've never met. "Almost . . . there."

A few more careful glances around corners, furtive dashes across intersections, and there it is. A five-story house looms ahead of us, tall, skinny, and gray like the rest of this skeletal city, its windows flickering yellow like wary eyes.

"What the hell, R?" Julie whispers, staring up at it. "This is . . ."

I pull her to the front door and we stand there in the shelter of the eaves, the roof rattling like military drums in the rain. "Can I . . . borrow your hat?" I ask without looking at her.

She doesn't move for a moment, then she pulls it off and hands it to me. Overlong and floppy, dark blue wool with a red stripe . . .

Mrs. Rosso knitted this for Julie's seventeenth birthday. Perry thought she looked like an elf in it and would start speaking to her in Tolkien tongues whenever she put it on. She called him the biggest nerd she'd ever met, and he agreed, while playfully kissing her throat and—

I pull the beanie low over my face and knock a slow waltz on the door, eyes glued to the ground like a shy child. The door opens a crack. A middle-aged woman in sweatpants looks out at us. Her face is puffy and heavily lined, dark bags under bloodshot eyes. "Miss Grigio?" she says.

Julie glances at me. "Hi, Mrs. Grau. Um . . ."

"What are you doing out? Is Nora with you? It's after curfew."

"I know, we . . . got a little lost on our way back from the Orchard. Nora's staying at my house tonight but um . . . can we come in for a minute? I need to talk to the guys."

I keep my head down as Mrs. Grau gives me a cursory appraisal. She opens the door for us with an annoyed sigh. "You can't stay here, you know. This is a foster home, not a flophouse, and your friend here is too old for new residency."

"I know, sorry, we'll . . ." She glances at me again. "We'll just be a minute."

I can't endure formalities right now. I brush past the woman and into the house. A toddler peeks around a bedroom door and Mrs. Grau glares at him. "What did I tell you?" she snaps, loud enough to wake the rest of the kids. "Back in bed right now." The boy disappears into the shadows. I lead Julie up the staircase.

The second story is identical to the first, except there are rows of preadolescents sleeping on the floor on small mats. So many now. New foster homes pop up like processing plants as mothers and fathers disappear, chewed up and swallowed down by the plague. We step over a few tiny bodies on our way to the stairs, and a little girl grasps feebly at Julie's ankle.

"I had a bad dream," she whispers.

"I'm sorry, honey," Julie whispers back. "You're safe now, okay?"

The girl closes her eyes again. We climb the stairs. The third floor is still awake. Young teens and patch-beard semiadults sitting around on folding chairs, hunched over desks writing in booklets and flipping through manuals. Some kids snore on stacked bunks inside narrow bedrooms. All the doors are open except one.

A few older boys look up from their work, surprised. "Wow, hey Julie. How's it going? You holding up okay?"

"Hey guys. I'm . . ." She trails off, and her ellipsis eventually forms a period. She looks at the closed door. She looks at me. Gripping her hand, I move forward and open the door, then shut it behind us.

The room is dark except for the faint yellow glow of streetlamps through the window. There is nothing in here but a plywood dresser and a stripped bed, with a few pictures of Julie taped to the ceiling above it. The air is stale and much colder than the rest of the house.

"R . . . ," Julie says in a quivery, dangerous voice. "Why the *fuck* are we here?"

I finally turn to face her. In the yellow dimness, we look like actors in a silent sepia tragedy. "Julie," I say. "That theory . . . about why we . . . eat the brain . . ."

She starts to shake her head.

"True."

I look into her reddening eyes a moment longer, then kneel down and open the bottom drawer of the dresser. Inside, under piles of old stamps, a microscope, an army of pewter figurines, there is a stack of paper bound together with red yarn. I lift it out and hand it to Julie. In so many strange and twisted ways, I feel like the manuscript is mine. Like I've just handed her my own bloody heart on a platter. I am fully prepared for her to claw it to shreds.

She takes the manuscript. She unties the yarn. She stares at the cover page for a full minute, breathing shakily. Then she wipes her eyes and clears her throat.

"'*Red Teeth*,'" she reads. "'By Perry Kelvin.'" She glances down the page. "'For Julie Cabernet, the only light left.'" She lowers the manuscript and looks away for a moment, trying to hide a spasm in her throat, then steels herself and turns the page to the first chapter. As she reads, a faint smile peeks through the tear tracks. "Wow," she says, wiping a finger across her nose and sniffling. "It's actually . . . kinda good. He used to write such dry and detached bullshit. This is . . . cheesy . . . but in a sweet way. More like how he really was." She glances at the cover page again. "He started it less than a year ago. I had no idea he was still writing." She flips to the last page. "It's not finished. Cuts off in the middle of a sentence. 'Outmanned and outgunned, certain of death, he kept fighting, because—'"

She rubs her thumbs into the paper, feeling its texture. She puts it near her face and inhales. Then she closes her eyes, closes the manuscript, and reties the yarn. She looks up at me. I am nearly a foot taller than her and probably sixty pounds heavier, but I feel small and featherweight. Like she could knock me down and crush me with a single whispered word.

But she doesn't speak. She sets the manuscript back in the drawer and gently slides it shut. She straightens up, dries her face with her sleeve, and embraces me, resting her ear against my chest.

"Thump-thump," she murmurs. "Thump-thump. Thump-thump."

My hands hang limp at my sides. "I'm sorry," I say.

With her eyes closed, her voice muffled by my shirt, she says, "I forgive you."

I raise a hand and touch her straw-gold hair. "Thank you."

These three phrases, so simple, so primal, have never sounded so complete. So true to their basic meanings. I feel her cheek move against my chest, her zygomaticus major pulling her lips into a faint smile.

Without another word, we shut the door on Perry Kelvin's room and leave his home. We descend the stairs past beleaguered teens, past tossing and turning kids, past deeply dreaming babies, and out into the street. I feel a nudge low in my chest, closer to my heart than my belly, and a soft voice in my head.

Thank you, Perry says.

. . .

I would like to end it here. How nice if I could edit my own life. If I could halt in the middle of a sentence and put it all to rest in a drawer somewhere, consummate my amnesia and forget all the things that have happened, are happening, and are about to happen. Shut my eyes and go to sleep happy.

But no, "R." No sleep of the innocent. Not for you. Did you forget? You have blood on your hands. On your lips. On your teeth. Smile for the cameras.

"JULIE," I SAY, bracing to confess my final sin. "I need . . . to tell you . . ."

BANG.

The stadium's field halogens flare like suns and midnight becomes daylight. I can see every pore in Julie's face.

"What the hell?" she gasps, whipping her head around. A piercing alarm further shatters the night's stillness, and then we see it: the Jumbotron is aglow. Hanging from the upper reaches of the open roof like a tablet descending from Heaven, the screen plays a blocky animation of a quarterback running from what appears to be a zombie, arms outstretched and clutching. The screen blinks between this and a word that I think might be:

BREACH

"R . . . ," Julie says, horrified, "did you *eat* someone?"

I look at her desperately. "No ch . . . no choi . . . no *choice*," I stutter, my diction collapsing in my state of panic. "Guard . . . stopped me. Didn't . . . mean. Didn't . . . *want*."

She presses her lips together, her eyes boring into me, then gives a single shake of her head as if banishing one thought, committing to another. "Okay. Then we need to get inside. God damn it, R."

We run into the house and she slams the door. Nora is at the top of the stairs. "Where have you guys been? What's going *on* out there?"

"It's a breach," Julie says. "Zombie in the stadium."

"You mean *him*?"

The disappointment in her reply makes me wince. "Yes and no."

We hurry into Julie's bedroom and she turns out the lights. We all sit on the floor on the piles of laundry, and for a while nobody speaks. We just sit and listen to the sounds. Guards running and shouting. Gunfire. Our own heavy breathing.

"Don't worry," Julie whispers to Nora, but I know it's for me. "It won't spread much. Those shots were probably Security taking him out already."

"Are we in the clear, then?" Nora asks. "Will R be okay?"

Julie looks at me. Her face is grim. "Even if they think the breach started from a natural death, that guard obviously didn't eat himself. Security will know there's at least one zombie unaccounted for."

Nora follows Julie's eyes to mine, and I can almost imagine my face flushing. "It was you?" she asks, straining for neutrality.

"Didn't . . . mean. Was . . . going . . . kill me."

She says nothing. Her face is blank.

I meet her stare, willing her to feel my crushing remorse. "It was my last," I say, straining to force language back into my idiot tongue. "No matter what. Swear to the skymouth."

A few agonizing moments pass. Then Nora slowly nods, and addresses Julie. "So we need to get him out of here."

"They shut everything down for breaches. All the doors will be locked and guarded. They might even shut the roof if they get scared enough."

"So what the hell are we supposed to do?"

Julie shrugs, and the gesture looks so bleak on her, so wrong. "I don't know," she says. "Once again, I don't know."

. . .

Julie and Nora fall asleep. They fight it for hours, trying to come up with a plan to save me, but eventually they succumb. I lie on a pile of pants and stare up at the starry green ceiling. *Not so easy, Mr. Lennon. Even if you try.*

It seems trivial now, a thin silver lining on a vast black storm-cloud, but I think I'm learning to read. As I look up at the phosphorescent galaxy, letters come together and form words. Stringing them into full sentences is still beyond me, but I savor the sensation of those little symbols clicking together and bursting like soap bubbles of sound. If I ever see my wife again . . . I'll at least be able to read her nametag.

The hours ooze by. It's after midnight but bright as noon outside. The halogens ram their white light against the house, squeezing in through cracks in the window shades. My ears tune to the sounds around me. The girls' breathing. Their small shifting movements. And then, sometime around two in the morning, a phone rings.

Julie comes awake, gets up on one elbow. In some distant room of the house, the phone rings again. She throws off her blankets and stands up. Strange to see her from this angle, towering over me instead of cowering under. I'm the one who needs protecting now. One mistake, one brief lapse of my newfound judgment—that's all it took to unravel everything. What a massive responsibility, being a moral creature.

The phone keeps ringing. Julie walks out of the bedroom and I follow her through the dark, echoing house. We step into what appears to be an office. There is a large desk covered in papers and blueprints, and on the walls various kinds of telephones are screwed to the drywall, different brands and styles from all different eras.

"They rerouted the phone system," Julie explains. "It's more like an intercom now. We have direct lines to all the important areas."

Each phone has a nametag sticker stuck below it, with the location Sharpied onto the blank. *Hi, my name is:*

GARDENS
KITCHENS
WAREHOUSE
GARAGE
ARMORY
CORRIDOR 2
GOLDMAN DOME
LEHMAN ARENA
AIG FIELD

And so on.

The phone that's ringing, a pea-green rotary-dialer covered in dust, is labeled:

OUTSIDE

Julie looks at the phone. She looks at me. "This is weird. That line is from the phones in the abandoned outer districts. Since we got walkie-talkies nobody uses it anymore."

The phone clangs its bells, loud and insistent. I can't believe Nora is still asleep.

Slowly, Julie picks up the receiver and puts it to her ear. "Hello?" She waits. "What? I can't under—" Her brow furrows in concentration. Then her eyes widen. *"Oh."* They narrow. *"You.* Yeah this is Julie, what do *you*—" She waits. "Fine. Yeah, he's right here."

She holds the phone out to me. "It's for you."

I stare at it. "What?"

"It's your friend. That fat fuck from the airport."

I grab the phone. I put the earpiece to my mouth. Julie shakes her head and flips it around for me. Into the receiver I breathe a stunned "*M?*"

His deep rumble crackles in my ear. "Hey . . . loverboy."

"What's . . . Where are you?"

"Out in . . . city. Didn't know . . . what would get with . . . phone, but had . . . to try. You're . . . okay?"

"Okay but . . . trapped. Stadium . . . locked down."

"Shit."

"What's . . . going on? Out there?"

There is silence for a moment. "R," he says. "Dead . . . still coming. More. From airport. Other places. Lots . . . of us now."

I'm silent. The phone wanders away from my ear. Julie looks at me expectantly.

"Hello?" M says.

"Sorry. I'm here."

"Well we're . . . *here*. What now? What should . . . do?"

I rest the phone on my shoulder and look at the wall, at nothing. I look at the papers and plans on General Grigio's desk. His strategies are all gibberish to me. I have no doubt it's all important—food allocation, construction plans, weapon distribution, combat tactics. He's trying to keep everyone alive, and that's good. That's foundational. But like Julie said, there must be something even deeper than that. The earth *under* that foundation. Without that firm ground, it's all going to collapse, over and over, no matter how many bricks he lays. This is what I'm interested in. The earth under the bricks.

"What's going on?" Julie asks. "What's he saying?"

As I look into her anxious face, I feel the twitch in my guts, the young, eager voice in my head.

It's happening, corpse. Whatever you and Julie triggered, it's moving. A good disease, *a virus that causes life! Do you see this, you dumb fucking monster? It's inside you! You have to get out of these walls and spread it!*

I angle the phone toward Julie so she can listen. She leans in close.

"M," I say.

"Yeah."

"Tell Julie."

"What?"

"Tell Julie . . . what's happening."

There's a pause. "Changing," he says. "Lots of us . . . changing. Like R."

Julie looks at me and I can almost sense her neck hairs standing on end. "It's not just you?" she says, moving away from the phone. "This . . . reviving thing?" Her voice is small and tentative, like a little girl poking her head out of a bomb shelter after years of life in the dark. It almost quivers with tight-leashed hope. "Are you saying the plague is healing?"

I nod. "We're . . . fixing things."

"But *how?*"

"Don't know. But we have to . . . do more of it. Out there . . . where M is. 'Outside.'"

Her excitement cools, hardens. "So we have to leave."

I nod.

"Both of us?"

"Both," M says, his voice crackling in the earpiece like an eaves-dropping mother. "Julie . . . part of it."

She eyes me dubiously. "You want *me.* Skinny little human girl. Out there in the wild, running with a pack of zombies?"

I nod.

"Do you grasp how insane that is?"

I nod.

She is silent for a moment, looking at the floor. "Do you really think you can keep me safe?" she asks me. "Out there, with them?"

My incurable honesty makes me hesitate, and Julie frowns.

"Yes," M answers for me, exasperated. "He can. And I'll . . . help."

I nod quickly. "M will help. The others . . . will help. Besides," I add with a faint smile, "you can . . . keep yourself safe."

She shrugs nonchalantly. "I know. I just wanted to see what you'd say."

"So you'll . . . ?"

"I'll go with you."

"You're . . . sure?"

Her eyes are distant and hard. "I had to bury my mom's empty dress. I've been waiting for this a long time."

I nod. I take a deep breath.

"The only problem with your plan," she continues, "is that you seem to be forgetting you *ate* someone last night, and this place is going to stay clamped shut until they find and kill you."

"Should we . . . attack?" M says. "Get you . . . out?"

I put the phone back to my ear, gripping the receiver hard. "No," I tell him.

"Have . . . army. Where's . . . battle?"

"Don't know. Not here. These are . . . people."

"Well?"

I look at Julie. She looks at the ground and rubs her forehead.

"Just wait," I tell M.

"Wait?"

"A little longer. We'll . . . figure it out."

"Before . . . they kill you?"

"Hopefully."

A long, dubious silence. Then: "Hurry up."

• • •

Julie and I stay up all night. In our rain-wet clothes we sit on the floor in the cold living room and don't say a word. Eventually my eyes sag shut, and in this strange calm, in what may be my last few hours on Earth, my mind creates a dream for me. Crisp and clear, alive with color, unfolding like a time-lapse rose in the sparkling darkness.

In this dream, *my* dream, I am floating down a river on my house-jet's severed tail fin. I am lying on my back under the blue midnight, watching the stars drift by above me. The river is uncharted because the maps have burned and the satellites have crashed, and I have no idea where it leads. The air is still. The night is warm. I've brought only two provisions: a box of pad thai and Perry's book. Thick. Ancient. Bound in leather. I open it to the middle. An unfinished sentence in some language I've never seen, and beyond it, nothing. An epic tome of empty pages, blank white and waiting. I shut the book and lay my head down on the cool steel. The pad thai tickles my nose, sweet and spicy and strong. I feel the river widening, gaining force.

I hear the waterfall.

. . .

"R."

My eyes open and I sit up. Julie is cross-legged next to me, watching me with grim amusement.

"Having some nice dreams?"

"Not . . . sure," I mumble, rubbing my eyes.

"Did you happen to dream up any solutions to our little problem?"

I shake my head.

"Yeah, me either." She glances at the wall clock and bunches her lips ruefully. "I'm supposed to be at the community center in a few hours to do story time. David and Marie are going to cry when I don't show up."

David and Marie. I repeat the names in my head, savoring their contours. I would let that dog eat my whole leg for the chance to see those kids again. To hear a few more clumsy syllables tumble from their mouths before I die. "What are . . . you reading them?"

She looks out the window at the city, its every crack and flaw brought into sharp relief by the blinding white light. "I've been trying to get them into the Redwall books. I figured all those songs and feasts and courageous warrior mice would be a nice escape from the nightmare they're growing up in. Marie keeps asking for books about zombies and I keep telling her I can't read nonfiction for *story* time, but . . ." She notices the look on my face and trails off. "Are you okay?"

I nod.

"Are you thinking about your kids at the airport?"

I hesitate, then nod.

She reaches out and touches my knee, looking into my stinging eyes. "R? I know things look bleak right now, but listen. You can't quit. As long as you're still breathe—sorry, as long as you're still *moving*, it's not over. Okay?"

I nod.

"Okay? Fucking say it, R."

"Okay."

She smiles.

"TWO. EIGHT. TWENTY-FOUR."

We jolt away from each other as a speaker in the ceiling blares out a series of numbers followed by a shrill alert tone.

"This is Colonel Rosso with a community-wide notice," the speaker says. *"The Security breach has been contained. The infected officer has been neutralized, with no further casualties reported."*

I release a deep breath.

"However . . ."

"Shit," Julie whispers.

". . . the original source of the breach remains at large within our walls. Security patrols will now begin a door-to-door search of every build-ing in the stadium. Since we don't know where this thing might be hiding, everyone should come out of their houses and congregate in a public area. Do not confine yourself in any small spaces." Rosso pauses to cough. *"Sorry about this, folks. We'll get it taken care of, just . . . sit tight."*

There's a click, and the PA goes quiet.

Julie jumps to her feet and storms into the bedroom. She pulls open the blinds, letting the floodlights burst through the window. "Rise and shine, Miss Greene, we're out of time. Do you remember any old exits in the wall tunnels? Wasn't there a fire escape somewhere by the skybox? R, can you climb a ladder?"

"Wait, what?" Nora croaks, trying to shield her eyes. "What's happening?"

"According to R's friend, maybe the end of this shitty undead world, if we don't get killed first."

Nora finally comes awake. "Sorry, *what?*"

"I'll tell you later. They just announced a sweep. We have maybe ten minutes. We need to find . . ." Her voice fades and I watch her mouth move. The shapes her lips make for each word, the flick of tongue against glistening teeth. She is holding on to hope but my grip is slipping. She twists at her hair as she talks, her golden tresses stiff and matted and in need of a wash.

The spicy smell of her shampoo, flowers and herbs and cinnamon dancing with her natural oils. She would never say what brand she used. She liked to keep her scent a mystery.

"R!"

Julie and Nora are staring at me, waiting. I open my mouth to speak, but I have no words. And then the front door of the house bangs open so hard it resonates through the metal walls all the way to where we're standing. Heavy, booted footfalls pound the stairs.

"Oh Jesus," Julie says in a panicked breath. She herds us out of the room and into the hallway bathroom. "Get his makeup back on," she hisses to Nora, and slams the door shut.

As Nora fumbles her compact out of her purse and tries to re-rouge my rain-stained face, I hear two voices out in the hall.

"Dad, what's going on? Did they find the zombie?"

"Not yet, but they will. Have you seen anything?"

"No, I've been here."

"Are you alone?"

"Yeah, I've been here since last night."

"Why is the bathroom light on?"

Footsteps pound toward us.

"Wait, Dad! Wait a second!" She lowers her voice. "Nora and Archie are in there."

"Why did you just tell me you're here alone? This is not a time for games, Julie, this is not a time for hide-and-seek."

"They're . . . you know . . . *in there*."

There is the briefest of hesitations. "Nora and Archie," he shouts at the door, his voice compressed and extremely loud. "As you just heard on the intercom there is a breach in progress. I cannot begin to imagine a worse time for lovemaking. Come out immediately."

Nora straddles me against the sink and buries my face in her cleavage just as Grigio yanks the door open.

"*Dad!*" Julie squeals, flashing Nora a quick look as she jumps off of me.

"Come out immediately," Grigio says.

We step out of the bathroom. Nora straightens her clothes and pats down her hair, doing a pretty good job of looking embarrassed. I just look at Grigio, unapologetic, limbering up my diction for its first and probably last big test. He looks back at me with that taut, angular face, peering into my eyes. There are less than two feet between us.

"Hello, Archie," he says.

"Hello, sir."

"You and Miss Greene are in love?"

"Yes, sir."

"That is wonderful. Have you discussed marriage."

"Not yet."

"Why delay. Why deliberate. These are the last days. Where do you live, Archie?"

"Goldman . . . Field."

"Goldman Dome?"

"Yes, sir. Sorry."

"What work do you do at Goldman Dome."

"Gardens."

"Does that work allow you and Nora to feed your children?"

"We don't have children, sir."

"Children replace us when we die. When you have children you will need to feed them. I'm told things are bad at Goldman Dome. I'm told you are running out of everything. It's a dark world we live in, isn't it, Archie."

"Sometimes."

"We do the best we can with what God gives us, don't we. If God gives us stones when we ask for bread, we will sharpen our teeth and eat stones."

"Or make . . . our own bread."

Grigio smiles. "Are you wearing makeup, Archie?"

Grigio stabs me.

I didn't even notice the knife coming out of its sheath. The five-inch blade sinks into my shoulder and pokes out the other side. I don't feel it and I don't flinch. The wound doesn't bleed.

"Julie!" Grigio roars, stepping back from me and drawing his pistol, his eyes wild in their deep sockets. "Did you bring the Dead into my city? Into my home? Did you let the Dead touch you?"

"Dad, listen to me," Julie says, holding her hands out toward him. "R is different. He's *changing*."

"The Dead don't change, Julie! They are not people, they are things!"

"How do we *know* that? Just because they don't talk to us and tell us about their lives? We don't understand their thoughts so we assume they don't have any?"

"We've done tests! The Dead have never shown any signs of self-awareness or emotional response!"

"Neither have *you*, Dad! Jesus Christ—R saved my life! He

protected me and brought me home! He's *human*! And there are more like him!"

"No," Grigio says, abruptly calm. His hands stop wavering and the gun steadies, inches from my face.

"Dad, please listen to me? Please?" She takes a step closer. She is trying to stay cool but I can tell she is terrified, and I hate myself for being the cause. "When I was at the airport, something happened. We sparked something, and whatever it is, it's spreading. The Dead are coming back to life, they're leaving their hives and trying to change what they are, and we have to find a way to help. Imagine if we could *cure* the plague, Dad! Imagine if we could clean up this mess and start over!"

Grigio shakes his head. I can see his jaw muscles tightening under his waxy skin. "Julie, you are young. You don't understand. We can stay alive and we can kill the things that want to kill us, but there is no grand solution. We searched for years and never found one, and now our time is up. The world is over. It can't be cured, it can't be salvaged, it can't be saved."

"Yes it *can!*" Julie screams at him, losing all composure. "Who decided life has to be a nightmare? Who wrote that fucking rule? We can fix it, we've just never *tried* before! We've always been too busy and selfish and scared!"

Grigio grits his teeth. "You are a dreamer. You are a child. You are your mother."

"Dad, *listen!*"

"No."

He cocks the gun and presses it against my forehead, directly onto Julie's Band-Aid. Here it comes. Here is M's everpresent irony. My inevitable death, ignoring me all those years when I wished for it daily, arriving only after I've decided I want to live forever. I close my eyes and brace myself.

A spatter of blood warms my face—but it's not mine. My eyes flash open just in time to see Julie's knife glancing off Grigio's hand. The gun flies out of his grip and fires when it hits the floor, then again and again as the recoil knocks it against the walls of the narrow hall like a ricocheting Super Ball. Everyone drops for cover, and the gun finally spins to rest touching Nora's toes. In the deafened silence she stares down at it, wide-eyed, then looks at the general. Cradling his gashed hand, he lunges. Nora snatches the gun off the floor and aims it at his face. He freezes. He flexes his jaw and inches forward as if about to pounce anyway. But then Nora pops out the spent ammo clip, whips a fresh one out of her purse, shoves it into the gun and chambers a round, all one liquid motion without ever taking her eyes off his. Grigio steps back.

"Go," she says, her eyes flicking to Julie. "Try to get out somehow. Just try."

Julie grabs my hand. We back out of the room while her dad stands there vibrating with rage.

"Good-bye, Dad," Julie says softly. We turn and run down the stairs.

"*Julie!*" Grigio howls, and the sound reminds me so much of another sound, a hollow blast from a broken hunting horn, that I shiver in my damp shirt.

• • •

We are running. Julie stays in front, leading us through the cramped streets. Behind us, angry shouts ring out from the direction of Julie's house. Then the squawk of walkie-talkies. We are running, and we are being chased. Julie's leadership is less than decisive. We zigzag and backtrack. We are rodents scrambling in a cage. We run as the looming rooftops spin around us.

Then we hit the wall. A sheer concrete barrier laced with scaffolding, ladders, and walkways to nowhere. All the bleachers are gone, but one staircase remains; a dark hallway beckons to us from the top. We run toward it. Everything on either side of the staircase has been stripped away, leaving it floating in space like Jacob's ladder.

A shout flies up from the ground below just as we reach the opening. "Miss Grigio!"

We turn and look down. Colonel Rosso is at the bottom of the steps, surrounded by a retinue of Security officers. He is the only one without his gun drawn.

"Please don't run!" he calls to Julie.

Julie pulls me into the hallway and we sprint into the dark.

This inner space is clearly under construction, but most of it remains exactly as it was abandoned. Hot dog stands, souvenir kiosks, and overpriced pretzel booths sit cold and lifeless in the shadows. The shouts of the Security team echo behind us. I wait for the dead-end that will halt us, that will force me to turn and face the inevitable.

"R!" Julie pants as we run. "We're going to get out, okay? We're *going* to!" Her voice is cracking, halfway between exhaustion and tears. I can't bring myself to respond.

The hallway ends. In the faint light creeping through holes in the concrete, I see a sign on the door:

EMERGENCY EXIT

Julie runs faster, dragging me behind her. We slam into the door and it flies open—

"Oh shhh—" she gasps, and whips around, grabbing on to the door frame as one foot dangles out over an eight-story drop.

Cold wind whistles around the doorway, where torn stumps of a fire escape protrude from the wall. Birds flutter past. Below, the city spreads out like a vast cemetery, high-rises like headstones.

"Miss Grigio!"

Rosso and his officers roll to a stop about twenty feet behind us. Rosso is breathing hard, clearly too old for hot pursuit.

I look out the door at the ground below. I look at Julie. I look down again, then back at Julie.

"Julie," I say.

"What?"

"Are you *sure* you want . . . to come with me?"

She looks at me, straining to force breath through her rapidly constricting bronchial tubes. There are questions in her eyes, maybe doubts, surely fears, but she nods. "Yes."

"Please stop running," Rosso groans, leaning against his knees. "This is not the way."

"I have to go," she says.

"Miss Cabernet. *Julie.* You can't leave your father here. You're all he has left."

She bites her lower lip, but her eyes are steely. "Dad's dead, Rosy. He just hasn't started rotting yet."

She grabs my hand, the one I shattered on M's face, and squeezes so hard I think she might break it even further. She looks up at me. "Well, R?"

I pull her to me. I wrap my arms around her and hold tight enough to fuse our genes. We are face-to-face and I almost kiss her, but instead I take two steps backward, and we fall through the doorway.

We plummet like a shot bird. My arms and legs encircle her, almost completely enveloping her tiny body. We crash through a roof overhang, a support bar tears into my thigh, my head bounces off a beam, we tangle in a cell phone banner and rip it in half, and then, finally, we hit the ground. A chorus of cracks and crunches shoots through me as my back greets the earth and Julie's weight flattens my chest. She rolls off me, choking and gasping for breath, and I lie there staring up at the sky. Here we are.

Julie raises herself on hands and knees and fumbles her inhaler out of her bag, takes a shot and holds it, supporting herself against the ground with one arm. When she can breathe again she crouches over me with terror in her eyes. Her face eclipses the hazy sun. "R!" she whispers. "Hey!"

As slow and shaky as the day I first rose from the dead, I lift myself upright and hobble to my feet. Various bones grind and crackle throughout my body. I smile, and in my breathy, tuneless tenor, I sing, "You make . . . me feel so young . . ."

She bursts out laughing and hugs me. I feel the pressure snap a few joints back into place.

She looks up at the open doorway. Rosso is framed in it, looking down at us. Julie waves to him, and he disappears back into the stadium with a swiftness that suggests pursuit. I try not to begrudge the man his paradigm—perhaps in his world, orders are orders.

So Julie and I run into the city. With each step I feel my body stabilizing, bones realigning, tissues stiffening around cracks to keep me from falling apart. I've never felt anything like this before. Is this some form of *healing*?

We dash through the empty streets, past countless rusty cars and drifts of dead leaves. We violate one-way streets. We blow stop signs. Ahead of us: the edge of town, the high grassy hill where the city opens up and the freeway leads elsewhere. Behind us: the relentless roar of assault vehicles gunning out of the stadium gate. *This cannot stand!* declare the steel-jawed mouths of the rulemakers. *Find those little embers and stomp them out!* With these howls at our backs, we crest the hill.

We are face-to-face with an army.

They stand in the grassy field next to the freeway ramps. Hundreds of them. They mill around in the grass, staring at the sky or at nothing, their gray, sunken faces oddly serene. But when the front line sees us they freeze, then pivot in our direction. Their focus spreads in a wave until the entire mob is standing at attention. Julie gives me an amused glance as if to say, *Really?* Then a disturbance ripples through the ranks and a burly, bald, six-foot-five zombie pushes his way into the open.

"M," I say.

"R." He gives Julie a quick nod. "Julie."

"Hiiii . . . ," she says, leaning into me warily.

Our pursuers' tires screech and we hear a rev of engines. They are very close. M steps up to the peak of the hill and the mob follows him. Julie huddles close to me as they sweep in around us, absorbing us into their odorous army, their rank ranks. It could be my imagination or a trick of the light, but M's skin looks less ashen than usual. His partial lips seem more expressive. And for the first time since I've known him, his neatly trimmed beard is not stained with blood.

The trucks barrel toward us, but as the swarm of the Dead rises into view on the hilltop, the vehicles slow down, then grumble to a stop. There are only four of them. Two Hummer H2s, a Chevy Tahoe, and an Escalade, all spray-painted military olive drab. The hulking machines look small and pitiful from where we stand. The Tahoe's door opens, and Colonel Rosso slowly emerges. Clutching his rifle, he scans row upon row of swaying bodies, weighing odds and strategies. His eyes are wide behind his thick glasses. He swallows, then lowers his gun.

"I'm sorry, Rosy," Julie calls down to him, and points at the stadium. "I can't do it anymore, okay? It's a fucking lie. We think we're surviving in there but we're *not*."

Rosso is looking hard at the zombies arrayed around him, peering into their faces. He's old enough that he's probably been around since the beginning of all this. He knows what the Dead are supposed to look like, and he can tell when something's different, no matter how subtle, subliminal, subcutaneous.

"You can't save the world by yourself!" he yells. "Come back and we can discuss this!"

"I'm not by myself," Julie says, and gestures at the forest of zombies swaying around her. "I'm with these guys."

Rosso's lips twist in a tortured grimace, then he jumps in his vehicle, slams the door, and revs back toward the stadium with the other three right behind. A brief respite, a quick suck of breath, because I know they aren't quitting, they *can't* quit, they're just gathering their strength, their weapons, their brute-force determination.

And well they should, because look at us. We are several hundred monsters and a hundred-pound girl, standing on the edge of their city with fire in our eyes. Deep under our feet Earth holds its molten breath, while the bones of countless generations watch us and wait.

W<small>E ARE MASSED</small> on the freeway on-ramp. Behind us, the city. In front of us, angular hills of alders and landscaped medians leading back toward the airport. Julie stands close by my side, looking a lot less confident than the brash revolutionary she just portrayed for Rosso. I put a hand on her shoulder and address the crowd.

"Julie!"

The crowd shivers, and I hear one or two sets of teeth snap. I raise my voice. "*Julie!* We keep her safe."

A few of them look tempted, but for the most part what I see in their eyes isn't hunger. It's the same fascination I saw back in the airport, intensified. More focused. They're not just looking at her, they're studying her. *Absorbing* her. Strange spasms ripple through their bodies every few seconds.

I catch M giving her a slightly different kind of stare, and I snap my fingers in his face.

"Come on," he says as if I'm being unreasonable.

I sit down on the concrete barrier, struggling to think. The noise of Rosso's trucks is still fading into the distance. Everyone is looking at me. Impatient stares from every direction. It's a look that says, *Well?* and I want to shout, *Well what?* I'm not a general or a colonel or a builder of cities. I'm just a corpse who wants not to be.

Julie sits next to me and puts a hand on my knee. I finally notice all the scrapes and bruises she acquired during our chuteless sky-dive. There's even one on her cheek, a shallow cut that makes her wince when she smiles. I hate it.

"You're hurt," I say.

"Not too bad."

I hate that she's hurt. I hate that she's been hurt, by me and by others, throughout the entire arc of her life. I barely remember pain, but when I see it in her I feel it in myself, in disproportionate measure. It creeps into my eyes, stinging, burning.

"Why did . . . you come?" I ask her.

"To help, remember? And to keep you safe."

"But why?"

She gives me a soft smile, and the cut on her cheek brightens with fresh blood. "Because I like you, Mr. Zombie." She wipes the blood away, looks at it, then smears it down my neck. "There. Now we're even."

Watching her sitting next to me, this blue-eyed angel surrounded by the drooling Dead, this fragile girl smiling with bloody lips into a highly uncertain future, I feel something surge in me. My vision blurs, and a wet trail streaks down my face. The burning in my eyes cools.

Julie touches my cheek and looks at her finger. She stares at me with such fascination I can't return her gaze. Instead I stand up and blurt, "We're going back to the airport."

The Dead look at me. They look at M.

"Why?" M says.

"Because it's where . . . we live. Where . . . we start."

"Start . . . what? War? Fight Boneys?"

"Not war. Not . . . that kind."

"Then what?"

As I stand there trying to answer, trying to distill the whirlwind of images in my head—music in the airport's dark halls, my kids coming out of their hiding places and dusting off their pinkening skin, a movement, a change—as I stand there dreaming, the hushed city air shivers with a scream. A frantic, gurgling howl like a cow thrashing around half-butchered.

Someone is coming toward us from farther down the freeway. He's running, but his lumbering gait betrays his biological status. M rushes out to meet the newcomer. I watch them converse, the newcomer waving his hands and gesturing in a way that creates a sinking feeling in my stomach. He is, without question, a bringer of bad news.

He merges into our crowd and M walks slowly back to me, shaking his head.

"What?" I ask.

"Can't . . . go home."

"Why not?"

"Boneys . . . going crazy. Coming in . . . from everywhere. Killing all who . . . differ."

I look at the newcomer. What I at first took for severe decomposition is actually severe injury, countless bites and claw marks. Farther down the road, there are more like him. Some are on the freeway, some stumble through the mud and grass in the medians, a widely dispersed crowd of hundreds.

"Ones like us . . . trying to escape," M continues. "And Boneys . . . chasing them."

Just as he says this, as if cued by the sound of their name, Death's publicists make their entrance. One, then two, then five and six spindly white shapes burst out of the distant trees and overtake two of the fleeing zombies. I watch the skeletons drag them down and hammer their heads against the pavement. I watch them stomp out their brains like so much rotten fruit. And I watch them multiply, rolling out of the trees and down the freeway slopes as far back as I can see, gathering on the road in a vast, clattering swarm.

"Oh fuck this . . . ," Julie whispers.

"New plan?" M inquires with forced calm.

I stand there in a trance of indecision. I am back in Julie's bedroom, lying next to her on a pile of her laundry, and she's saying, *There's nowhere left, is there?* And I am grimly shaking my head, telling her that the entire world is now covered in death. In the back of my awareness I can hear the rumble of SUVs, a lot more than four, barreling down Main Street to snuff me out and drag Julie back to their concrete tomb, embalm her like a princess and lay her down for eternity in some fluorescent-lit ossuary.

So here we are. Trapped in the gap between the cradle and the grave, no longer able to fit in either.

"New plan!" M says, jolting me out of my reverie. "Go into . . . city."

"Why the hell would we go in there?" Julie says.

"Lead Boneys in. Let Living . . . clean up."

"Wrong," she snaps at him. "Security doesn't discriminate between Boneys and Fleshies. They'll wipe you all out equally."

"We'll . . . hide," M says. He points down the freeway slope to a wide valley of rambler homes and grassy roundabouts gone to seed. It's the northern extremity of the suburbs where Julie and I nested for a night, once upon a time in a mildewed fairy tale.

"What, just hide out and hope Security and the skeletons deal with each other?"

M nods.

Julie pauses for two seconds. "That's a terrible plan, but okay, let's go." She turns to run, but M puts his hand on her shoulder. She claws it off and whirls on him. "What are you doing? Don't fucking touch me!"

"You . . . go with R," M says.

"What?" I ask him, perking to attention, and he fixes his dry gray eyes on me as he strains for language.

"We draw them . . . this way. You take her . . . that way."

"Excuse me?" Julie squeaks. "He's not 'taking me' anywhere, why the fuck would we split up?"

M points to a bruised and bleeding gash on her arm, then the cut on her cheek. "Because you're . . . fragile," he says in a surprisingly tender voice. "And . . . important."

Julie looks at M. She says nothing. She and I have somehow found ourselves outside the rim of the crowd, and everyone is watching us. The Boneys are close enough now for us to hear them. The scraping of their brittle feet and the low, warbling hum of whatever dark energy powers them. The shadowblack marrow seething in their bones.

I nod to M and he nods back. I take Julie's hand. She resists briefly, keeping her eyes on the crowd, then she turns and looks at me, and we run. M and the others disappear from view as we scramble down the embankment and dash into the crumbled downtown streets. The old ghosts in my head rise from their sleep and run alongside us, eagerly cheering us on.

Something unknown to us, something we've never seen. Memory can't overtake the present; history has its limits. Are we all just Dark Age doctors, swearing by our leeches? We crave a greater science. We want to be proven wrong.

• • •

Within minutes we hear the battle. Machine-gun fire that echoes down the narrow canyons of the streets. Muffled explosions that thump in our chests like distant bass music. The occasional shriek of a Boney, so shrill and piercing it conducts across the distance like electricity through water.

"Should we hide out in one of those?" Julie asks, pointing out a few brick and steel towers. "Just wait it out?"

I nod but I hesitate in the street. I don't know why I hesitate. What else is there now but hiding?

Julie runs to the nearest building. She tries the door. "Locked."
She crosses the street to an apartment complex. "Locked." She approaches an old brownstone and rattles the door. "This might—"
A window shatters above her; a skeleton scuttles down the wall
like a spider and drops onto her back. I sprint across the street and
grab the creature by the spine to wrench it off of her, but its pointy
fingers are digging into her flesh like barbs. With both hands I grip
its skull and strain against it as it tries to bury its teeth in her neck.
Despite its withered neck tendons, the thing is unbelievably strong.
Its jaws snap, inching toward her.

"Against . . . wall!" I grunt at Julie. She stumbles backward and
slams the skeleton against the brick. Its strength falters just long
enough for me to twist its head away from her and bash it against
the window ledge. The skull cracks. The eyeless face squeezed
between my palms seems to look right at me. And although its
expression is a permanent grin, I can hear its outraged screams in
my head:

STOP. STOP. WE ARE THE SUM OF EVERYTHING.

I bash it against the brick again. The skull cracks wider and the
creature's grip on Julie weakens.

*YOU WILL BECOME US. WE WILL WIN. ALWAYS HAVE,
ALWAYS W—*

I wrench the thing to the pavement and ram my shoe through
its face. The bones clatter to rest. The hum goes quiet.

I'm about to grab Julie and force my way through the brownstone's rickety door when something happens that I don't understand. The skull under my foot twitches, and as the crushed brain
disintegrates, the jaw falls open and releases a wretched, mournful
call like an injured bird. It sounds nothing like the bone hum or
the horn roar or the skeleton's screaming voice, and I wonder with
horror if this is the human being it once was, the last gasp of its
freeze-dried soul dissolving into the void. The hairs on my neck
stand up. Julie shivers. And as if in response to this plaintive wail, a
sound begins to rise in the distant streets. A scrabbling clatter from

all directions, a circle of noise tightening in on where we stand. I catch a flicker of motion in the corner of my eye and I look up. The windows of all the buildings are filled with hollow faces. Their naked teeth grin through the glass, leering down like a nightmare jury.

"What is happening?" Julie pleads, exhaustion washing over her face.

I don't want to answer. I'm worried that she is near the brink, and the answer I have is not hopeful. But looking up at the self-satisfied skulls behind those windows, I see no other conclusion. "I think they want . . . *us,*" I say. "You and me. They know . . . who we are."

"Who *are* we?"

"Ones who . . . started it."

"Are you shitting me?" she explodes, her eyes darting down the streets as the marching clatter gets louder. "Are you telling me these things hold *grudges?* They're going to *hunt us down* because we accidentally started a little scuffle in their stupid haunted-house airport?"

Julie, Julie, Perry whispers inside my head. I can hear him smiling. *Look at me, babe. Look at R's face and read it there. It's not a grudge. These creatures are far too pragmatic to care about revenge. They're onto you. It's not because you started this scuffle, it's because they know you're going to finish it.*

Julie's look of panic freezes in sudden comprehension. "Oh my God," she whispers.

I nod.

"They're *afraid* of us?"

"Yes."

She considers this a moment, then nods rapidly and looks at the ground, chewing her lip, eyes flicking back and forth. "Okay," she says. "Okay, okay, yes, I've got it. Come on."

She grabs my hand and runs. Directly toward the sound of the oncoming mob.

"What are . . . you doing?" I pant as I run behind her.

"This is Main Street," she says. "This is where Dad's troop met me when I drove home. Right around that corner should be . . ."

It's there. The old red Mercedes, parked halfway into the street, just sitting there waiting for us like a faithful chauffeur. And three blocks ahead: the Boneys' front line, pouring into the street and racing toward us with single-minded purpose. We jump into the car, Julie starts it, and we make a screeching U-turn, weaving in and out of the abandoned vehicles that litter the street—the city's final traffic jam. The Boneys rush in behind us, loping forward with the relentless commitment of the Reaper himself, but we're losing them.

"Where are . . . we going?" I ask as the potholed pavement rattles my jaw.

"Back to the stadium."

I look at her with wide eyes. "What?"

"If the skeletons are after us, specifically *us*, then they'll chase us there, right? They'll give up on the rest of your people and come after us. We can lead them right to the gates."

"And . . . then what?"

"We hide inside while Security takes care of them. There's no way they're going to breach the stadium walls, unless they can fly or something." She glances at me. "They can't fly, can they?"

I look ahead through the windshield, gripping the dash as Julie careens through the ruined streets at extremely unsafe speeds. "Back to . . . the stadium," I repeat.

"I know what you're thinking. It sounds like suicide for you, going back, but I think we can get away with it."

"How? Your dad—"

"My dad wants to kill you, I know. He's just . . . he can't see things anymore. But I think Rosy can. I've known him since I was a kid; he's practically my grandpa, and he's not blind, no matter what he looks like in those glasses. I'm pretty sure he gets what's going on."

Having lost the Boneys in the tangled side streets, we circle back around to Main, slipping through an unfinished section of Corridor 1. Inside the concrete walls, the street is swept clean of cars and debris, pointing toward the stadium straight as a runway. Julie drops into low gear and accelerates until the antique engine rattles. The stadium roof rises on the horizon, rearing up like some monolithic beast. *Climb into my mouth,* it teases. *Come on, kids, don't mind the teeth.*

With certain death rattling behind us, we fly through the heart of the city toward death slightly less certain. Soon we hear an all-too-familiar sound. The rev of big engines and the popcorn of gunfire, but close now, no longer muffled by distance. As the corridor walls dissolve into collapsed concrete and bent rebar frames, the view opens up, and Julie and I stare in horror.

Citi Stadium is already under siege. As if anticipating our plan, separate streams of Boneys are rushing toward the walls from other parts of the city, leaping over cars and scrambling on all fours like skeletal cats. Bullets and bombs blow out storefronts and topple traffic lights as Security does its job, but the skeletons are replenishing from every direction, needing no help from the group advancing behind us. My mind flashes back to the last time I was in this car. Frank and Ava joyriding through their Golden Age romance, a warm bubble of blossoms and birdsong and smiling eyes in Technicolor blue. Was this fiery hellscape there all along, swirling just outside our bubble? These swarms of demons clawing to get in?

This is wrong. It's all wrong. I stare at the growing horde as if I've never seen a walking corpse before. Where are they all coming from? With everything I thought I knew about our decomposition process, there is no accounting for these numbers. It usually takes *years* for us to fully shed our flesh. Even if they're answering some call to arms and pouring in from nearby cities . . . there just shouldn't be this many.

Is this the new face of the plague? Stronger, crueler, gaining traction and speed? Is the hole in the hourglass widening?

Julie looks at me with fresh fear in her eyes. "Do you think . . . ?"

"Don't," I tell her. "Just keep going. Too late . . . to change plans."

She keeps going. She swerves around grenade craters, bounces over curbs, drives on the sidewalk and crashes into pedestrian Boneys like a reeling drunk. Elegant Mercey is starting to look like a crumpled roadside tragedy.

"There!" she shouts suddenly. "That's him!" She revs toward the gate, blaring on the horn. As we get closer I recognize Colonel Rosso standing at the main doors, calling out orders from behind a blockade of armored Suburbans. Julie skids to a stop in front of the trucks and jumps out of the car. "Rosy!" she yelps as she runs toward the doors with me just behind. "Let us in let us in!"

The soldiers raise their rifles, looking at me and then at Rosso. I prepare myself for the bullet that will enter my brain and put an end to all this. But Rosso waves a hand at them. They lower their weapons. We run to the doors and the soldiers close their circle around us, taking aim at our pursuers.

"Miss Cabernet," Rosso says, perplexed. "You saved the world already?"

"Not quite," she pants. "Ran into some snags."

"I see that," he says, surveying the army of dirty yellow bones flooding in through the remains of the corridor.

"You guys can handle them, right?"

"I think so." He watches as his men take down the first wave, then fumble to reload before the next one crashes. "I hope so." He starts to pull open the massive door, then stops and looks at me. "Is what your father said true?" he asks Julie in a very calm voice. "Is this boy what I think he is?"

"Let us in, Rosy. He's my friend."

"Did he kill the guard?"

Julie takes his veiny hand and squeezes it. "Rosy. Please. Please trust me right now."

With his other hand on the door, Rosso stares at me, his squinty eyes unreadable. I stare back. Silently, he opens the door a crack and steps aside. Julie pecks him on the cheek and slips in through the gap. I hesitate at the threshold. The colonel and I regard each other for a moment. Then I give him a nod, he returns it slowly, and I follow Julie inside.

• • •

Once again we are skulking through the rat-maze streets of the stadium, fugitives no matter where we go. Julie speed-walks, scanning street signs, making decisive turns. Her breath sounds tight but she doesn't stop for her inhaler. Bloody and dirty, clothes torn and lungs wheezing, she and I have never been a better match.

"Where are . . . you going?" I ask.

She points at the Jumbotron. A picture of Nora's face is blinking on the screen with a sequence of words:

NORA GREENE

ARMED ASSAULT

ARREST ON SIGHT

"We're going to need her," Julie says. "Whatever happens next, I want to make sure she's with us, not locked in the locker rooms."

I look up at Nora's huge, pixelated face. Her cheerful grin seems incongruous on a wanted poster. "Is that why . . . we came back?" I ask the back of Julie's head. "For her?"

"Fifty-fifty."

A faint smile creeps onto my face. "You have . . . plans," I say in my best attempt at an insinuating tone. "Not just . . . keeping safe."

"I really thought I was finished with this place," she says without slowing down, and leaves it at that.

We stick to the stadium's edges, following the wall around the perimeter. Anchored to the concrete above us, the thick steel support cables twang like sci-fi lasers as the buildings sway and creak in the breeze. The muddy streets are empty. Security forces are probably all outside dealing with the Boneys, while the civilians huddle in their flimsy homes waiting for it to be over. The early evening sky is hazy orange, with high-altitude clouds rippling past the sun. It would be almost peaceful if not for the armies outside, sending their argument through the walls like inconsiderate neighbors.

"I have an idea where she might be," Julie says as she leads us through a dark doorway. "We used to hang out in the walls a lot when we were younger. We'd sit in the VIP rooms and pretend we were celebrities or something. The world was mostly over by then, so it was fun imagining we still mattered."

We ascend several long flights of stairs into an upper level. Most of the doors appear sealed off, but Julie doesn't bother with any of them. She finds a narrow gap in the wall that's been covered over with plastic sheeting, and we squeeze in through a girl-sized tear.

We are in what appears to be the stadium's luxury skybox. Expensive leather chairs lie on their sides around cracked glass tables. Silver snack trays offer clumps of dry mold. On the bar, tumblers wait next to purses like patient boyfriends, unaware that their dates are never coming back from the bathroom.

Nora is sitting in front of the huge viewing window that angles out over the stadium's distant floor. She takes a sip from the bottle of wine in her hand and gives us a big smile. "Look," she says, pointing at the Jumbotron flashing her face. "I'm on TV."

Julie runs over to her and hugs her, spilling a little wine in the process. "You're okay?"

"Sure. Why'd you come back?"

"Have you picked up what's going on outside?"

A distant grenade-blast punctuates the question.

"Lots of skeletons?"

"Yeah. They chased me and R here. They're hunting us."

Nora waves at me. "Hi, R."

"Hi."

"Want some wine? It's an '86 Mouton Rothschild. I'd describe it as yummy, with notes of fucking delicious."

"No thanks."

She shrugs and looks back at Julie. "Hunting you? Why?"

"We think they know what we're trying to do."

A pause. "What are you trying to do?"

"I'm not sure. Fix the world?"

Nora's face looks exactly like Julie's last night on the phone with M, listening to the news she never thought she'd hear. "Really?" she says, the wine bottle dangling between her fingers.

"Yeah."

"How?"

"We don't know yet. We're just going to try. We'll figure it out while trying."

At that moment the Jumbotron goes blank, and the stadium's huge, ceiling-mounted speakers crackle to life. A familiar voice booms across the sky like an insane god.

"Julie. I know you're here. This tantrum you are throwing will end now. I will not let you become your mother. Soft flesh is eaten by hard teeth. She died because she refused to harden."

Down on the ground below, I can see the few remaining guards staring up at the speakers, looking at each other uneasily. They can hear it in his voice. Something is wrong with their commander in chief.

"Our world is under attack and this may be the last of our last days, but you are my priority. Julie. I can see you."

As his words reverberate through the speakers I feel the chill of eyes on my back, and I turn around. On the far opposite side of the stadium, I can just make out the shape of a man standing behind the glass of the dark announcer's booth, gripping a microphone. Julie stares bleakly across the distance.

"When every real thing decays there is nothing left but principle and I will hold to it. I'm going to reset things back to right. Wait, Julie. I'll be there soon."

The speakers click off.

Nora hands the wine bottle to Julie. *"L'chaim,"* she says quietly.

Julie takes a drink. She hands it to me. I take a drink. The wine's bright red spirits dance around in my stomach, oblivious to the somber stillness in the room.

"What now?" Nora says.

"I don't know," Julie snaps before Nora finishes asking. "I don't know." She grabs the bottle from me and takes another long pull.

I stand in front of the viewing window and gaze out over the streets and rooftops below, that microcosmic parody of urban contentment. I'm so weary of this place. These tight rooms and claustrophobic hallways. I need some air.

"Let's go to the roof," I say.

The girls both look at me. "Why?" Julie says.

"Because it's . . . the only place left. And because I like it there."

"You've never been there," Julie says.

I look her in the eyes. "Yes I have."

There is a long silence.

"Let's go up," Nora says, glancing uncertainly from Julie to me. "It's probably the last place they'll look, so it'll at least . . . I don't know . . . buy us some time."

Without breaking eye contact with me, Julie nods. We travel through the dark corridors, which grow less and less crowd-friendly, more and more industrial as we go. Our path ends at a ladder. White light streams down from above.

"Can you climb this?" Nora asks me.

I grasp the ladder and tentatively pull myself up. My hands tremble on the cold steel, but the skill is there. I advance another rung, then look down at the girls. "Yes," I say.

They come up behind me and I ascend, *climbing a ladder*, rung after rung like I've done it a hundred times. The feeling is exhilarating, even better than the escalators, my own numb hands drawing me up toward daylight.

We emerge from a hatch doorway, and we're on the roof. The smooth panels shine white under the setting sun. Structural beams arch overhead like sculpture. And there's the blanket, damp and maybe a little mildewy from weeks of rain, but laid out exactly as I remember it, bright red against the white roof.

"Oh Lord . . . ," Nora whispers, looking out at the surrounding city. The ground below is alive with skeletons, now outnumbering Security by vast margins. Have we miscalculated? Have we erred? In my head I can hear Grigio exulting as they scale the walls and flood through the gates to kill every last person. *You dreamers. You ridiculous children. You dancing grinning fuckups. Here is your bright future. Your earnest, saccharine hope. How does it taste dripping from the neck of everyone you love?*

Perry! I call out into my head. *Are you there? What do we do?*

My voice echoes like a prayer in a dark cathedral. Perry is silent.

I watch the skeletons kill and devour another soldier, then I turn away. I block out the screams, the explosions, the compressed pops of sniper fire from the tier just below us. I block out the skeletons' hum, even though it's now an immense chorus, howling in stereo from every direction. I block all this out and sit on the red blanket. While Nora paces the roof watching the battle, Julie walks slowly to the blanket and sits next to me. She tucks her knees against her chest, and we both look out at the horizon. We can see the mountains. They're blue like the ocean. They're lovely.

"This plague . . . ," Julie says in a very soft voice. "This curse . . . I have an idea where it came from."

The clouds are thin and pink overhead, stretched out into delicately textured swirls. A bracing cold wind whips across the roof and makes us squint.

"I don't think it's from any spell or virus or nuclear rays. I think it's from a deeper place. I think we brought it here."

Our shoulders are pressed together. She is cool to the touch. As if her warmth is retreating, curling deep inside her to escape the extinguishing wind.

"I think we crushed ourselves down over the centuries. Buried ourselves under greed and hate and whatever other sins we could find until our souls finally hit the rock bottom of the universe.

And then they scraped a hole through it, into some . . . dark place."

I hear pigeons cooing somewhere in the eaves. Starlings zip and dive against the distant sky, pretty much unaffected by the end of our silly civilization.

"We released it. We poked through the seabed and the oil erupted, painted us black, pulled our inner sickness out for everyone to see. Now here we are in this dry corpse of a world, rotting on our feet till there's nothing left but bones and the buzz of flies."

The roof shudders under us. With a low, grinding rumble, the entire expanse of steel begins to move, sliding shut to shield the people inside from what is quickly becoming a full-scale invasion. As it booms closed, footsteps clang toward us from the ladder. Nora pulls Grigio's pistol out of her purse and rushes to the hatch.

"What do we do, R?" Julie finally looks at me. Her voice is shaky, her eyes are raw, but she doesn't surrender to tears. "Are we stupid to think we can do anything? You made me start hoping again, but here we are, and I think we're about to die. So what do we do?"

I look into Julie's face. Not just at it, but into it. Every pore, every freckle, every faint gossamer hair. And then the layers beneath them. The flesh and bones, the blood and brain, all the way down to the unknowable energy that swirls in her core, the life force, the soul, the fiery will that makes her more than meat, coursing through every cell and binding them together in millions to form *her*. Who is she, this girl? What is she? She is everything. Her body contains the history of life, remembered in chemicals. Her mind contains the history of the universe, remembered in pain, in joy and sadness, hate and hope and bad habits, every thought of God, past-present-future, remembered, felt, and hoped for all at once.

"What do we do?" she pleads, confounding me with her eyes, the vast oceans in her irises. "What do we have left?"

I have no answer for her. But I look into her face, her pale cheeks,

her red lips bright with life and tender as an infant's, and I understand that I love her. And if she is everything, maybe that's answer
enough.

I pull Julie into me and kiss her.

I press her lips against mine. I pull her body against mine. She
wraps her arms around my neck and squeezes me hard. We kiss
with our eyes open, staring into each other's pupils and the depths
inside them. Our tongues taste each other, our saliva flows, and
Julie bites my lip. I feel the death in me stirring, the anti-life surg-
ing toward her glowing cells to darken them. But as it reaches the
threshold, I *halt* it. I hold it back and hammer it down, and I feel
Julie doing the same. We hold this thrashing monster between us in
a relentless grip, we bear down on it together with determination
and rage, and something happens. It changes. It warps and squirms
and twists inside-out. It becomes something altogether different.
Something new.

A surge of ecstatic agony rushes through me, and we fall back
from each other with a gasp. My eyes are aching with some deep,
twisting pain. I look at Julie's and see that her irises are shimmer-
ing. The fibers twitch, and their hue begins to change. Vivid sky
blue fades to pewter gray—but then hesitates, flickers, and flashes
back as gold. A brilliant shade of solar yellow that I have never
seen before on any human being. As this happens, my sinuses
ignite with a new smell, something similar to the life energy of
the Living but also vastly different. It's coming from Julie, it's her
scent, but it's also *mine*. It rushes out from us like an explosion of
pheromones, so potent I can almost see it.

"What . . . ," Julie whispers, staring at me with her mouth slightly
open, "just happened?"

For the first time since we sat down on this blanket, I look
around and see my surroundings. Something has changed on the
ground below. The armies of skeletons have stopped advancing.
They stand completely motionless. And it's hard to tell from this
distance, but they all seem to be looking directly at *us*.

"Julie!"

The voice shatters the unearthly stillness. There is Grigio, standing in front of the ladder hatch while Rosso clambers up behind him, breathing hard and keeping his eyes on the general. Nora sits slumped against the hatch with her hands cuffed to the ladder, her bare legs sprawled against the cold steel roof. Her gun lies at Grigio's feet, just out of reach.

Grigio's jaw muscles look tight enough to burst. When Julie turns and he sees her changed eyes, his entire body clenches. I can hear his teeth grinding.

"Colonel Rosso," he says in the driest voice I have ever heard. "Shoot them."

His face is ashen, the skin dry and flaky.

"Dad," Julie says.

"Shoot them."

Rosso glances from Julie to her father. "Sir, she's not infected."

"Shoot them."

"She's not infected, sir. I'm not even so sure the *boy* is infected. Look at their eyes, they're—"

"They're *infected*!" Grigio barks. I can see the shape of his teeth under his pursed lips. "This is how the infection travels! This is how it works! There is no—" He chokes off his words as if deciding he's said enough.

"Sir . . . ," Rosso says.

Grigio draws his pistol and points it at his daughter.

"John!" Rosso grabs Grigio's arm and wrenches it down, grappling for the gun. With trained precision Grigio twists Rosso's wrist and snaps it, then jabs him hard in the ribs. The old man falls to his knees.

"Dad, stop!" Julie screams, and he replies by cocking the gun and taking aim once again. His face is empty now, expressing absolutely nothing. Just skin stretched over a skull.

Rosso stabs a knife into his ankle.

Grigio doesn't cry out or visibly react. But his leg gives under him, and he topples backward. He slides down the roof's steep slope, rolling and twisting, fingers grasping for purchase on the smooth steel. His gun spins past him and drops over the edge, and he nearly follows it—but he stops. His hands cling to the rim of the roof as the rest of him dangles over the drop. All I can see are his white-knuckled fingers and his face, tight with exertion but still eerily impassive.

Julie runs to help him, but the slope is too steep and she starts to slip. She crouches there and stares at her father, helpless.

Then a curious thing happens. As Grigio's skinny hands clutch the roof edge, another set of fingers rises up and clamps down over his. But these fingers have no flesh. Just dry bone, yellowed and browned by dust and age and ancient blood from ancient murders. They grip the roof, digging into the steel, and hoist up a grinning, humming skeleton.

It is not fast. It doesn't leap or sprint. It moves leisurely, lacking the relentless, bloodthirsty drive that pursued us through the city. And despite the desperation of that pursuit, it seems in no hurry now to get to me or Julie. It doesn't even seem to notice us. It bends over to hook its claws into Grigio's shirt and drags him up onto the ledge. Grigio struggles to stand, and the skeleton hauls him to his feet.

Grigio and the skeleton regard each other, their faces inches apart.

"Rosy!" Julie screams. "Fucking shoot it!"

Rosso is struggling for breath, clutching his wrist and ribs, unable to move. He gives Julie a look that pleads forgiveness, not just for this failure but for all the failures leading to it. All the years of knowing and not acting.

The skeleton takes hold of Grigio's arm gently, tenderly, as if leading him into a dance. Then it pulls him close, gazes into his eyes, and bites a chunk out of his shoulder.

Julie shrieks, but everyone else is dumbstruck. Grigio doesn't fight. His eyes are wide and feverish, but his face is a blank mask as the creature chews into him, taking slow, almost sensual bites. Pieces of flesh fall through its hollow jaw and hit the roof.

I am transfixed. I stare at Grigio and the skeleton in rapt horror, trying to grasp what I'm witnessing. They are perched there on the edge of the roof, silhouetted against a smoldering sky of pink clouds and sickly orange haze, and in that otherworldly light, their figures are indistinguishable. Bones devouring bones.

Julie sprints to the hatch. She picks up Nora's gun and points it at the skeleton. It finally looks at her, finally acknowledges our presence, and rears back its head to release a roar, a piercing blast like the trumpets at the end of time, rusted and broken and forever out of tune.

Julie fires. The first few shots miss completely, then a bullet snaps off a rib, a clavicle, a hip bone.

"Julie."

She pauses, the gun trembling in her hands. Her father stares at her vacantly as the blood drains from his body. "I'm sorry," he says in a quiet murmur.

"Dad, push it off you! *Fight it!*"

Grigio closes his eyes and says:

"No."

The skeleton grins at Julie, and eats her father's throat.

Julie screams with all the anguish and rage in her battered young heart and fires one more time. The creature's skull vanishes in a burst of dust and bone shards. With its fingers still embedded in Grigio's shoulders, it reels backward and tips off the edge of the roof.

Grigio goes with it.

They fall together, entangled, and Grigio's body shudders in the air, convulsing. Converting. His remaining flesh peels away in the wind, dry scraps floating up like ashes, leaving the pale bones underneath, and there is a message in those bones that I'm finally able to read. A warning etched into each femur, each humerus, each grasping metacarpal:

This is the plague. This is the curse. So potent now, so deeply rooted and ravenous for souls, no longer content to wait for death. Now reaching out and simply taking what it wants.

But a decision has been made today. We will not be robbed. We will cling tight to what we have, no matter how hard the curse pulls. We will fight it.

On the ground below, the Boneys watch Grigio's remains plummet to earth and shatter. They stare at the fragments in the dirt, those little white shards, broken and inconsequential. Then all at once, with movements devoid of purpose or intent . . . they wander off. Some walk in circles, some bump into each other, but little by little they disperse and disappear into the buildings and trees. I feel a tiny thrill creeping through me. What signal have they received? Between the fall of those bones and the strange new energy pulsing out from this rooftop like radio waves, is there a notice blaring loud in their empty skulls? An announcement that their time is over?

Julie lets the gun fall from her fingers. She inches her way to the edge of the roof and crouches there, gazing down at the pile of bones below. Her eyes are red, but there are still no tears. The only sound on the roof is the wind, whipping at the tattered remnants of state and country flags. Rosso watches Julie for a moment, then unlocks Nora's cuffs and helps her to her feet. Nora rubs her wrists and they share a look that makes words unnecessary.

Julie makes her way over to us with dazed, dragging steps. Rosso touches her shoulder. "I'm so sorry, Julie."

She sniffs, staring down at her feet. "I'm okay." Her voice is like her eyes, raw and wrung out. Now that I have the ability, I want to do her crying for her. Julie has become an orphan, but she is much more than the tragic waif that word implies. Her grief will catch up to her eventually and demand its due, but for the moment she is here with us, alive and standing.

Rosso brushes his left hand against her hair, tucking a lock behind her ear. She squeezes his callused palm against her cheek and offers a faint smile.

Rosso turns his attention to me. I can see his eyes flicking left and right, studying my irises. "Archie, was it?"

"Just R."

He puts his hand out to me, and after a moment's confusion, I put out mine. Rosso shakes my broken hand, enduring his broken wrist with a fierce grimace. "I don't know exactly why," he says, "but I'm thrilled to know you, R."

He walks back to the hatch.

"Will we be having a community meeting tomorrow?" Nora asks.

"I'm going to announce it as soon as I get down this ladder. We have some urgent developments to address." He looks out at the retreating skeletal army. "And I'd certainly love to hear your take on just what the hell happened today."

"We might have some theories," Nora says.

Rosso descends the ladder, gripping carefully with his left hand. Nora looks at Julie. Julie nods. Nora smiles at her, then at me, then disappears into the hatch.

We are alone on the rooftop. Julie squints up at me, studying me as if she's never seen me before. Then her eyes widen, and she takes in a sharp breath. "Oh my God," she says. "R, you're . . ." She reaches up and peels the Band-Aid off my forehead. She touches the place where she stabbed me on the day we first met, ages ago, last month.

Her finger comes away red.

"You're *bleeding!*"

As she says this I begin to notice things. Sharp points of pain all over my body. I *hurt*. I pat myself down and find my clothes sticky with blood. Not the dead black oil that once clogged my veins. Bright, vivid, living-red *blood*.

Julie presses her hand into my chest so hard it's almost kung fu. Against the pressure of her palm, I feel it. A movement deep inside me. A *pulse*.

"R!" Julie nearly shrieks. "I think . . . you're *alive!*"

She pounces on me, wrapping herself around me and squeezing so hard I feel my semihealed bones creaking. She kisses me again, tasting the salty blood from my lower lip. Her warmth radiates into my body, and I feel a rush of sensations as my own warmth finally pushes back.

Julie goes still. She releases me and pulls back a little, glancing downward. A wondering smile creeps across her face.

I look down at myself, but I don't need to. I can feel it. My hot blood is pounding through my body, flooding capillaries and lighting up cells like Fourth of July fireworks. I can feel the elation of every atom in my flesh, brimming with gratitude for the second chance they never expected to get. The chance to start over, to live right, to love right, to burn up in a fiery cloud and never again be buried in the mud. I kiss Julie to hide the fact that I'm blushing. My face is bright red and hot enough to melt steel.

Okay, corpse, a voice in my head says, and I feel a twitch in my belly, more like a gentle nudge than a kick. *I'm going now. I'm sorry I couldn't be here for your battle; I was fighting my own. But we won, right? I can feel it. There's a shiver in our legs, a tremor like the Earth speeding up, spinning off into uncharted orbits. Scary, isn't it? But what wonderful thing didn't start out scary? I don't know what the next page is for you, but whatever it is for me I swear I'm not going to fuck it up. I'm not going to yawn off in the middle of a sentence and hide it in a drawer. Not this time. Peel off these dusty wool blankets of apathy and antipathy and cynical desiccation. I want life in all its stupid sticky rawness.*

Okay.

Okay, R.

Here it comes.

living

Nora Greene is in the square by the stadium's main gate, standing with General Rosso in front of a huge crowd. She is a little nervous. She wishes she had smoked before coming out today, but it seemed inappropriate somehow. She wanted a clear head for this occasion.

"Okay, folks," Rosso begins, straining his reedy voice to reach the back of the assembly spilling out into the far streets. "We've prepared you for this as best we could, but I know it may still be a little . . . uncomfortable."

Not everyone in the stadium is here, but everyone who wants to be is. The rest are hiding behind locked doors with guns drawn, but Nora hopes they'll come out eventually to see what's going on.

"Let me just assure you once again that you are not in any danger," Rosso continues. "The situation has changed."

Rosso looks at Nora and nods.

The guards pull open the gate, and Nora shouts, "Come on in, guys!"

One by one, still clumsy but walking more or less straight, they wander into the stadium. The Half-Dead. The Nearly-Living. The crowd murmurs anxiously and contracts as the zombies form a loose line in front of the gate.

"These are just a few of them," Nora says, moving forward to address the people. "There are more out there every day. They're trying to cure themselves. They're trying to cure the plague, and we need to do whatever we can to help."

"Like *what?*" someone shouts dubiously.

"We're going to study it," Rosso says. "Get close to it, knead it and wring it until answers start to emerge. I know it's vague, but we have to start somewhere."

"Talk to them," Nora says. "I know it's scary at first, but look them in the eyes. Tell them your name and ask them theirs."

"Don't worry," Rosso says. "Each one will have a guard assigned to them at all times, but try to believe that they won't hurt you. We have to entertain the idea that this will work."

Nora steps back to let the crowd come forward. Cautiously, they do. They approach the zombies, while wary guards keep rifles trained. For their part, the zombies are handling this awkward experience with admirable patience. They just stand there and wait, some of them attempting affable grins while trying to ignore the laser dots jittering on their foreheads. Nora moves to join the people, crossing her fingers behind her back and hoping for the best.

"Hi there."

She turns toward the voice. One of the zombies is watching her. He steps forward from the line and gives her a smile. His lips are thin and slightly mangled under a short blond beard, but they, along with countless other wounds on his body, appear to be healing.

"Um . . . hello . . . ," Nora says, glancing up and down his considerable height. He must be well over six feet. He's a little heavyset, but his muscular arms strain his tattered shirt. His perfectly bald head gleams like a pale gray pearl.

"I'm Nora," she says, tugging at her curls.

"My name is Mm . . . arcus," he says, his voice a velvety rumble. "And you're . . . the most beautiful woman . . . I've ever seen."

Nora giggles and twirls her hair faster. "Oh *my*." She reaches out a hand. "Nice to meet you . . . Marcus."

• • •

The boy is in the airport. The hallways are dark, but he's not scared. He runs through the shadowed food court, past all the unlit signs and moldy leftovers, half-finished beers and cold pad thai. He hears the rattle of a solitary skeleton in an adjacent corridor and quickly changes course, darting around the corner without pausing. The Boneys are slow now. The moment the boy's dad and stepmom first came back here, something happened to them all. Now they wander aimlessly like bees in winter. They bump into walls and stand motionless, obsolete things waiting to be replaced.

The boy is carrying a box. It's empty now, but his arms are tired. He runs into the connecting overpass and stops to get his bearings.

"Alex!"

The boy's sister appears behind him. She's carrying a box, too. She has bits of tape stuck all over her fingers.

"All done, Joan?"

"All done!"

"Okay. Let's go get more."

They run down the corridor. As they hit the conveyer, the power comes back on and the belt lurches under their feet. The boy and the girl are running barefoot at the speed of light, flying down the corridor like loping deer while the morning sun drifts up behind them. At the end of the corridor they nearly collide with another group of kids, all holding boxes.

"All done," says a boy whose charcoal skin is turning warm brown.

"Okay," Alex says, and they run together. Some of the kids still wear tatters. Some of them are still gray. But most of them are alive. The kids lacked the instinctual programming of the adults. They had to be taught how to do everything. How to kill easily, how to wander aimlessly, how to sway and groan and properly rot away. But now the classes have stopped. No one is teaching them, and like perennial bulbs dried up and waiting in the winter earth, they are bursting back to life all on their own.

The fluorescent lights flicker and buzz, and the sound of a record needle scratches onto the speakers overhead. Some enterprising soul has hijacked the airport PA system. Sweet, swooning strings swell into the gloom, and Francis Albert Sinatra's voice echoes lonely in the empty halls.

Something wonderful happens in summer . . . when the sky is a heavenly blue . . .

The dusty speakers pop and sizzle, short out and distort. The record skips. But it's the first time in years this place's inert air has been stirred by music.

As the kids run to the Arrivals gate to get fresh boxes, fresh rolls of tape, they pass a pale figure shambling down the hall. The zombie glances at the Living children as they run past, but doesn't pursue them. Her appetite has been waning lately. She doesn't feel the hunger like she used to. She watches the kids disappear around the corner, then continues on her way. She doesn't know where she's going exactly, but there's a white glow at the end of this hallway, and it looks nice. She stumbles toward it.

Something wonderful happens in summer . . . when the moon makes you feel all aglow . . . You fall in love, you fall in love . . . you want the whole world to know . . .

She emerges into the waiting area of Gate 12, flooded with bright morning sunlight. Something in here is different than before. On the floor-to-ceiling windows overlooking the runways, someone has taped small photos to the glass. Side by side and stacked about five squares high, they form a strip that runs all the way to the end of the room.

Something wonderful happens in summer . . . and it happens to only a few. But when it does . . . yes when it does . . .

The zombie approaches the photos warily. She stands in front of them, staring with mouth slightly agape.

A girl climbing an apple tree. A kid spraying his brother with a hose. A woman playing a cello. An elderly couple gently touching. A boy with a cat. A boy crying. A newborn deep in sleep. And one older photo, creased and faded: a family at a water park. A man, a woman, and a little blond girl, smiling and squinting in the sun.

The zombie stares at this mysterious and sprawling collage. The sunlight glints off the nametag on her chest, so bright it hurts her eyes. For hours she stands there, motionless. Then she takes in a slow breath. Her first in months. Dangling limply at her sides, her fingers twitch to the music.

· · ·

"R."

I open my eyes. I am lying on my back, arms folded behind my head, looking up at a flawless summer sky. "Yes?"

Julie stirs on the red blanket, scooting a little closer to me. "Do you think we'll ever see jets up there again?"

I think for a moment. I watch the little molecules swim in my eye fluids. "Yes."

"Really?"

"Maybe not us. But I think the kids will."

"How far do you think we can take this?"

"Take what?"

"Rebuilding everything. Even if we can completely end the plague . . . do you think we'll ever get things back to the way they were?"

A lone starling swoops across the distant sky, and I imagine a white jet trail sketching out behind it, like a florid signature on a love note. "I hope not."

We are silent for a while. We are lying in the grass. Behind us, the battered old Mercedes waits patiently, whispering to us in sizzles and pings as its engine cools. Mercey, Julie named it. Who is this woman lying next to me, so overflowing with life she can grant it to a car?

"R," she says.

"Yeah."

"Do you remember your name yet?"

On this hillside on the edge of a crumbled freeway, the bugs and birds in the grass perform a tiny simulation of traffic noise. I listen to their nostalgic symphony, and I shake my head. "No."

"You could give yourself one, you know. Just pick one. Whatever you want."

I consider this. I thumb through the index of names in my brain. Complex etymologies, languages, ancient meanings passed down through generations of cultural traditions. But I'm a new thing. A fresh canvas. I can choose what history I build my future on, and I choose a new one.

"My name is R," I say with a little shrug.

She twists her head to look at me. I can feel her sun-yellow eyes on the side of my face, as if they're trying to tunnel into my ear and explore my brain. "You don't want to get your old life back?"

"No." I sit up, folding my arms over my knees and looking down into the valley. "I want this one."

Julie smiles. She sits up with me and faces what I'm facing.

The airport spreads out below us like a thrown gauntlet. There was no global transformation after the skeletons surrendered. Some of us are on our way back to life, some are still Dead. Some are still lingering here at the airport, or in other cities, countries, continents, wandering and waiting. But to fix a problem that spans the globe, an airport seems like a good place to start.

We have big plans. Oh yes. We're fumbling in the dark, but at least we're in motion. Everyone is working now; Julie and I are just pausing for a moment to enjoy the view, because it's a beautiful day. The sky is blue. The grass is green. The sun is warm on our skin. We smile, because this is how we save the world. We will not let Earth become a tomb, a mass grave spinning through space. We will exhume ourselves. We will fight the curse and break it. We will cry and bleed and lust and love, and we will cure death. We will *be* the cure. Because we *want it*.

ACKNOWLEDGMENTS

Thank you, Cori Stern, for discovering my stories at the bottom of the Internet swamp and making me write this book, which has changed my life. Thank you, Laurie Webb and Bruna Papandrea, for pushing it out into the world. Thank you, Joe Regal, my brilliant agent, for helping me shape it into what it's become. Thank you, Nathan Marion, for supporting all my artistic endeavors throughout the years, for believing in them and me even when both seemed crazy.